Erin's Rebel

I0687599

by

Susan Macatee

Erin's Rebel

Cover Art by *Nicola Martinez*

The Wild Rose Press
PO Box 708
Adams Basin, NY 14410-0706
Visit us at www.thewildrosepress.com

Publishing History
First American Rose Edition, 2009
Print ISBN: 1-60154-520-7

Published in the United States of America

The sound of her name on his lips made her skin tingle. She tore the paper off the package. At the sight of the brooch, her breath caught.

"Do you like it?" he asked anxiously. "I had it made just for you."

Eyeing him, she had a hard time finding her voice. This was Erin O'Connell's brooch, the very one that had sent her back in time. It shone in her hands, new and unworn from time and wear.

What did this mean? She must be following Erin O'Connell's footsteps. As far as she knew her being here hadn't changed anything. Will was still destined to die this year.

"I didn't mean to upset you, Erin. If you don't want the brooch—"

"No." She clasped the pin against her chest as the meaning of his gift sank in. "It just means so much to me."

His look of concern softened into a lopsided grin. "I'm happy you feel that way."

"Thank you, Will." She slipped the brooch into the pocket of her wrapper, then stood on her toes, lifting her arms to circle his neck. She kissed his cheek, inhaling his musky scent.

His mouth was on hers, hot and urgent. The softness of his moustache and chin beard tickled her lips. She opened to him, her tongue slipping inside to taste him thoroughly. He groaned, pressing the length of his body against her.

Fourth place - 2006 Valley Forge Romance Writers'
Sheila Contest

Third place - 2005 San Francisco Area RWA's
Sharp Synopsis Contest

Dedication

To my mom. I love sharing books with you.

And to all my men: my sons,
Shaun, Chris and Ryan

And to my hero: my husband, Walt

I love you all.

Chapter One

Erin Branigan had finally found the man of her dreams.

Unfortunately, he'd died over one hundred and forty years ago.

On a warm, bright day in mid-June, she stood in a small, church cemetery in a rural area outside Mason, Virginia. Vivid dreams of a handsome, Civil War soldier had sent her here, but they had also driven a wedge between her fiancé, Rick Meyers, and her. To solve this mystery, she'd called off her wedding two and a half months before. And now today, she hoped what she learned in this graveyard would put a halt to her nightly visions.

Erin kneeled beside the weathered granite headstone of the Confederate captain and traced her finger over the inscription. *William James Montgomery; Born September 20, 1833; Died November 23, 1864.* Despite the warmth of the day, she shivered, recalling the dark-eyed man and her intense, sometimes sensual dreams. After taking a deep breath, she rose, brushed off her jeans, and snapped a few photos.

"Here's his wife." The caretaker, who'd introduced himself as John, tipped the bill of his black Orioles cap toward the stone beside Montgomery's.

Erin glanced at it. *Anne Eugenia Montgomery; Born October 3, 1838; Died September 15, 1861.*

"She was so young," she said.

The caretaker lifted his cap and ran a liver-spotted hand through his thinning, gray hair. Replacing the hat, he turned to indicate the old, stonewalled church. "The records show she died shortly after William enlisted in the Confederate Army."

Erin nodded. Her grandmother had told her some of this story. The couple had a daughter, Amanda, and a stillborn son. They were also buried here, along with Amanda's husband and their children.

She fingered the engraved silver frame of the brooch pinned to the lapel of her beige, cotton blazer. As she glanced at the clear summer sky, a light breeze ruffled her cropped hair. Sparrows, perched in the oaks overlooking the plots, twittered. Such a beautiful day to recall such sadness.

"My grandmother told me her great-aunt Erin O'Connell knew William Montgomery. She met him during the war. This brooch was given to her by the captain." She clasped the oval frame, surrounding tightly woven chocolate-brown hair. "It's supposed to be a lock of his hair."

"Well, I'll be." John admired the pin. "Where's this great-aunt buried?"

"In Pennsylvania in a small town named Candor. It's just north of Gettysburg. My grandmother lived there, but she died last week." Her voice broke as she recalled the dear lady.

"Sorry to hear that."

She cleared her throat. "That's why I've come here. It was one of her last requests that I find this man's grave. In addition to the brooch, she had an old Bible and photos of both her great-aunt and William Montgomery." She lifted the photos she carried with her.

"My God! She looks just like you."

Erin smiled. "There are a few minor differences." In fact, she'd found the family resemblance unnerving, especially since Captain Montgomery resembled the soldier in her dreams. "Grandma also told me Erin O'Connell had been a Federal spy."

John arched his brows and let out an appreciative

whistle. "What a great story! Researching the past is fascinating. You say you're from Philadelphia?"

"Yeah. I'm a reporter for the *Philadelphia Inquirer.*"

"Well, then, feel free to go through all the records we have." He gestured at the church. "It should be all in a day's work for you."

****

On her return trip to Pennsylvania later that night, Erin couldn't shake the eerie feeling she'd experienced after going through the ledger. The facts she'd uncovered only added to her sense of unease. As her dreams combined with the historic facts, a feeling of insanity invaded her mind.

On her drive south, the winding two-lane highway through north-western Virginia had been so open and scenic in daylight. Now in the darkness, the heavily forested road and lack of traffic caused chills to slither through her as she mulled over her discoveries. She should have left earlier but had found it difficult to pull herself away. Erin had discovered the man for whom she'd been searching. But would finding his grave finally end the dreams, or would this just make things a helluva lot worse?

The moist scent of impending rain sifted through the window she'd left cracked open. Hopefully, any shower would be light. She didn't look forward to a long drive in heavy rain, especially on an unfamiliar road. After two, quick flashes of lightning and rumbles of thunder, the first drops of rain hit the windshield. A deluge followed, forcing her to flick the wipers on high.

A sudden vibration shocked already frayed nerves. Where did that come from? Her cell phone was in her purse on the adjoining seat, so it hadn't come from that. The hair brooch on her lapel? When she fingered it, a sharp pulsation shot up her arm.

"What the hell?" She jerked her hand.

Despite the strange sensation, Erin remained

3

focused on the road. Nothing ahead or behind her but forest. Dark, *creepy* forest encased in sheets of rain. Unable to see, she considered pulling over but wasn't sure she wanted to stop *there*.

As the vibration increased, she almost skidded off the blacktop. She grasped at the clasp, trying to yank the pin off her jacket.

Headlights glared in the distance and grew brighter. She had to concentrate on regaining control of the car. Tires squealed as a truck slid into her path on a rain-slicked curve.

"Oh, shit!" Heart pounding, she jerked the steering wheel to avoid a collision. She hydroplaned off the highway and swerved onto the shoulder—too late to see the tree dead in front of her.

Impact rolled as a film in slow motion. The sound of crunching metal, smell of rubber and gasoline, and a jolt through her system were the last things she remembered.

Chapter Two

Confederate Camp in Northern Virginia
June 18, 1863

A scream pierced the air. Men's shouts woke Will Montgomery from a deep slumber and dreams of his home and Anne.

What in damnation? Black coated the interior of his tent, making it impossible to see. What time was it anyway? Snatching up his trousers, he yanked them on over his under drawers. Emerging from the tent, he struggled to see in the ink-black darkness. No moonlight shone, and only a few, lone stars flickered through the dense clouds. The shuffling of heavy boots and the sound of men's angry voices drew his attention a few yards past the laundress' tent.

Had it been Mrs. O'Connell? A lantern glowed near her tent. Upon investigation, he found two men standing over what appeared to be a woman lying in a heap of calico skirts and petticoats. One of the men held a mare by the reins; the other hefted a lantern.

"What happened?" Will said.

"The lady fell from the horse, sir," the private holding the animal answered.

Kneeling at the woman's side, he tilted her face toward him. He motioned to the other soldier. "Bring the lantern closer."

Mrs. O'Connell, a young widow serving as one of the camp's new laundresses, lay limp and still. What the hell had the laundress been doing on a horse in the dead of night? He gazed at her placid face. Long, red-gold lashes brushed against her rounded cheekbones, ghostly pale in the candlelight. Blood oozed from one delicate nostril. Her bosom rose and fell gently, drawing his gaze to the swell of her breasts.

The first day the Irish woman had arrived in camp, feelings stirred in him he'd thought died with Anne. After his wife's death, he'd vowed not to give his heart to another woman. Losing her had torn out his soul.

"What happened?" Will addressed the thin private with the lantern.

The soldier glanced at his companion and shrugged. "We think the horse reared up, sir. Then we heard her scream and came a-runnin' just in time to see her hit the ground."

Will nodded. Could be she'd imbibed a bit too much tonight. He'd heard the new laundress kept a bottle of whiskey in her tent, but so far, he hadn't witnessed any improprieties.

He studied the motionless figure. Doc Matthews could determine the extent of her injuries. As he lifted her, he smelled no hint of alcohol, but a feminine scent overwhelmed him. Soap and something sweet he couldn't identify.

He hadn't held a woman for two years. The softness of her curves increased the yearning he'd been denying. Leaving the other men to tend to the horse, he carried her across the camp to Doc.

****

Erin groaned. Her head and neck hurt like hell, and so did her nose. In fact, everything hurt. What had happened? She reached to the back of her head, where her fingers closed around a damp cloth. When she opened her eyes, a sharp pain knifed through her skull.

Focusing her thoughts, she recalled flashes of a dark, rainy highway. A truck hurtling toward her. The tree.

She turned her head and squinted into the yellow-white glow of a lantern. She wasn't in her car but lying flat on her back.

Someone moved beside her. A man with a heavy drawl spoke. "Are you all right, ma'am? Can you speak?"

She stared at him. Was she in a hospital? No. The gangly, sandy-haired man with the handlebar mustache wasn't wearing scrubs. He appeared to be in his early thirties and was dressed in an oversized, striped blue and white shirt draped over tan wool pants with a set of suspenders dangling to his knees. This sure wasn't an emergency room.

"Where am I?" she croaked. "What happened?" Blinding pain shot through her skull, again.

"You were thrown from a horse. Do you remember?"

"Horse?" She shook her head, then the sharp pain stopped her. "Ow, everything hurts."

The man pried the damp cloth from her hand and pressed it against the back of her head. "I don't feel any broken bones, but you've got a nice sized lump right here. I reckon you have a nasty headache. Just what were you doing on that mare this hour of night?"

"I wasn't on a horse," she said. "I've never been on a horse in my life. It was a car crash. I hit a tree when that truck slid in front of me."

"A bad fall like that could have affected your mind, Mrs. O'Connell." The man eyed her. "You're not making a lick of sense."

"O'Connell? No. I think you've made a mistake, Doctor." She scrutinized him. "You *are* a doctor, aren't you?"

He grinned. "Now I know your mind has been affected. I'm Doc Matthews. We met two weeks ago when you first came to camp."

"I've never seen you before in my life."

Prickles of fear shot through her. When she made to rise, her legs tangled around mounds of material.

She stared down the length of her body. Was she wearing a long dress?

"Where am I?" Leaning on one arm, she glanced around and studied the walls of the spacious, white canvas tent. With the pain in her head making it difficult to see, she blinked to bring things into focus. Only then did she fully notice her surroundings. She lay on a canvas wood-frame cot while other, empty cots stood in rows along one wall of the tent. A long, wooden table with spindle-back chairs occupied the opposite corner. An oil lantern on the table illuminated the interior. Assorted corked bottles of colored glass, in various sizes and shapes sat beside—what looked like—antique medical instruments. Had she stumbled into some kind of reenactment? A friend of hers from the paper had been into Civil War reenacting. She'd visited his camp, and it had looked like this.

Cradling her aching head between her hands, she blinked, squeezing out tears that obscured her vision. On the edge of the table sat a pile of cream-colored ceramic plates, bowls, a few teacups, two pitchers, and an assortment of wood-handled utensils.

"Where am I?" she repeated. She struggled to untangle her feet from the skirts and reach the floor. She gasped. Not only did she wear a dress, but her white sneakers had been replaced with black leather lace-up boots. "Why am I dressed like this? Where are my clothes?"

A long strand of red-gold hair flowed over her shoulder. She reached up and realized it was attached to her head. The close-cropped style she normally wore was gone. Her fingers brushed over long, loose strands tumbling over the nape of her neck. She pulled out hairpins stuck in the thick, tangled mass.

Alarmed, she pushed herself to her feet. The momentum caused her to sway, and a bout of nausea made her stomach churn.

Doc reached out to steady her. "Whoa there,

ma'am. Don't go running off so all-fired fast." He pressed her back into a seated position on the cot.

Through the haze of pain, something clicked in her memory. "Did you call me Mrs. O'Connell? My name is Erin...Erin Branigan."

The doctor frowned. "Your Christian name is Erin, but your married name is O'Connell. Could Branigan be your maiden name? Hitting your head could've caused a lapse in your memory."

"There's nothing wrong with my memory. I'm Erin Branigan. I've never been married. I was in a car accident on my way home."

"Railcar? That don't make a lick of sense. Far as I heard, you never left camp."

"No—I mean—I don't understand any of this." A knot formed in her stomach.

"The blow to the head has affected your memory. Just rest a spell, and everything will come back to you."

"I don't know who the hell you think I am. I just want to know where I am and how the *hell* I got here. I have to get back home."

The man backed up a step and raised his hands, palms out. "Calm down, ma'am. There's no cause for cussing. And what happened to your brogue?"

"My what?"

"Your choice of words is odd, too. I'm having a hard time catching your meaning."

Is this guy for real? He obviously understands English.

But another thought sent a chill down her spine. What had happened to her car? It could still be back on the road, or already been towed. The vehicle would be traced to her, and her mother would be notified as next of kin. Her mom would be frantic when the police can't locate her.

Her cell phone must still be in the car, along with the rest of her belongings. But where were her clothes?

"Listen, Mr.—ah—Doc," she said. "I need to make a phone call. My mother will be worried sick. I guess I should call the local police, too."

His brow furrowed. "I thought you said your mother lived in Ireland. And what in tarnation is a phone call?"

She sighed in exasperation. "Don't you have a cell phone?"

A blank expression took over his face.

"I've heard you re-enactors can be strict, but there must be a pay phone somewhere around here."

He shook his head. "You should rest, ma'am. I'll mix up a headache powder for you. You'll feel a mite better once you get some sleep." After lifting her ankles onto the cot, he pushed against her shoulders, forcing her to lie down.

As he walked away, she glared at him. No way could he force her to stay.

While he occupied himself with the colored bottles on the table, she rose and steadied herself as a wave of pain coursed through her. Her head spun, and she nearly plopped back down. But sheer determination pushed her forward. Edging toward the open tent flap, she peered outside. Until her vision refocused, everything appeared fuzzy.

Where the hell am I?

After glancing back to be sure he wouldn't try to stop her, she eased through the canvas flaps. Rows of different sized tents surrounded her in the rosy glow of dawn. A large tarp overhead shielded the tent's entryway. Two black cast iron grates sat a few feet beyond the tarp. Burnt logs nestled among cinders sent wafts of white smoke into the air, while cast iron skillets and pans sat atop one of the grates. The scent of wood smoke reminded her of nights spent beside a cozy fireplace at her grandmother's house in Candor.

Tents were lined up in a partially cleared area with a few trees standing among them. A handful of men dressed like Doc, in loose shirts and gray or tan trousers held up with suspenders, milled about. This had to be a reenactment. If one of them could drive her back to her car...but on second thought, the car would be in no condition to drive. She had to get hold of her mother.

One man with straight, copper-colored hair touching his collar and a full beard crouched over a grate where flames crackled. The contents of his pan sizzled. The smell of bacon sent a wave of nausea through her. She doubled over, afraid she might retch.

"Ma'am," someone called, startling her. "I'm mighty pleased to see you're up."

She turned in the direction of the deep voice. *Am I dreaming?* She licked her dry lips as she stared into the dark eyes that had haunted her dreams.

"Ma'am? You look a might peaked."

As he moved closer, her knees turned to jelly. Strong, hard-muscled arms embraced her, offering support. Her head spun. She lifted a hand to stop the motion and encountered wool, a double row of metal buttons and a rock-hard chest. The enticing aroma of sandalwood mixed with a musky, masculine scent, plus a tinge of wood smoke invaded her senses. Had she hit her head harder than she'd thought?

She gazed at his lightly tanned face. Firm lips tilted upward slightly at the corners surrounded by a thin chocolate-colored mustache curving into a neatly-trimmed beard covering only his chin. Thick, dark hair brushed his collar and curled from beneath a broad-brimmed black hat. Her pulse raced as she leaned against his long, solid frame. Night after night in her dreams she'd run her hands through those curls.

"How can you be here?" she murmured.

"Pardon me, ma'am?"

"I don't understand." She tried to wrench from his grasp, but he gathered her close, lifting her into his arms. "What are you doing?"

"Taking you back where you belong." He carried her to the tent entrance where Doc peered out.

"Will, what the devil is going on?"

"I assume you didn't give Mrs. O'Connell permission to leave."

"I did not." He scowled. "I told you to rest."

The dark-haired man carried her inside and laid her on the cot. She propped herself on an elbow to get a better view of the man Doc called Will. Broad shoulders tapered into a narrow waist accentuated by the cut of his gray frock coat trimmed in gold braid.

"Who the hell *are* you?" she asked.

"Pardon me, ma'am?"

His gaze chilled her blood. He looked exactly like the man in the antique photo she'd found between the pages of her grandmother's Bible. If he were the man in the photo, where was she? Maybe the crash had killed her, and she was now in the afterlife. And like the man who called himself Doc, this man had *also* called her Mrs. O'Connell. Grandma Rose's great-aunt. Something wasn't right.

Unable to voice her fears, she stared open-mouthed at the man.

"Will," Doc said. "I think Mrs. O'Connell's having trouble with her memory."

"Her memory?"

"The fall from the horse," Doc explained, "seems to have affected her memory—even her speech. Her nose was bleeding a bit, and she has a fair-sized lump on the back of her head."

Will frowned.

Erin's mind reeled. This couldn't be the same man she'd researched.

The men looked at her, waiting for a response.

"How many times do I have to tell you?" she said. "I was never on a horse." She squeezed her eyes shut as the pain increased, then blinked furiously so she could focus.

Doc glanced at Will as if to confirm his diagnosis, then pressed a cool, damp towel against her forehead.

"Ma'am." Will removed his hat. "I would advise you to stay put until Doc says you can go back to your tent."

"I don't have a tent," she grated between clenched teeth.

The men exchanged glances.

"It's worse than I thought," Doc said.

"You say the fall affected her speech?" Will scowled.

"There's no other way to explain it."

"What's wrong with the way I talk?" she asked.

"You've lost your lilting brogue, for one thing," Will said, "unless that was an act."

She stretched out on the cot, as her stomach lurched again. "Look. All I want to do is go home."

"*This* is your home," Will said, "since you signed on as camp laundress two weeks ago. Or have you forgotten that, too?"

"No, you don't understand—"

"Are you having second thoughts, Mrs. O'Connell?"

"I told you, I'm not—" She froze in mid-sentence. They would never believe she wasn't Erin O'Connell.

Despite the pain slicing through her head, she slowly sat up. "I need a mirror."

Doc glanced at Will.

"A mirror!" she repeated. Her heart hammered in overdrive, and her head felt ready to explode. Doc rummaged among the contents on the table, producing a small, wood-framed hand mirror.

Blinking back the blinding pain, she stared at her reflection. Her own eyes stared back, wide and bright blue. The face was hers, yet it wasn't. The cheeks were a bit rounder. Her skin was pale. No make-up. Red-gold hair tumbled over her shoulders.

Touching her neck, she noted the maroon-checked dress she wore was topped with a starched, white collar stained with blood. She fingered a small, ivory-stoned brooch at her throat.

In the photo, her Civil War relative had worn her hair parted in the center and pulled back off her face, but otherwise, she was looking at a live portrait of her great-great-great-aunt. Erin O'Connell – Federal spy.

Chapter Three

Jake Wagner straddled his camp stool then lowered himself, perching a tin plate of bacon and runny eggs on his knees. His mug of chicory coffee sat at his feet. As he raised his fork to dig in, Charlie Ross lumbered up beside him, settling his bulky frame on a stool across from Jake.

"Smells mighty good." Charlie licked his lips and grinned, exposing a row of large, brown teeth nearly hidden in his long, wiry beard.

Jake glanced sidelong at the big man whose thick, black hair stood out in disarray under his wide-brimmed, black felt hat. "And it's all mine." He waved his fork over the food. "It's the last of my meat ration for the week."

Charlie chuckled. "I'm not here to beg. Jest wanted to sit for a spell and commune."

After stabbing his fork into his eggs, Jake shoved them into his mouth and chewed in earnest. Smoke from his fire pit drifted along the row of tents toward the wooded area that fringed camp. His gaze lifted to the couple picking their way around smoking grates.

Erin O'Connell clasped the arm of Captain Montgomery. He covered her small hand with his as she nodded at something he said. Jake scowled.

Following his gaze, Charlie said, "Reckon you best keep watch on that sweetheart of yours. Montgomery outranks you, and the ladies all say he's mighty handsome."

"She's not my sweetheart. That Irish woman's nothing but a whore."

The big man guffawed. "You've no cause to be

15

jealous, then."

"Jealous? Why in tarnation would I be jealous?"

"She *is* mighty pretty. And willing—so you say? How much does she cost?"

Jake squinted at the couple's backs as they angled toward the laundress' tent.

"I don't pay her nuthin'," he grumbled.

"She gives it away for free?" Charlie's eyes widened.

"Not to the likes of you." Jake glared at Erin's retreating back. In truth, the woman hadn't allowed him to as much as touch her. She'd just made vague promises of things to come. But he wasn't about to admit that.

He lifted his cup and gulped the brew that passed for coffee. Since the Yankee blockade, decent coffee no longer existed in the South.

"Did you hear the ruckus last night?" Charlie pulled out a cigar, unwrapped it, and then struck a match against the heel of his brogan.

"Ruckus?"

Charlie lit the cigar, then took a puff before answering. "Dead drunk again, were you?"

Jake tried to recall where he'd been last night. He did remember waking up with an empty bottle of whiskey in his bedroll.

Charlie nodded. "I wager you finished off that bottle you wuz carryin' around. That's why you didn't hear nuthin'."

Jake rolled his eyes. "Just tell me what the hell happened."

"That Irish washer woman fell off her horse in the dead of night. Woke up half the camp."

He frowned. Erin was on a horse? Had she been going out to meet her Federal contact?

"What happened to her?"

"She done blacked out. Captain Montgomery took her to the hospital tent. Reckon Doc fixed her up."

Jake inclined his head. Captain Montgomery and Erin O'Connell. An unlikely pair if he ever saw one. He'd have to scrounge up some laundry for washing today so he could find out what the hell was going on.

****

After being deposited in what Captain Montgomery had said was her tent, Erin glanced at the interior of the A-shaped canvas structure. A cot with a thin, lumpy mattress topped with coarse, wool blankets and a worn patchwork quilt occupied a small space. In one corner of the tent, a small wooden table stood and held a wood-framed hand mirror, comb, brush, and hairpins. A heavy, gray cloak and cloth bonnet dangled from a peg screwed into the post supporting the tent. Looking homemade, a small, braided rug covered straw spread over the dirt floor. *Home sweet home.*

Thinking back to the captain, she recalled his hard, muscular arm beneath the sleeve of his coat and shivered. Doc had called him Will. He had taken her hand and threaded it through the crook of his elbow as he'd escorted her to this tent. While they moved through the row of tents, Captain Montgomery took care to keep her skirts from brushing against smoking fires that rose from shallow dug-out pits along the way. He'd also sternly warned her to stay off horses. As if she'd even consider climbing onto one.

Moving closer to the cot, her booted foot hit something hard beneath it and pulled her thoughts from the image and sandalwood and leather scent of Will Montgomery. Crouching, she found a ceramic, lidded pot and a large, brown trunk beneath the bed.

"There should be something here to help me make sense of this," she muttered. She gazed at the pole running across the top of the tent. "How the hell did this happen? Grandma Rose, are *you* responsible for sending me here?"

Erin recalled the day Grandma Rose had died.

She'd entered the bedroom and found her grandmother sleeping. Not wanting to disturb her, she eased herself out of the room, until a whispery voice called her back.

"Erin—child—is that you?"

"Yes, Grandma, it's me." She stepped back to the bed and took the old woman's frail hand. Cool, dry skin covered her grandmother's fragile bones.

"There's something I must show you," Grandma Rose said.

With a trembling hand, her grandmother pointed to a tin box resting on the bedside table.

Erin opened the box and lifted out the silver-framed brooch containing dark woven hair and a photo of Erin O'Connell. She gasped as she'd stared at the old photograph. Except for the woman's hair parted in the center with a knot in the back and plumper cheeks, the woman could have been her.

Erin sank to the lumpy cot in her tent and raised a hand to her face. How had this happened? Everything was too real to be a dream. If only she could talk to Grandma Rose again. She'd always suspected Grandma was a mystic, although Mom had scoffed at such things.

When Erin had been a child, Grandma told her she was a descendent of practitioners of a mysterious Celtic sect. But her mother had been far too pragmatic to entertain the old woman's stories of the supernatural, telling Erin her grandmother liked to spin fanciful tales.

Now, she wondered, could Grandma have some kind of influence on events beyond the grave? Maybe the trunk would shed light on the situation.

Kneeling, she pulled the heavy chest out and opened it. A blue patterned dress sat neatly folded on top. She lifted it out and rifled through the other contents—long cotton slips with wide ruffles at the hem, a few aprons, a thick green and blue plaid shawl, and a corset. She held the white cotton garment, decorated with pale blue ribbons, and stretched it out before her.

"All right, Grandma, just what did you get me into?"

She laid the corset on the cot, then resumed her search. She pulled out several pairs of white cotton stockings, three white cotton, capped-sleeved shifts that looked like nightgowns, and two pairs of long, flat, stretchy white bands. *What the hell are these?* At the bottom of the trunk, her fingers brushed against something hard. Pulling the object from beneath mounds of clothing, she gasped in delight at the sight of a hardback book. Her fingers skimmed over the plain, deep blue leather cover. After opening it, she noted ragged edges where the first few pages had been torn out. The remaining pages had been penned with small, neat, cursive handwriting. Her hands stilled as she studied the script. The penmanship looked familiar. She could almost believe she'd written this, although she'd never before seen this journal.

Her heart thudded, and she tried to focus on the words.

"Hello, Miss Erin?"

Startled, she shut the book and shoved it back under the cot.

"Are you there?" A female voice with an Irish brogue preceded a round, cheerful face, peering into the tent. "Sorry to disturb you, but Doc told me you'd be needing help."

Erin closed the trunk and pushed it under the bunk to hide the book. She'd have to read it later when she had some privacy. She stood and pulled back the tent flap. A small, plump woman with light brown hair covered with a white cap resembling a handkerchief beamed at her.

"Help with what?" Erin frowned.

The woman brushed her hand over her apron. "Doc told me you had a bad fall last night and lost yer memory."

"Oh—ah—yes, I can't remember a thing." She eyed the woman, who nodded. "And you are?"

"I'm Brigid Malone. Me husband's Sergeant Thomas Malone. I do a great deal of the cooking in camp."

Erin glanced at the table and large wooden tub set up under the tarp outside her tent. "And what do I do?"

Brigid gasped. "You poor dear. Why, yer one of the camp laundresses." She clucked her tongue. "Then 'tis true. You really cannot recall a thing."

Erin shook her head, figuring she should just play along.

"Well, then, I'll help you start yer fire. We'll brew some tea and cook breakfast—then we'll boil the water for the laundry."

Erin nodded. She *was* hungry. And another thought—bathroom facilities.

Brigid helped her locate her chamber pot and the paper put aside to use with it. She also showed her where to empty it. Erin recalled camping a few times when she'd been a teen, but most of those campgrounds had flush toilets. Except for one time they had to use an outhouse. She shuddered at the memory. This was even worse. She had to go in a pot and clean up the best she could with no running water. And the paper provided was coarse and scratchy.

How in the hell was she supposed to live like this? She wanted to go back to her city apartment, her job, her friends. This sucked!

Before she left, Brigid stoked the fire pit with kindling and helped Erin locate her box of matches.

Later, she sat under her tarp, chewing on the hoecakes the Irishwoman had helped her cook. The hot food fortified her body but did nothing for her spirits. Seeing no way out of this mess, she had to use her wits to stay on top of things.

If she really *was* in the past, and after seeing Captain Montgomery she had no doubt of that, could there be a way to return home? Had the car accident brought her here, or had it been the brooch? As she recalled the ominous vibration, a chill went through her. Where *was* the brooch? *Think, Erin, think.* At the time of the accident, the jewelry had been pinned to her blazer. But she didn't have her blazer. That meant the brooch was still in the future.

Grandma, I need you. Her eyes stung with unshed tears, and a lump rose in her throat. She seldom cried but was on the verge now. She didn't want to be here. She wanted to go home.

Chapter Four

When Captain Montgomery had escorted Erin O'Connell to her tent early in the morning, Jake took notice. But more important than that, he must confront her about where she had planned on going last night.

After getting her the position of camp laundress two weeks before, he'd been feeding her information about officers and plans for troop movements. Although he'd joined the Confederate Army the second year of the war, he felt no allegiance to the State of Virginia or "The Cause." After his pa had kicked him out, an Army recruiter convinced him army life would be a way to earn pay and keep a roof over his head—although that roof was made of canvas. He didn't care. Memories of the leaky roof of the shack he'd grown up in outside Mason assured him he'd made the right decision.

His mother had run off when he was three, leaving his pa with four boys to raise alone. And Pa's way of dealing with boys was to use his fists or any other implement he could lay his hands on to beat some sense into his disobedient offspring.

Yes, his present life suited him fine, as long as he could escape being hit by Yankee bullets. And he had found a way to make it better when he befriended the man who'd been in camp two months before posing as a photographer but who was actually a Federal spy. That Yankee had promised him money and other benefits if he simply appointed Erin O'Connell to the position of laundress.

Once he agreed, Jake was rewarded with the

excitement of espionage and the promise of sampling the Irish woman's charms. All he had to do was supply military information she could send to her Yankee contacts.

He struck a match against the heel of his brogan and lit a hand-rolled cheroot. The day had passed quickly, and he still hadn't had the chance to talk to her. First, that busybody Brigid Malone had shown up. Then he'd been assigned duties that took up the rest of the day. He'd just completed his last assignment for today, assigning men for picket.

The overcast sky and the lateness of the hour cast the camp into near darkness. The tip of his cheroot glowed red, the only illumination around. Everyone must be asleep, including the laundress.

He hesitated for a moment, then eased his way to her tent. He'd find out what the hell she was up to. He had every right, since they were in this together. If caught helping her, he'd be shot as a traitor.

Glancing around to be sure no one saw him, he crept around her tent. He ground his cheroot under his boot and ran his hand along the canvas until he found the slit. Feeling along the edge, he felt the ties that held the tent closed and fastened from the inside. He inserted his fingers and worked the knot until it came loose, then untied the other strips above and below it to lengthen the opening.

Jake allowed his vision to adjust before edging forward in the dark interior. He banged up against the edge of a table and stifled a curse.

The cot creaked, as a body shifted.

Jake froze, holding his breath, then slid a hand against smooth wax in the shape of a long tallow candle set in a metal stand. Pulling out a match, he struck it and held it to the wick. A soft glow illuminated the interior.

A form lay on the cot beneath a worn patchwork quilt. At the top of the cot, a shock of red-gold hair cascaded over the covers. He bit his lip, itching to run his fingers through the loose, silken strands.

She moaned and turned over, her face exposed. He focused on her mouth, wondering how those generous lips would taste. The woman was no virgin. She'd told him she'd been married. Mr. O'Connell had died of scarlet fever before the war started, leaving his wife of two months, newly arrived from Ireland, in dire straits.

He knelt before the cot and leaned toward her lips. Her sweet scent intoxicated him as his mouth came within a breath of hers.

Her eyes opened wide. She inhaled sharply, then let out an ear-splitting shriek. Afraid she'd wake others, he grabbed her shoulders and pressed his lips to hers. She fought like a wildcat—the way he liked it. He took his fill of her honey-sweet mouth before she pushed him away.

Gaping at him, her blue eyes wide, she said, "Who *are* you? And what the *hell* are you doing here?"

****

Heart hammering, Erin stared at the man who held her pinned to the cot. At first, she'd thought he was trying to smother her. Once she realized his mouth was pressed against hers, outrage overtook fear. Even after she'd pushed him off, the taste of tobacco and whiskey on his breath made her gag.

"I need to talk to you now. I couldn't allow you to scream." He grinned as if that explained everything.

She clutched the quilt to her chest, realizing she'd seen this man before. Long, dark lashes shaded his pale eyes and copper-colored brows. A memory surfaced of a soldier sitting near an open fire.

"I saw you yesterday."

"And I saw you," he said, "being escorted by the *captain*." He nearly spat the word. "And then I hear tell of the goings-on last night."

She stared at him. "Do I know you?"

After a brief hesitation, he asked, "What kind of game are you playing now, woman? What in tarnation happened to your brogue, or was that part of your spy cover?" His fingers bit into her shoulders.

"Ow!" She wriggled, trying to free herself. Who the hell did he think he was? "Let me go."

He lifted his hands from her and stood.

Gathering the quilt, she rose to a seated position. She needed time to think—to clear her head. And she needed this man out of here.

"If you must know," she said, "I don't remember anything about last night."

His ice-blue gaze narrowed. "Were you drunk?"

"I don't drink."

"The hell you don't." He rolled his eyes.

She ignored his statement. "When I fell, Doc thinks I lost my memory."

"About last night?"

"About everything."

He scowled. "Are you saying you don't know who I am?"

"No—I don't remember you." This guy was really starting to piss her off.

He shook a dirt-streaked finger at her. "If you're lying..."

"I'm telling you the truth. I don't even know who I am." She wrapped the quilt around her and rose to face him. He stood only a few inches taller than she—not as tall as Captain Montgomery. Why had she made *that* comparison? The idea of having the captain in her tent, instead of *this* bastard, sent a thrill through her.

"I don't understand this at all," he complained. "You don't sound like yourself."

"I think you should leave, now." Erin glared into his ice-cold eyes. Her pulse raced, and she found breathing difficult. What would she do if he said no?

"I'll leave. But you best take care what you say to the captain." He pushed open the tent flap and

25

disappeared into the night.

She stood a moment longer, trying to control her breathing then sank back onto the cot. She watched the open flap, half expecting him to return. Sighing, she pushed back her newly acquired mass of hair. This was all too real. Somehow, she now occupied Erin O'Connell's body. If she only knew what had happened to her own body back in the future. She could be dead. Or lying in a hospital in a deep coma. And how was she supposed to get back after she did whatever she was expected to do?

A scene from the movie, *Back to the Future*, flashed through her mind. Things she did here could have an effect on her own or her family's future.

Her gaze rose to the open tent flap. A light breeze waved the canvas back and forth. She rose and poked her head outside. The man had disappeared. She tied the flaps back together, then paced the confined interior.

Who was he to Erin O'Connell? She didn't even know his name. But he knew her. She wiped the edge of the quilt across her mouth to erase his rancid taste. She didn't know if she'd get any more sleep tonight. She just hoped to God he didn't come back.

Chapter Five

"Miss Erin?"

Erin groaned as the lilting voice pierced through her dream. Or had it been a nightmare? She'd dreamt she was lost in a forest. Men with rifles chased her...

She rolled over and slid off the narrow bunk. "What the hell?"

"Miss Erin?"

She glanced in the direction of the voice. Light slivered through the opening in the canvas. "Oh, no," she groaned. "I'm still here." She dragged her aching body from the rug covering the dirt floor. Remembering she only wore a loose cotton chemise, she grabbed the tattered quilt from the floor and wrapped it around her shoulders before unlacing the ties that held the tent closed.

When she peered out, Brigid's round face greeted her.

"I heard a crash," the Irish cook said. "Are you all right?"

"Oh...ah...I fell off my bunk."

Brigid blinked. She hesitated a moment before saying, "Doc asked me to look in on you to see if yer recollection had come back a'tall."

Erin shook her head. Since she seemed to be stuck in this God forsaken time, the loss of memory story would be her only salvation.

"You'll be needing help setting up the laundry, then?"

She nodded. "Ah...yeah." Brigid had told her she was a laundress. She wondered what doing laundry in this century entailed as she eased out of the tent

27

opening.

The Irish woman's gaze dropped. Her face reddened when she stared at Erin's bare feet. "You'll be wanting to dress before you come out of there. You don't want the men in camp to be seeing too much."

"Oh." Erin backed up. "I guess I'll put something on then."

Brigid smiled. "I'll bring you some kindling for yer fire while yer dressing."

"Okay," Erin called. She studied the dress and petticoats she'd discarded the night before. A fine sheen of dirt covered the clothing. She wanted something clean to put on. Jeans and a tee shirt were what she preferred, but she doubted she'd find those items here.

Sighing, she reached under the bunk and brought out the trunk. She'd hoped the past day and a half had been a bad dream. But, somehow, she was still here. Well, she could do nothing but get dressed. She needed to uncover more information to discover a way to get back to where she belonged.

She pulled out a brown calico dress with a starched white collar. Beneath it were two cotton petticoats. How many was she supposed to wear? When undressing last night, she'd found she'd been wearing three. She eyed the white, boned corset. No way was she putting that on.

By the time she slipped into one of the petticoats, tied it at her waist and settled the dress over her head, Brigid had returned. Erin slid on a pair of stockings, tied on a pair of those flat, stretchy things she'd discovered were garters when she'd undressed last night, and stepped into and laced up her shoes. She lifted the tent flap to find the Irish cook crouched before the fire pit, adding bits of kindling.

"Do you recall where you left yer matches?"

"Ah, yes, I think so." Erin wasn't sure where she'd tossed the matches after Brigid had helped her locate them on the table in her tent yesterday, but she managed to find the container on the table amid a pile of clothing.

Reaching into the box, Brigid removed a thin wooden match. She struck it against the log she'd placed in the fire pit yesterday. After the kindling caught, she rose and wiped her plump hands against her apron. "I'll fetch me teapot and a few biscuits I saved from last night's meal. We'll have a bite to eat before we head down to the stream."

"The stream?"

"To fetch the water for washing," Brigid said.

"Oh, sure." Erin shrugged. She didn't like the sound of that. *This totally sucks! Just how far away is this stream, and how much water do we have to carry?* She watched the cook scurry to her tent.

She eyed two tin buckets sitting upside down alongside her tent. They'd need more than that to fill the large wood laundry tub.

Once Brigid returned and they'd eaten, she instructed Erin to bring along the buckets by the tent and produced two more. Erin followed her down to the stream, where they filled the containers before lugging them up the slope. After they poured the water into a large copper pot hanging from a cast iron rail over the fire, the Irishwoman brought out a large bar of lye soap from a wood box set beside Erin's tent. While the water heated, soldiers arrived bearing soiled shirts.

Erin rubbed her aching arms. She anticipated a long, hard day ahead of her and wished there was a way she could transport a modern washing machine from the twenty-first century.

****

Will ducked into his tent and sifted through the folded, crumpled papers he'd found yesterday after he'd escorted Mrs. O'Connell to her tent. The pages had obviously been torn from a journal. The writer had penned a list of recent and future Confederate troop movements. He studied the small, neat handwriting looking for any clue as to the writer's identity. They likely had a spy or traitor amongst them.

Mrs. O'Connell had only been here two weeks. Sergeant Wagner had appointed her laundress, claiming she was a recently widowed relative who desperately needed the money. He'd noted Wagner's comings and goings to her tent at all hours and wondered about their relationship. But he hadn't given a thought to them being involved in espionage. The sergeant could be a trial at times—insubordinate and late for roll call. He'd been caught drinking while on picket duty. And he'd had his share of punishment.

Wagner wasn't much different from many of the men. They'd left their homes to defend the rights of Virginia to govern itself and not be dictated to from Washington. But camp life wasn't an easy way to live, and the time between battle engagements could be endless. Men sought diversions any way they could.

Will folded the papers and stuffed them into his leather haversack. He'd turn the pages in to the colonel. But without proof, did he want to cast suspicion on Mrs. O'Connell and the sergeant? He wouldn't voice his doubts to the colonel, but he'd keep an eye on them. If they had anything to do with the papers, maybe they'd trip up, and he'd catch them.

A loud, male voice outside drew Will from his tent.

"I told you, woman, I want what I was promised. You won't put me off again."

He glanced a few yards down the row of military tents toward the laundress' tent. Wagner held Mrs. O'Connell's forearms.

"Let go!" She struggled against the sergeant's grip.

Will's jaw tightened when he strode down the path to face the couple. "Is there a problem here, Sergeant?"

Wagner released Mrs. O'Connell. "She owes me money, sir."

The woman glared at Wagner.

"I'm sure you'll get your money when Mrs. O'Connell gets paid," Will reassured.

"But sir—"

"She wasn't able to work yesterday due to her injuries. You should be a bit more understanding of your own relation."

Wagner dropped his gaze. "Yes, sir."

"Dismissed, Sergeant."

Wagner saluted and stalked off without looking back.

Mrs. O'Connell hadn't moved or spoken during the exchange. Will's gaze drifted over her. She wore a bib apron pinned to her worn, calico workdress. Her hair was now arranged in her usual bun.

"Are you all right, ma'am?" She seemed fragile. He longed to put his arms around her and reassure her.

She brushed her hands over her apron. "I'm fine."

"If he hurt you," he continued, "I'll see that he's punished."

She glanced in the direction Wagner had taken and scowled. "I can handle him."

He doubted that. He'd seen Wagner drunk and knew how mean he could get. "If you don't mind my asking, ma'am, how are the two of you related?"

Her mouth dropped open. He didn't consider it an unusual question, since a sergeant normally appointed his wife, or one of his other relatives as laundress and took a cut of her pay.

"He's a cousin," was all she said.

"Well, cousin or no, if he bothers you again, you come to me."

She smiled. Her teeth were small, even and white, surrounded by lush, pink lips. He wondered what it would be like to kiss her. He had a hard time drawing his gaze from her mouth.

Whoa, I don't know anything about this woman. Getting involved with her will likely bring me nothing but trouble.

"Thank you," she said. "I'd better be getting back to the laundry."

Will tipped his cap. "Ma'am." He watched her return to the washtub. She rolled up her dress sleeves, exposing the ivory skin of her forearms.

He admonished himself as he turned away. *Don't get sweet on a camp laundress, especially one who could turn out to be a Yankee spy.*

****

After a meal of salt pork and corn the men had been permitted to pick from a local farm, Will spotted Wagner leaning against a wide oak tree at the edge of camp. The sergeant puffed on a cheroot.

Will watched him, and anger bubbled up inside. What hold did he have on Erin O'Connell? Maybe a talk with the man would shed light on their situation.

Wagner's eyes widened, then narrowed when Will approached. He tossed his cheroot to the grass and ground it out with the toe of his brogan.

"I'd like a word with you, Sergeant," Will said.

Wagner straightened. "Sir?"

"Mrs. O'Connell has not been herself since she fell off the horse."

"Ah..." Wagner hesitated. "She does seem to be having a hard time recollecting things."

"Perhaps if she were to return home, a familiar setting might jar her memory."

Wagner glanced away. "She don't have a home to go to. That's why she's here."

"But surely, your family—"

"My family?" The sergeant shook his head. "I have no family I care to associate with." He raised his gaze to Will. "She has nowhere else to go, sir."

The bleakness of Wagner's statement caused Will's chest to tighten. Mrs. O'Connell had no one but this man?

He dismissed the sergeant but noted the intense glare in the man's eyes as he turned to go. He was dangerous. Will didn't know Mrs. O'Connell's true relationship with Wagner, but he was damned if he'd allow him to hurt her again.

Chapter Six

Erin arrived at the medical tent that evening cradling a peach pie Brigid helped her make that afternoon after she'd hung laundry to dry. Doing anything in this century took so much time and effort; she was amazed these people had any leisure time at all. When Doc dropped by to invite her to share his evening meal, she couldn't resist the opportunity, hoping she could pump him for more information about Erin O'Connell's past. Brigid didn't know anything about her, other than she was a widow.

After reading the journal entries, she learned Erin O'Connell had tolerated Wagner for the information he provided. But a later entry revealed that her Civil War relative had been more than a bit attracted to Captain Montgomery, although he showed no indication of reciprocating her feelings. She suspected the woman had a secret crush on him.

And she couldn't blame her. That afternoon, when he'd come to her rescue, she'd forced herself to breathe after having been literally swept off her feet three days before into his strong arms.

In her dreams, she'd had a romantic relationship with the handsome captain. Maybe the dreams were some kind of psychic connection to Erin O'Connell's spirit, and she'd been experiencing her relative's life.

Hopefully, Doc could help her learn who she was supposed to be in this century, so she'd at least have a clue how to act. She could hardly tell anyone she'd come from the future. They'd lock her up in the insane asylum.

The savory smell of chicken stew wafted from the

cast iron pot hanging above the fire pit by Doc's tent. He leaned over and stirred the contents with a long-handled wooden spoon, straightening his long, thin frame when she approached. He wore a voluminous, long-sleeved cotton shirt covered with a gray wool vest and appeared overdressed for this humid, summer night.

Erin held out the pie. "I promised dessert."

He nodded. "Apple?"

"No, peach."

He raised his eyebrows in approval. "I've got a loaf of bread on the table. Just set that down there, while I dish out the stew."

The table he indicated was small, covered with a blue checked tablecloth. Two wooden chairs sat on either side. He'd set places for two with metal pie tins, forks, spoons, knives, and mugs. A loaf of sourdough bread and small jar of strawberry preserves sat in the center. As Erin made a place for the pie, he approached with a ceramic bowl of stew. He divided it between the two pie tins, then set the bowl aside.

Doc pulled out one of the chairs for her. "I'll be right back." He brought a pitcher from his tent, then poured lemonade into her glass. When he poured his own drink, she lifted her glass and took a sip. Sour and a bit warm. She grimaced. He didn't seem to notice.

She studied the man as she ate. Brigid had told her the young doctor was married and expecting his first child. She started with polite conversation about his wife, Josephine, and his home in Richmond before she steered the conversation to herself.

By the time she cut into the pie, she'd learned she was an Irish immigrant, had been widowed before the war started, had no children, and Sergeant Wagner had appointed her laundress as a favor to the family.

After swallowing a bite of the pie, she said, "You wouldn't happen to know how Sergeant Wagner and I are related."

"He's a relative of your late husband's family."

"Oh." After reading the journal entries about Jake, she had to suppress a shudder. She didn't believe he was related to Erin O'Connell at all. And she knew exactly what he wanted from her.

If she inhabited Erin O'Connell's body, she was in a precarious position. The woman had been a Yankee spy, and she was in a Confederate camp. Jake was somehow involved in the espionage.

That snake had a hold on her.

****

After the meal, Doc escorted Erin to her tent. She genuinely liked the pleasant, gangly man. Although they'd just met, she felt comfortable with him, as if they were old friends. He'd even admitted that his Christian name was Jeremy, though everyone here called him Doc.

When she'd asked him to call her Erin, he'd seemed embarrassed but agreed to call her that when no one else was around. He'd beamed when he talked about his wife and the baby he looked forward to seeing.

After he left, she pulled back her tent flap but stopped when she caught movement out of the corner of her eye. She turned to glance behind her. Men milled about, talking and laughing. Then she saw Jake headed straight for her. She groaned inwardly.

Just what I need. Another confrontation with him. She had the urge to hide in the tent but knew he'd follow her. Not a good idea.

"Miss Erin." He removed his broad-brimmed hat. "I've been wanting to apologize for my behavior two nights ago."

She studied him. Just what was going on here?

"Go on," she prodded.

He smiled. She guessed the man was used to charming his way out of any situation. "Well, I thought we needed to speak...in private," he added.

She crossed her arms over her chest. "About what?"

His eyes widened. "Not out here. Someone might hear."

"And they won't in there?" She gestured toward the tent.

"Why are you being so damned ornery?"

"Because of what you tried to do two nights ago."

"Well, how was I to know you'd lost all recollection of me," he explained.

"So, sneaking into my tent is a regular thing with you?"

"You always appreciated my nightly visits before." His boyish grin turned into a leer.

After reading Erin O'Connell's journal, she doubted that. "I'm tired. I've been washing all day, and I need to get some rest." She reached for her tent flap, planning to enter the tent and shut him out.

"I'll rub your tired back...and anything else that needs rubbing."

"I don't think so." She pushed past him into the tent. When she turned to fasten the ties, he pushed his chest against her and forced his way inside. She opened her mouth to scream, but his callused palm silenced her.

"You got this post because of me, and I want what's due me." His voice, though quiet, held an ominous tone.

Her heart pounded furiously, as she considered the best way to get out of this situation. Agitating him could be a big mistake. She couldn't count on Captain Montgomery coming to the rescue again. He drew her to him, nuzzled her cheek, then kissed her throat. Fighting the urge to kick him in the groin, she stilled against him. Maybe she could pacify him, then steer him into a conversation that would reveal more about how they were involved.Hesitantly, he moved his hand from her mouth and stroked her cheek.

She forced herself to smile. "I'm sorry," she said. "I still can't remember much. You'll have to clue me in."

He took a step back and tilted his head as if trying to come to a decision. "That brogue you used to have was fake, wasn't it?" When she didn't answer, he continued, "Reckon you don't recollect who your Yankee contact is."

She shook her head. "I don't remember having a Yankee contact. Don't you know who he is?"

"No. I supply you with information. You're the only one who knows the contact. This isn't good." He bit his thumbnail. "What'll we do now?"

"Doc said my memory could come back in time," she said.

He scowled. "I'm taking a big risk by helping you. If I'm found out, they'll likely shoot me."

"Then why are you doing it?" she demanded.

"Great God Almighty! For the money. Why else would I stick my neck out?"

"What money?"

"The money your Yankee contact gives you for the information I supply." He threw up his hands.

She shrugged. "Oh, well, until I remember who this person is..."

"I've missed your company these past few nights, sweetheart." His grin widened, and his arms encircled her waist.

"Please," she said, "I've got a fearful headache. Can't we do this another time?"

He pulled back and scowled. "Tarnation, woman. What's wrong with you now?"

"Just give me a little time. I'll make it up to you. I promise." She traced her finger along his collar.

"When?"

"When my head feels better." Although she wanted to retch, she kept her tone light. "You know...the fall."

"That's another thing." His gaze bore into her. "Just where were you sneaking off to that night?"

"I can't remember."

He frowned. "All right. I'll give you time, but not too long, you hear?" He stroked her cheek.

She wanted to pull away, but nodded, relieved he bought her story. When he left, she wondered just how long she could hold him off.

Chapter Seven

Early the next day, Erin knelt over the washtub and arched her aching back. She glanced over at a well-dressed, dark-haired woman holding the hand of a little girl.

The child looked up at the woman. "Aunt Jenny, where's Papa?"

"We'll find him, Amanda," the woman said.

The young girl, who appeared to be four or five, caught Erin's attention. The child's large blue eyes and auburn hair, styled in two long braids hanging like thick ropes from beneath her calico bonnet, made her look like a doll.

Erin rose stiffly and carried an armload of wet shirts to a clothesline strung between two, wide oaks. She started to hang the shirts. The child pulled from the woman's grasp and raced toward Erin.

"Ma'am, could you help me find my papa?"

"Young lady, mind your manners!" the woman scolded.

Erin smiled. She wiped her hands on her brown, paisley apron, then crouched to meet the girl's height. "Hello, my name's Erin."

The child frowned. Twisting one of her braids, she said, "I'm Miss Amanda Montgomery."

"Montgomery?" Erin rose and scrutinized the well-dressed woman standing beside the girl. "Are you Captain Montgomery's wife?"

"No, I'm his sister, Miss Jenny Montgomery. This is his daughter."

Turning back to the child, Erin said, "Amanda's such a pretty name."

Amanda scrunched up her face. "What kind of name is Erin?"

"Amanda!" Jenny reprimanded.

"It's all right," Erin said. She crouched again to the girl's eye level. "It's an Irish name. It means *from Ireland*. I'm named after my great-great-great aunt." Rising, she glanced around. "Your mother didn't come with you?"

"My momma went to heaven," Amanda said.

Jenny shook her head.

"Papa!" Amanda called.

Looking up, Erin watched Captain Montgomery approach. His stern expression lightened into a broad smile when he caught sight of his daughter.

"Go see your papa," Jenny prompted the child.

When Amanda ran to her father, Jenny said her goodbyes to Erin and headed toward the row of tents where a group of young privates and corporals gathered around a man playing the harmonica. A lean, clean-shaven, dark-haired soldier engaged in a lively conversation with another private turned toward her.

As Jenny smiled and waved at the soldier, she boldly approached the knot of men and boys. The dark-haired private pushed his way through them to meet her and take her hand. As he led her away from the group, the other men snickered. Did the captain know about the young soldier and his sister?

Erin glanced toward Will. With animation, Amanda bounced in his arms. The sight of the child's exuberance and the tenderness the captain displayed toward her brought a smile to Erin's face.

****

By evening, Erin's arms ached, and her shoulders weren't much better. Hell, her entire body hurt in places she'd never felt before.

What I wouldn't give for a hot shower. All she had to look forward to was a sponge bath with the pot of water she'd set over the fire to heat and after that, sleep on a hard canvas cot.

She examined her hands, dismayed at how rough and red they were, her nails worn and ragged. But if her theory was correct, these weren't her hands. This wasn't her body.

Where *was* her body? Maybe she'd died in the crash and had already been buried. If that were true, she had no way to go back to her old life. And Mom had just lost her own mother. How was *she* dealing with this? If only she could let her mother know what had happened.

Maybe this was some form of Hell.

Despite what she'd already learned, she needed more information on Erin O'Connell. But she was in a Confederate camp. Finding information about a woman employed by the Federal government might be difficult. Those she'd asked in camp didn't seem to know the whole story. Even Jake hadn't revealed enough to help.

Damn. Why had this happened? She was a journalist. Now, she was reduced to doing laundry in a washtub. This wasn't fair. If this were a dream, at least she'd have the hope of waking up. But this wasn't a dream. For some unknown reason, she was stuck here.

Once the water had fully heated, she lifted the pot from the grate and entered her tent, where she had a pan, linen towel, and a bar of castile soap laid out.

After removing her dress, petticoats, and stockings, she pulled the chemise over her head. She loosened and dropped her drawers, then sponged herself off, allowing the warm, soapy water to refresh and soothe her. Gratefully, she inhaled the relaxing warmth, trying to ease her discomfort. But this was no substitute for the hot shower she craved. She didn't even like to go camping. And here she was trapped in a century that didn't have electricity or running water. Even a modern toilet would be welcome.

Instead of relaxing her, the sponge bath caused more agitation. She worked the linen washrag over her legs and grimaced at the hair covering her calves. Women didn't shave in this time period, yet when she'd undressed her first day here, she'd found the amount of hair on her underarms and legs alarming. Even knowing her clothing would hide the hair didn't content her. *She* knew it existed.

But she'd decided to resign herself since the only razor existing in this time period was the straight edge. She hated to think of what that would do to her skin. Plus, her leg hair wasn't coarse, it was fine and silky.

While she washed, she recalled her meeting with Captain Montgomery's sister. She'd known from her prior research he'd been a widower since just after the war started and he had a daughter, but the sight of the auburn-haired child had startled her. His stern expression had evaporated when he'd seen Amanda—definitely a doting father.

After drying herself, she slipped a clean cotton chemise over her head. She reached for the paisley, robe-like garment she'd found hanging in her tent, the one Brigid had called a wrapper. Before she could slide her arm into the sleeve, a shadow against the canvas startled her. She froze and stared at a man's silhouette. Too late, she realized she'd forgotten to tie up the flap.

Frantically, she scanned the interior for a weapon. She reached for the candleholder, but before she could grasp it, Jake pushed his way inside.

His face was flushed. She smelled whiskey on his breath. He waved a half-empty bottle in front of her. "Bring out your mugs," he slurred. He set the bottle on her table, tipping it so it fell and dripped amber liquid onto her rug.

Alarmed he'd appeared here again in this condition, she lifted her wrapper to shield herself when he retrieved the bottle. "I apologize, Miss Erin, for my clumsiness." He swayed before her, grinning.

Her heart thudded, and she tried to reason out what to do. She wouldn't put it past this bastard to force himself on her in his inebriated state. No matter what it took, she had to get him out of here *now*.

His eyes widened when he took in her state of undress. "I see you're all ready for me."

"No," she stated. "I'm going to sleep now."

"You promised me," he said harshly. "You'll give me what I want, woman." Grabbing her forearm, he tried to wrench the wrapper from her.

She pushed and knocked him off balance. She wasn't about to be pinned down by him, again. Rushing past him, she slid through the tent opening. He grabbed her by the wrist and tightened his grip when she tried to wrench free.

"What's going on here?"

Erin glanced up into Captain Montgomery's eyes as he sprinted to her side.

Straining, she tried to loosen Jake's grip. His arm was half-way out of the flap, hand still circled around her wrist. Montgomery grabbed Jake's hand and pried it from her arm. She moved aside, and he yanked the sergeant out.

Jake's mouth flew open when he saw who had hold of him.

"I told you to stay away from her, Wagner."

"But sir...she owes me."

"I don't care what she owes you. I don't want to catch you laying your filthy hands on the lady again. The next time I see you anywhere near her, I'll put you on report."

"Yes, sir." When the captain released his grip on Jake, he scurried off as fast as he could move without looking back.

Erin watched him go, then met the gaze of her rescuer. Only then did she realize she still wore her chemise and nothing else. She crossed her arms over her chest.

"Ma'am, I suggest you go inside. And I would advise you not to be inviting drunken men into your tent."

"I didn't invite him." Her face flushed at his accusation. "He forced his way in."

The captain looked her over, but said nothing.

Erin flung back her tent flap and slipped inside. She watched Will Montgomery's broad back as he strode away in the early twilight, wondering what kind of woman he thought she was.

Chapter Eight

The next morning after Erin dressed and prepared for another grueling day of washing laundry, Captain Montgomery surprised her with a visit.

Great. She noted the bundle in his arms. *He's bringing more dirty clothes for me to wash.* The sight of him dressed in a gray jacket that fell just below his lean hips, over tan trousers and a gray cap perched on his chocolate brown hair, made her breath catch. Her pulse raced as the reality before her converged with the dreams she'd had.

Had her subconscious mind known him? She'd never seen his photo until Grandma Rose had shown it to her. But she'd known him in her dreams. In the months before her impending wedding, the dreams had become more vivid and intimate. Even though this man was a stranger, she felt she'd known him all her life.

He removed his cap and stopped just outside the edge of the tarp she sat under. "Ma'am."

She nodded, for her vocal chords were too taut to speak.

"I wanted to apologize for invading your privacy last night." A blush crept up his lightly tanned cheeks. "I can't abide any man harming a woman, even if the two are related or even wed."

She gazed up into his dark eyes. Up close they were a deep, chocolate brown. He was so damned attractive in that uniform. Clearing her throat, she found her voice. "I appreciate what you did, Captain. That man's been harassing me."

"I suspected as much. Wagner doesn't seem to

know how to be respectful to a woman."

She had trouble finding the words to reply. The aroma of sandalwood and his unique masculine scent that had floored her when he'd carried her into Doc's tent left her flabbergasted.

"I'd warned Wagner to stay away from you," he said.

"He was so drunk, I don't think any warning would have stopped him."

"He didn't hurt you—"

She shook her head, noting the concern in his eyes. "All I could think to do was get out of the tent."

"That was wise, ma'am."

She glanced at the bundle he still held. "Are those for me?"

He grinned. "If you don't mind, ma'am. I have two shirts that need washing."

"My pleasure." When he handed her the clothes, their hands briefly touched. Electricity shot through her. She caught his gaze.

His eyes widened. He swallowed and backed away a few steps, then tipped his cap.

"Ma'am." He turned away.

She watched him cross the camp and disappear from sight. If a reason existed for her coming to this time period, it had to be Will Montgomery. But why had this happened? Would she ever go back to her old life, or was she stuck here forever?

Although she'd tried to hold her emotions in check, the tension that had been building for the last few days caused her eyes to burn at the prospect. A sob built at the back of her throat. She dropped the clothing she'd been sorting in the basket and scurried into the privacy of her tent.

****

When Will returned to his tent, he found one of his soiled shirts hanging on a stool outside.

May as well get this one washed, too. The thought

of seeing Mrs. O'Connell again so soon brought a smile to his face. He hadn't had any reason to smile for the past two years.

Amanda was the only bright spot in his life, now. But sometimes, she reminded him too much of her mother, Anne. One look at that cherubic face and the hurt would come back as strong as the day he'd lost his wife to pneumonia. After two years, guilt from not being with her when she passed still consumed him.

Since her death, he'd found the army to be pure escape, until the death of his younger brother. Living in the large house they'd shared with his parents and Jenny, as well as Amanda, made it impossible to move forward. The place was a daily reminder of all he'd lost.

Now, he found himself in danger of becoming attracted to a woman he hardly knew and was likely involved with another man. His loneliness had caused him to fall for the first, pretty face available. If he were smart, he'd keep his distance from the woman, but seeing her threatened proved too much to ignore.

He started back to her tent, steeling himself to keep his emotions in check. He only needed her laundering services and planned to deliver the shirt and leave.

Mrs. O'Connell wasn't outside her tent where he'd left her. Perhaps she'd gone inside or left on an errand. He hesitated, trying to decide what to do, but heard a stifled sound from inside the tent. He drew near the canvas and listened. The muffled sound of sniffles turned to sobs. It had to be Mrs. O'Connell. Should he intrude? He considered leaving the shirt outside, but the thought of her alone, crying her heart out, was too much for him. After a moment of hesitation, he pulled the tent flap and peered inside. Mrs. O'Connell sat on her bunk, her face buried in her apron.

"Ma'am?"

She glanced up and quickly wiped her flushed

face. "Yes?" Her voice cracked.

He eased his way into the tent. "I beg your pardon for the intrusion, but I heard you and feared Sergeant Wagner may have come back and hurt you."

She shook her head, then turned away as if embarrassed.

"I'm sorry...I didn't mean..." He lifted the soiled shirt he held. "I forgot this."

She turned toward him. "Just leave it..." Her face crumpled. More tears dropped from beneath reddened eyelids.

"Ma'am?" He set the shirt on her table and stepped to where she sat, reaching his hand out to rest on her slender shoulder. He felt an overwhelming need to protect this woman, but being here in her tent was highly improper. He'd be wise to take his leave. *Now.*

Her slim frame heaved beneath his hand. He couldn't leave her in this state. "Tell me how I can help you."

She shook her head. "No one can help me." Her lower lip quivered.

His heart twisted. He'd avoided women since Anne had died. He wouldn't allow himself to be hurt like that again. But the sight of this woman alone and in tears broke through his resolve. He dropped to one knee drawing one of her small hands into his.

Wrapping his other arm around her, he pulled her against his chest. She reached an arm around his back clutching him as if her life depended on it and sobbed into his shirt. He allowed her to cry a few minutes more. Her enticing scent and the feel of the soft feminine bosom pressed against him set his pulse racing.

He reached into his coat pocket and pulled out his handkerchief, handing it to her.

After she dabbed her eyes and blew her nose, she drew a deep breath and straightened her shoulders. "I'm sorry." She stood, extracting herself from his arms. "I don't even know you."

He rose to face her. "It was my pleasure, ma'am. I just wish you'd tell me what's wrong."

She smiled at him. "I suppose you'd fix my problem if you could." Saying nothing more, she bit her lower lip drawing his gaze to her generous mouth. Much time had passed since he'd felt a woman's kiss, other than the perfunctory kisses bestowed by his female relatives. Despite the urging of his brain to leave, he leaned toward her. His lips touched hers, tentatively at first, then when she didn't protest or pull away, he deepened the kiss and devoured her sweet taste. She tasted of apples and cinnamon mixed with salty tears. She'd likely been helping Mrs. Malone with the baking. His thumbs brushed the wetness from her cheeks.

Her arms circled his neck, pulling him closer. He sighed, relishing her womanly softness as she leaned against him. No. He couldn't do this. Not with her. He removed himself from her embrace. "Begging your pardon, ma'am. I shouldn't be here."

She frowned. Her lips parted, but she didn't speak.

"I'd best be going now." He stepped outside and left without looking back. What had he been thinking? This woman would bring him nothing but trouble.

Chapter Nine

A week later, after traveling north with the army, Erin unpacked her supplies and prepared for the onslaught of men with shirts in need of laundering. Every morning when she woke, she hoped she'd find herself in her city apartment in a soft bed complete with air conditioning, running water, a stocked refrigerator, and a microwave.

Since that hadn't happened, she had no choice but to come along with the troops, for she had nowhere else to go. Also, being in Pennsylvania, she now felt closer to home. Her only trepidation was they were now camped north of Gettysburg. The thought of being involved in a bloody battle over the next few days scared the shit out of her.

The trip had been grueling. She'd traveled in a wagon over bumpy, rural roads. When she couldn't take the jostling any more, she'd get out and walk. At least, the trip had given her a break from the constant laundering. She swore she'd grown new muscles she hadn't known she had, and her hands were cracked and sore.

On those occasions when out of sheer exhaustion she'd fallen asleep in the wagon, she dreamed of highways. Smooth, paved highways where she drove along at high speed on pneumatic rubber tires. A bump would jolt her out of her dream, and she'd find herself still in the nineteenth century. Then despair kicked in. Would she ever get back to her old life?

Captain Montgomery remained a big piece of the puzzle. Before Grandma Rose had died, she'd told Erin she would find her destiny in the past. But it hadn't made any sense, so she had chalked it up to an old woman's ramblings. But now that she was in the past, she realized what Grandma told her was important. Maybe she had to accomplish something to get back to her own time. But what?

Although Will Montgomery had been avoiding her, her heart still raced every time she caught a glimpse of him. After he'd kissed her, she knew without a doubt she'd come back in time for him. She brushed a finger over her lips as the memory of that kiss made her crave more.

Why did she have to fix things here? What connection did she and Will have?

Banishing her troubled thoughts, she put her tent in order with the help of a few women and young privates. She sat on a camp stool under the shade of her canvas tarp to take a breather. While she fanned herself, enjoying the light summer breeze, an elderly woman caught her attention. She must be a visitor from town.

The woman was small, almost birdlike, and well-dressed. She wore oval spectacles perched on her long nose and carried a black parasol trimmed in lace and a dainty crocheted bag that dangled from the waistband of her skirt.

Erin watched, too tired to move. The woman studied her, then approached. She opened her mouth, revealing a gaped-tooth smile.

"Can I help you?" Erin asked.

"I'm looking for Mrs. O'Connell." Her voice was high and thin.

"That's me."

The woman leaned in close. Erin caught the aroma of roses. "Your contact will meet you tonight."

"My what?"

"Shh." The woman glanced from side to side. "Someone might hear."

"Are you sure you've got the right person?" Erin

frowned.

"You *are* the laundress from Ireland?" She waited as Erin digested the question.

Her reporter's instincts kicked in. Erin O'Connell had been a Yankee spy. Best to play along and see what information she could obtain.

"Where am I to meet this person?"

The woman's brow furrowed. "You don't sound like you're from Ireland."

"I've done a lot of traveling."

Looking doubtful, the woman continued, "To the west of camp...just outside. You'll have to avoid being seen by the pickets."

Erin nodded as if all this was routine. "How will I know him?"

"He'll call you by the name *Robin*."

"All right."

"And you're to bring the book with you."

"Book?"

"We need any new information you've gathered," the woman stated matter-of-factly.

"I lost it," Erin lied, "on the trip north."

By the way the woman's eyebrows drew together, Erin feared she was in for a scolding. "You mustn't be so careless, dear, the Reb's wouldn't hesitate to send you to prison, or worse, if you're caught."

Erin nodded. "I'll be careful in the future, but what should I do for now?"

"I'll inform your contact. If he still wants to see you, he'll get a message to you."

Without another word, the woman hobbled off.

Erin's thoughts went to the journal still inside her trunk. Was that the book they wanted? Nothing of consequence in there would help the Yankees, and she wasn't sure she'd want to give it to them, anyway.

She was curious about who this contact was, but did she really want to get herself involved in espionage? The fear of being caught and locked up in a

Confederate prison was all the deterrent she needed. She had enough problems.

****

July 3, 1863

Will gazed across the field toward the rise called Cemetery Ridge. Yankee troops waited on the opposite side of the open expanse. His regiment had been ordered to march through the field and attack the Federal line. But they would come under fire long before they reached the other side.

After two days of fighting, he and his men were hot, hungry, and tired. He surveyed his company where they stood alongside the rest of the regiment. A few leafed through small copies of the Bible, while others whispered prayers. He frowned when he caught sight of Sergeant Wagner weaving his way toward the rear.

"Sergeant!" Will called. "Resume your post."

"Yes, sir." Wagner moved to his spot up front. He glared at Will but said no more.

Kevin Donnelly, the young Irishman for whom his sister had set her cap, was among the group whispering prayers. Will watched Donnelly make the sign of the cross.

Will's thoughts turned to Amanda. He'd promised his daughter he'd return. An image of the child's auburn plaits and round, baby-face flashed through his mind. She'd already lost her mother. He had to survive.

Confederate cannon fire jolted him from his reminiscence of home. The troops waited within the tree line for another hour, the shade providing some respite from the hot, humid summer day.

While the cannonade continued, his thoughts drifted to Erin O'Connell. He still felt guilty for kissing the laundress, but her vulnerability and pain brought his protective instincts to the fore. And, Lord help him,

Mrs. O'Connell was a beautiful woman. If he survived this battle and wasn't wounded badly enough to be discharged from the army, he'd have to decide what his feelings were regarding her.

After the cannons quieted, the order, "Forward. March," echoed down the line. Raising his sword, he repeated the order as he led his men into the open field. They marched part of the way in silence long after the drums and cheers of the artillery men faded behind them. At the midway point, the explosions of Yankee shells and men screaming in pain lent a nightmarish quality to the long trek.

Stoically, he continued forward, although his insides quaked. Men fell to the ground around him. He urged on the soldiers still with him. When they drew near the Yankee troops, blue forage caps and kepis appeared above the rock barricade the Yankees erected. His thoughts again drifted to Erin O'Connell. Her soft, ripe body and sensual lips. He shook his head. Anne. If he was about to die, he should be thinking of Anne, but he had trouble recalling an image of her face.

As the Yankees rose, preparing to fire, he shifted his sword to his left hand and grasped the butt of his pistol. Adrenaline surged as he shouted to his men to fire at will. He fired off a few shots himself before something hard slammed into his side. Knocked flat on his back, he stared at the smoke-filled sky. Erin O'Connell's face appeared before everything around him went black.

Chapter Ten

A sharp pain shot up Erin's left side. She gasped and gripped the edge of the table to keep from falling.

Brigid appeared behind her. "Are you feeling all right?"

Erin ran her hand down the side of her bodice. The pain had stopped. "I'm fine."

Wounded men lay around her on every available cot and on the floor, wherever there was room. The stewards had begun laying them outside on the grass.

She raced from man to man, keeping herself busy to avoid thinking about Captain Montgomery. But something had happened to him, of that she was sure. Since she could do nothing about it, she concentrated on comforting and helping whomever she could. If she could beam these soldiers to a twenty-first century hospital, so many who were dying could be saved.

Erin was surrounded by moans, screams, hushed voices trying to comfort, and shouted orders from surgeons. Her senses reeled. The sight of so much blood as well as the sickening coppery smell, threatened to send her running from the scene of all this carnage.

Although she tried not to worry about the captain, she checked every new arrival. He could be lying out on the field dead. What would she do if he died? She wondered if she'd return to her own time if that happened, or be trapped here forever. After sharing that kiss with him, however brief it had been, she couldn't stand the thought of his being hurt.

"I need a nurse over here!" Doc called.

Erin looked up to find him motioning to her. She

gulped and raced over to where he stood. Another surgeon had his hands clamped on an unconscious man's leg where he lay on a wooden door propped between two crates the doctors used for surgery.

"What do you want me to do?" she asked.

Doc looked her in the eye. "We've got to take this man's leg. Hold his artery so he doesn't bleed to death."

She nodded but felt the blood drain from her face.

"Can you do it?" His frown bored into her.

Grimacing, she nodded again. "I can do it." He wouldn't have asked her if he had someone else. She wouldn't let him down.

He nodded, and the other surgeon, a dark-haired man named Nate Edwards, showed her where to clamp her fingers.

"Don't ease up or let go," he instructed her, "until I say you can."

"I understand." Fighting down a wave of nausea, she tried not to think about what she held as warm, slick blood covered her hand. The artery throbbed against her finger.

Instead, she studied the face of the man lying on the improvised operating table. His skin had turned ghastly gray, but his features looked serene. He reminded her of a marble statue, except for the fuzzy beard covering the lower part of his face.

She couldn't help but wonder if he had a wife, children, or a sweetheart waiting at home. She tried not to watch what the two doctors were doing, but the grind of the bone saw and the scent of fresh blood kept her stomach jumping.

I can't pass out. If she let go, it would be over for this poor soul. She'd told Doc she could do this, although, God knows what she was thinking at the time.

After what seemed like hours, Doc told her they'd finished. She had trouble straightening her numb fingers and felt lightheaded when she looked down at her hand covered in warm blood. She would not pass out, nor would she throw up. But she had to get the blood off her. Searching for an unused basin and bar of soap, she scrubbed her hands until her fingers' tingling indicated the feeling had returned.

When she was finished, a few volunteers from town arrived to help. She spent the rest of her time dispensing water and washing men's faces and hands. Doc finally told her she'd done enough for today and insisted she go to her tent to rest. Before leaving, she scanned the faces of all the new arrivals, looking for Captain Montgomery. She didn't think she could sleep until she found him.

A vision of him lying in a smoke-filled field covered in blood flashed into her mind. On the way to her tent, she carefully looked over the soldiers as they returned to camp, hoping to spot him. She found only a handful of broken, discouraged men. None of them recalled seeing the captain since the battle.

When she pulled back the flap of her tent, she distinctly heard Grandma Rose's voice. "Find him," Grandma urged, "or all is lost."

The whispery voice caused a shiver to run down her spine. What did that mean? He wasn't supposed to die until 1864. Had her coming here altered things? Sinking onto her bunk, she dropped her head into her hands and tried to decide what to do.

If he wasn't in camp, he must still be on the battlefield. Maybe he was already dead...or he could be hurt, unable to move. Grandma wanted her to find him, so that was what she was going to do.

After settling her cloth bonnet over her hair, she picked up the canteen beside her bunk. The sounds of battle had quieted. Hoping the fighting was done for the day, she stopped by Brigid's tent and filled the canteen with the water the cook had drawn for supper.

Erin headed for the battlefield. The afternoon heat

caused her to feel the full weight of her many layers of clothing. She surveyed the field, wishing she could strip down to her chemise.

Two pickets stopped her. "Where you headed, ma'am?" one of the soldiers asked.

"I need to find someone. He could be hurt or dead."

The pickets exchanged glances. The younger one, a smooth-cheeked boy, said, "I wouldn't go out there yet."

"But the fighting's over," she protested.

The older picket, short, stocky, with a wiry-beard, said, "We still heard some shootin' over yonder. It ain't safe, ma'am."

She scanned the field. Men's bodies, dead horses, and wounded men crying piteously for help covered the landscape. Gesturing angrily, she said, "None of those men are capable of shooting anyone."

"But the Yankees—"

"I'm not afraid of Yankees."

The men eyed each other again. The older one looked at her and said pointedly, "Go, if you want to, but if the Yankees shoot you, it will be your funeral."

She almost laughed aloud. "It certainly will."

The men parted to let her pass. She slowly made her way across the vast open field.

How will I ever find him? She threaded her way through prone bodies, stopping every time a man called out for water. She searched for Will, fearing she'd find him among the dead.

The heat, combined with the stench of gunpowder and the scent of blood nearly caused her to collapse, but she had to keep going, had to find him.

"Please...please, ma'am, help me." She turned at the sound of the pitiful voice. A stocky, heavily bearded man lay on the ground at her feet. She gasped, then covered her mouth when she looked at where his legs should have been. Two bloody stumps poked out from his shredded trousers.

Following her gaze, he said, "I know I'm not long for this world. I don't want to die alone. If you could jest sit here with me until it's over, I'd be much obliged."

Erin bit her lip. She needed to find Will but couldn't refuse this man's plea. No one else moved nearby. The stretcher- bearers, who'd started to collect the wounded, hadn't made it this far. She sat beside the man, facing away from the bloody stumps.

"What's your name?" she asked.

"Earnest Watkins."

"Are you married, Earnest?"

"Yes, ma'am. She's the prettiest gal you've ever seen."

"Any children?"

"I got three. I got a tintype if you'd like to see."

"Of course."

He fumbled in his pocket.

She learned forward to help him fish out a small photo. She scanned the innocent, baby faces. Two boys and a girl. She imagined their mother waiting for this man to come home and wondered how the woman would bear this. Her eyes misted over.

"They're beautiful children." She handed the picture back.

He nodded proudly.

"I only wish I could see them one more time in this life."

"You will," she lied. She helped him tuck the photo into his pocket, against his heart.

Earnest sighed. "I can't fool myself. I know I've lost a lot of blood. Even if I could survive, I'd be no good to them like this." He gestured to his legs. "I'm a farmer," he explained.

She nodded, blinking back tears. "Where are you from?"

"North Carolina." He smiled weakly. "I only hope my wife can take my body back there when this is over. I'd like to rest back home."

"I'm sure she will." But she doubted a woman with three, small children could travel that far and back in this time period.

"I can't rest here." He glanced around fearfully.

"You'll get back." She patted his shoulder.

"I want to be buried on my farm. Under the magnolia tree."

Erin nodded, not sure what else she could say. His face turned white as marble. She didn't think he could last much longer. She took his hand in hers.

"Ellie, is that you?" he whispered.

She looked around. No one else was in sight.

"I know you'll take good care of the children," he said.

He thought she was his wife. "The children will be fine," she assured him. "Don't you worry. Rest."

"I love you, Ellie," he rasped.

His hand slipped from hers. He was gone. She closed his eyes and covered his face with the kepi that lay beside him. Standing over him and recalling her Roman Catholic upbringing, she made the sign of the cross and said a silent prayer for his soul.

She felt drained and exhausted but was determined to continue her search for Captain Montgomery. She only hoped that, if he'd died and it hadn't been instantaneous, someone had been with him as she'd been with Earnest.

Close to the Federal lines, she found Yankees and Rebels lying side by side, atop one another. She feared she'd never find him in this chaos. She spent several minutes comforting soldiers, both Confederate and Federal. The men were grateful for a sip of water, a smile, and a kind word.

Erin wanted to offer all of these men encouragement but knew most of them wouldn't survive long enough to make it back to the hospital. One young Union soldier kept calling her Harriet. He promised her they'd marry as soon as he mustered out of the service. Another impossibly young Rebel thought she was his mother. He cried and pleaded with her to take him home.

She couldn't take much more of this misery. Tears streamed down her cheeks. Fearing she'd never find the captain, she made the decision to go back. Defeated, she rose and gathered her skirts to start the long hike back to camp.

One of the stretcher-bearers, a young, hospital steward named Matt, stopped her. "Ma'am, the captain over yonder asked me to get you."

She peered at the boy's freckle-spattered face. "The captain?"

"Yes, ma'am."

"Where is he?" She glanced around.

He pointed. "Right there, ma'am."

After thanking him, she followed his gesture. Several men lay in a cluster. None of them moved. Her heart thumped wildly. She frantically searched among the men, whose faces she didn't recognize. Most of them appeared dead.

Looking back in the direction the boy had gone, she found he had disappeared. Could he have been mistaken? None of the men around her seemed capable of speech.

This is hopeless.

She walked a few feet, then froze. A man in Confederate uniform lay belly down, his face turned to the side, revealing a familiar profile, with dark brown hair. She sucked in a breath and held it.

Crouching, she touched his face. Cold. Too late. In despair, she covered her face with her hands. She'd lost him. And with that, any hope of accomplishing whatever she'd been sent here to do.

"What am I supposed to do now?" she said aloud.

A low moan answered her.

"Captain?" She touched his face and held her palm

close to his lips. His breath faintly fanned against her hand.

Erin rolled him onto his back. Before she could do anything, he moaned again. A bright red stain covered his left side over the gray of his frock coat. She recalled the sudden pain she'd felt back at the hospital. Was there some psychic connection between them?

She laid her head against his chest. He had a faint, rapid heartbeat, and he was breathing. He needed help and fast. If she'd been home, she would've used her cell phone to call 911. She couldn't let him die.

After opening his frock coat, she parted the ruined fabric of his muslin shirt. Blood seeped from a gaping hole in his side. She tore the ruffle off one of her petticoats and pressed the fabric against his chest, then pressed the bloodied coat back against it to hold the cloth in place.

When she took his hand, he gasped and opened his eyes. "Mrs. O'Connell?" he croaked.

She stroked his cheek and smiled. "It's me, Erin. Can't you call me Erin?"

He tried to move, causing another moan to escape his lips. "You've been shot in the side," she said. "I don't know how bad."

"Doc'll fix me up," he murmured. "Get me to Doc." He closed his eyes.

"Captain? Will?" She shook him, but he didn't move. "You can't do this to me, you hear?"

A group of stretcher-bearers approached. She signaled to them. Impulsively, she leaned down and kissed him on the lips. The coldness of his mouth alarmed her.

Chapter Eleven

Jake leaned against a wide oak, furiously puffing on a cheroot. He'd nearly been killed today and for what? When that fool Lee ordered the march across that wide-open field, he'd tried to find a way to duck out. He didn't plan on dying for a cause he didn't believe in.

If it hadn't been for Captain Montgomery catching him, he could have hid until the battle was over. And if Montgomery hadn't been wounded, he'd likely be up on charges of desertion. At least, he was still in one piece with no one around to punish him.

Now, to make things worse, his arrangement with Erin O'Connell had gone awry. Ever since she'd fallen from that mare, she'd been a different woman—cozying up to Montgomery...acting haughty and refined like she was too good for him. She didn't even speak the same. This wasn't good. If that bitch had thoughts of betraying him...

She hadn't returned to her tent for hours. Spotting Brigid Malone, he casually asked if she'd seen Erin.

The dumpy Irish woman scowled. "She's helping with the wounded, but I don't think she'll be wanting to see the likes of you tonight."

Jake kept his expression bland, tipped his cap, and strode off. He knew the Irish cook hated him. He drew near the barn. The surgeons used it as a medical facility, since the hospital tents had filled to capacity the day before. The scent of blood caused him to stop short.

Men, who'd been left lying in the open yesterday, had been taken inside as heavy rain started to fall. He moved to the entrance and peered in.

Inside was chaos. Men moaned and screamed in pain. Doctors, nurses, and stewards rushed about trying to help in any way they could.

He grimaced at the sound of a bone saw coming from the back of the barn. He backed away from the horrific scene, but not before catching sight of the slender back of a woman with a reddish-gold bun. She bent over dispensing water to a cluster of men lying on a pile of hay. He watched until Erin lifted the bucket and moved toward where he stood.

Her eyes widened when she saw him. Before she could pass him, he grasped her arm. She strained against his grip.

"I need to get more water." She held the empty bucket for him to see.

"I'd like a word with you first," he ground against her ear.

"But they need me—"

Ignoring her protest, Jake yanked her outside into the rain. "Let me go!" She dropped the bucket.

Jake glanced inside the barn. No one noticed him pull her outside. After shoving her under the canopy of a wide oak, he spun her around to face him. "I want to know what's going on between you and Captain Montgomery."

Her eyelids narrowed to slits. "Nothing's going on. He's been wounded, and he's lying in there barely alive." She flung her free arm toward the barn.

"I need to know you won't betray me," he said. "Remember, I know who and what you are."

Before she could reply, one of the drummer boys stepped out, lifting the bucket she'd dropped. The lad's blond eyebrows rose when he spotted the two standing in the rain.

"Ma'am, they said I should fetch the water right quick."

Erin glanced at Jake. "Leave it out to catch the

rain water," she told the boy. "Bring the other bucket, too."

"Yes, ma'am." He left the bucket out in the open and disappeared inside.

She looked at Jake. "I'll talk to you about this later."

He nodded, releasing her arm. He'd wait until later when they had privacy. Before he could issue a final warning, the boy reappeared with a second bucket he placed beside the first. Erin and the boy disappeared inside, leaving Jake alone. He strode to his tent. Once things calmed down, he'd see to it she reveal everything. Or on second thought, maybe he should take matters into his own hands. He needed knowledge of all her activities, so he'd have evidence to hold against her, if she ever had any thoughts of betraying him.

****

Sitting near his cot, Erin stared at the captain who appeared to be sleeping after his surgery. Doc had dug out the lead ball and stitched the jagged wound. For now, the best thing she could do was keep the area clean. She carefully removed Will's bandage by first soaking it with water from the basin she'd placed beside him. With the bandage wet, she snipped it off with a small pair of scissors. Exposing the bright red wound, streaked with a dark zigzag edge, she looked for any sign of infection. *If I only had some sort of antibiotic. Even an ointment*! Infection could be a death sentence, especially in his weakened state.

Seeing no pus and catching no putrid smell, she breathed a sigh of relief. She gently washed the side of his chest moving beyond the edge of the wound, ending at his narrow waist. Glancing at his face every few seconds, she looked for any indication she caused him pain.

Using a linen towel to dry the area, she rebandaged him with the help of one of the musicians serving as a medical steward. Settling him back on the cot, she touched his cheek where a few days stubble roughened his face. His eyes remained closed.

"Will?" she whispered.

He reached a hand toward her.

She clasped it in both of hers.

"Anne," he rasped.

Erin glanced around in surprise. She'd grown used to being mistaken for other women, but this man meant something to her.

"His wife." Doc had sidled up beside her. "She died just after the war started."

Erin nodded, glancing at the captain. "How did she die?"

"Pneumonia. She'd given birth to a stillborn son shortly after Christmas of '60. The birth had weakened her, and she never fully recovered."

"He left when she was sick?"

"At first, she had nothing life threatening. She stayed with his parents and the servants. Just after he left for camp, she came down with the grippe, which progressed to croup. Will wasn't able to obtain a furlough to go to her. His parents assured him they'd care for her. Told him his duty was to defend Virginia."

"That's awful."

"He got the telegram that she was deathly ill after Manassas. By the time he got home, she was gone."

Erin tightened her grip on his hand. "He told you all of this?"

Doc shook his head. "My wife, Josie, had known Anne since childhood. We know Will's family."

"And the little girl?"

"Amanda. She was three when Anne died. Will's sister, Jenny, and his parents care for her now."

Erin gazed at Will's face. His brow furrowed as if he were in pain or dreaming of something unpleasant. "How bad is he, Doc?"

"If we can keep the wound from getting infected,

he should recover. Fortunately, nothing vital was hit."

Nodding, she vowed to personally clean his wound. If her purpose in being here was to keep this man alive, she had her work cut out for her.

****

Hours later, Doc woke her. She'd fallen asleep sitting at the edge of Will's cot with her head resting on a side table, where she'd left her basin and rags.

"Go back to your tent and get some sleep. You're no good to anyone like this."

Erin shook off the grogginess. A few hours stretched out on her cot sounded like a good idea.

As she crossed the camp to her tent, the heavy rain that fell revived her. Pulling back the canvas, she gasped. Her table and bunk had been upended, and the trunk gaped open, its contents spread everywhere. What could she have that anyone could want? She reached into the trunk, only then realizing the journal was gone.

Chapter Twelve

That evening Jake sat in his tent hunched over a lantern while rain pelted the canvas. He'd set the lamp on a flat block of wood away from the bedding and canvas and draped his rubber sheet over the opening of the small tent to keep the rainwater out.

Erin O'Connell's journal proved to be very interesting reading, although he had a bit of trouble with her small handwriting. Pages that had been torn out most likely contained the information she'd gathered on troop movements. But what he found most interesting were the entries regarding him. Seems the woman tolerated him for what information she could get. Furthermore, she *was* attracted to Captain Montgomery.

As he deciphered Erin's scribbling, his thoughts drifted to the woman who'd taught him to read. As a boy, he hadn't had any formal education, and at the age of fourteen, his father had farmed him out to do chores for a widow who, before her marriage, had been a schoolmarm. The woman had taught him not only how to read but had taken him into her bed for further education. He still held fond memories of her.

He turned his attention back to the journal. The last entry was dated the tenth of June. Nearly three weeks had passed since she'd written anything. He counted back, trying to recall how long it had been since she'd fallen from the horse. Everything had changed that night, but why? He had a hard time believing the woman had lost her memory.

He squinted against the lantern's glare to study the script. Although no military entries remained, notes on her involvement with him could possibly implicate her as a spy. Why had she made such personal entries? She was nothing but a foolish bitch.

Unfortunately, if anyone else found this book, he would be branded as her accomplice. A traitor. He sucked on his lower lip. There had to be something he could hold against her. He'd just keep this book in a safe place. If need be, he'd have to burn it.

But if she switched her allegiance and tried to betray him, he now had the means to bring her down with him.

****

Will drifted in and out of consciousness. One minute he was in the barn surrounded by wounded soldiers, the next he marched on a hot, blazing battlefield. Explosions tore men to shreds, but he plodded on. This was his duty, to defend...defend what? He thought of Amanda. The child had already lost her mother. If he should fall, she'd be alone.

Doc's voice brought him back to the barn. "Wake up, Will."

He opened one eye. The doctor's thin face appeared even more haggard than the last time they'd spoken. "You need rest," Will said.

Doc laughed. "You don't look all that well yourself."

"How bad is it?"

"You'll live. Just don't expect to be up and walking any time soon."

Will grimaced as he stretched his protesting muscles.

Doc glanced toward the barn entrance. "I do believe I see your own personal nurse."

He twisted his head to see to whom Doc was referring. Erin approached carrying something wrapped in a towel.

"Can he have soup, Doc?" she asked.

"I reckon so. Just take it slowly."

Erin wore her hair pulled back off her face and coiled into a bun. She perched on a stool by his cot holding the bundle in her lap. When she unwrapped it, the aroma of chicken broth teased his nostrils.

Her gaze fastened on his face. "Are you hungry?"

"Starved." He grinned.

She returned his smile. "I brought you some broth."

"Go right ahead." Doc said. "I'm off to get a few hours sleep."

Once the doctor left, she slowly spooned the liquid into his mouth. The warm flavor of chicken felt wonderful against his dry throat. But the real healing power came from the beautiful angel feeding him.

****

Four months later, the army camped on a farm near Winchester, Virginia. When the Confederates had retreated from Gettysburg, Doc made sure Will wasn't left behind. Over the past few months, as he'd slowly recovered, Erin had made it her personal mission to nurse him back to health, and in so doing, they'd grown close. But she still worried over her former life and wondered if she'd ever get back. What would happen if she did?

At night alone in her tent, she relived flashes of the dreams she'd had in the months before coming here. But these were more vivid than any dreams she'd had before. In those dreams, they were lovers, but she couldn't give herself completely to him. The shadow of betrayal and loss clouded those dreams turning them to nightmares from which she wanted nothing more but to escape.

****

Two weeks later, Erin stood before her washtub agitating soiled clothes with a long stick containing points on the end. Brigid called it a *dolly*. The day in, day out physical toil was wearing her down. No showers, no modern conveniences, living outdoors day after day, not to mention her diet, which was sadly lacking. What she wouldn't give for a pizza. Would she have to endure this life forever, or was it possible to return to her time?

Will slowly recovered from his battle wounds, although he remained in the hospital under Doc's care and was unfit to return to duty. Doc had suggested he take a furlough, and Will considered it. An uneasy feeling washed over her as she wondered where it would leave her if he left camp.

She hung the laundry to dry, frustrated that clothes dryers didn't yet exist, then returned to the medical tent to check on him. She found him propped on pillows reading the local newspaper. His face looked a bit thinner, his skin pale, and his formerly clean-shaven cheeks had acquired a dark growth.

"You're looking better today," she said. "Have you been eating?"

"Yes, ma'am." He ran a hand across his jaw. "I could use a shave, though."

"Don't look at me." She hoped he wasn't suggesting she do it.

He frowned at her. "You've never shaved a man before?"

She shook her head.

"Not even your husband?"

She nearly blurted out that she'd never been married. "I don't remember."

"You haven't regained memory of your past?"

"Just snippets here and there," she lied. In truth, she used what she knew of Grandma's historical records she'd read in the future and the stories Grandma had told her. The rest came from the journal. The journal that was now missing.

She suspected Jake had taken it. Believing it would only make things worse, she didn't want to confront him. Fortunately, he'd stayed away from her. But she had a feeling he was plotting something, and it wouldn't bode well for her.

Catching Will's expectant gaze, she said, "You don't want *me* to shave you."

"I can't think of a better luxury than to be shaved by a lovely woman."

Her skin tingled at the compliment, but she kept her cool. "Flattery will get you nowhere. I'll probably cut you."

"Why don't you collect my shaving kit from my tent and a basin and mirror. We'll do this together."

"When I cut your throat, don't blame me."

Within his tent, a masculine scent clung to everything. She found what she believed was his shaving kit—a razor in a pouch on the table beside his cot along with a mug and small mirror.

Upon returning, she propped him up, held the mirror, and set the mug and basin on a table beside him. He expertly lathered his cheeks and shaved the new growth, then used a small pair of scissors to trim his mustache and chin.

She bit her lip. The man of her dreams in the flesh performing such a masculine task quickened her heartbeat.

"You can lower the mirror now." The corner of his lip quirked into a half-smile. "I'm finished."

"Oh, okay." Erin flushed and set the mirror on the table, embarrassed he'd caught her staring.

"Getting ready for your furlough?" Doc asked.

So intent upon Will, Erin hadn't noticed his approach.

"Furlough?" she asked.

"Doctor's orders. He needs time to recover at home." To Will, he said, "Spend some time with your family and your little girl."

Will nodded but didn't look happy.

Erin's thoughts raced ahead to how she'd manage without him.

"I'll go if Mrs. O'Connell agrees to accompany me."

Startled by his comment, she stared at him. "Why would you want *me* to go?"

"You've been my nurse since I was wounded."

"But I'm sure your mother, or sister..."

"I want you," he said.

Want me? A thrill raced through her at his choice of words. But, of course, he obviously meant as nursemaid.

She bit her lip. "I'll have to think about it." After catching Doc's puzzled expression, she left to ponder what this meant. Although she wanted to stay with Will and believed she should, she worried about what that bastard, Jake, would say about it.

Chapter Thirteen

Mason, Virginia

Erin gazed at the white, green-shuttered house at the edge of town. She'd visited Will's grave in this very town over one hundred forty years in the future. The sensation of *déjà vu* caused a shudder.

Will shifted in the carriage and leaned toward her. "Are you cold, ma'am?"

She glanced at him. "Ah, no. I'm fine." She turned back to the house, the image of his gravestone too impossible to bear.

Although glad the dusty, bumpy ride was over, she was reluctant to leave the carriage. She'd already met Jenny and Amanda and looked forward to seeing them again but wondered what Will's parents were like. He jumped down from the carriage with a grunt, then moved to her side, offering her a hand.

"You're not recovered yet," she protested. When he didn't move away, she scowled. "I can get down by myself."

His eyebrows lifted, but he backed away. She jumped to the ground but found to her embarrassment her skirts still attached to the carriage.

I hate these clothes! If I could only find a pair of jeans that fit. And a nice, airy tank top.

"Allow me, ma'am." He reached for her dress and petticoats to pull them from the carriage frame.

A blush crept from her chest to the crown of her head, and she hoped no one, especially Will, had caught a glimpse of her crotchless drawers. She eyed him, noting that his light tanned complexion turned slightly pink.

Once she was loose, they stepped through the black wrought-iron gate. The door burst open, and a small form raced toward them.

"Papa!" Amanda flew into Will's stomach. He grunted.

"Careful, sweetheart," Erin said. "Your papa's side still hurts."

Amanda's mouth puckered into a frown. Erin glanced at Will. He caught her gaze and shook his head. She guessed Amanda hadn't been told he'd been wounded.

"Does the rest of your family know?" she whispered as the child ran inside calling for Jenny.

"They know what they need to know," he warned.

"Will!" Jenny screamed. "I can hardly believe you're here." She rose on tiptoe to plant a kiss on her brother's cheek. "And Miss Erin, I'm so glad you came. Come along, and I'll give you the tour."

Erin turned toward Will. "I think I should see that your brother's settled first."

"Tillie and Isaac will see to him," Jenny said. A tall, black man followed by a wide-hipped, black woman strode toward Will in welcome.

"You see." Jenny linked her arm with Erin's, leading her away.

Just inside the entry door, a row of hooks, set on a horizontal post, lined the wall to their left. She suspected these were for any outer clothing the family wore in the colder months. To the right, a large table flanked by chairs sat in the center of the room on a rectangular shaped Persian-style carpet. The walls were papered in a red and cream floral pattern. Heavy mahogany colored curtains, decorated with long gold tassels, framed the windows, and a crystal chandelier hung over the table.

Straight ahead a staircase led to the upper floors. To the left a pair of heavy wooden doors stood open, leading into a room Jenny called the parlor.

The tiny room made Erin's head spin. She'd never seen so much furniture crammed into one space. A fireplace dominated the outside wall. Vases filled with dried flowers adorned the cream-colored mantle. Small, assorted knickknacks and family photos covered any remaining space. She moved slowly through the cramped area afraid one false move would spell disaster.

Cleaning this room must be a nightmare! She'd never bother, and the dust would sit there for years. Probably why they didn't have many things. And why, she thought with a glance at Jenny, they had help.

"Do you spend much time in here?" Erin asked.

"Of course not," Jenny said. "The parlor is only for entertaining." She eyed Erin in a peculiar way.

The seating area consisted of two chairs and a settee, all wood framed, upholstered in plush materials of blue, red, and beige. Another set of heavy, mahogany-colored curtains with gold tassels lined the windows, and a piano sat in the corner. Small tables set about the room held more knickknacks. The dark blue patterned carpet contrasted with the red-orange walls and orange-cream ceiling. Her eyes hurt. Was this clash of colors fashionable now?

The tour continued through the kitchen, while Jenny prattled on about...was she talking about wallpaper? At least this room was a little more esthetic, containing a black cast-iron stove, another fireplace, pots and pans, and a long butcher-block table. They toured the mud room, ending on the second floor with Jenny's bedroom.

This room contained a large canopy bed in the center with a matching cream-colored, lace-trimmed coverlet. A wardrobe with intricate scrolling sat beside a dressing table equipped with assorted personal toiletries. Across from the window, flanked with blue velvet curtains, hung a portrait of Jenny. Her dark center-parted hair was plaited and framed her face, ending in ringlets resting on her shoulder. Her eyes placidly surveyed the room as a white nosegay adorned her lap. Her sky blue dress added to the tranquility of the portrait.

The bedroom was so unlike Erin's room in her small apartment. No TV, computer, DVD player, phone or file cabinet. This was almost as bad as being stuck in an army camp.

"Isaac and Tillie can set a bath for you up here if you'd like before dinner," Jenny offered.

"A bath. In a real tub? With soap, lots of towels and hot water?" Erin asked. The idea of immersing herself in soapy water was intoxicating.

"I can't imagine what it must be like for a woman to live in an army camp day after day."

"It's great to finally have a solid roof over my head." Erin dropped her gaze stamping her foot against the wool carpet. "And floor."

Jenny laughed. "I'm so glad you came home with Will. It'll be like having a sister."

While Jenny summoned the servants to prepare the tub, Erin's anticipation of her first real bath in months eased her anxiety about meeting Will's parents.

Later, as she soaked in the hot, lavender scented water, her thoughts drifted to where this relationship with Will would lead and how she could change history to prevent his premature death.

****

Will greeted his mother with an obligatory kiss on the cheek.

"Where's Father?" he asked.

"He's been at the bank all day in meetings." She waved her small, thin hand as if dismissing his father's activities as trivial. "He should be arriving shortly."

She snapped her fan open and fluttered it before

her thin, drawn face. She still dressed in black from head to toe. Will had hoped in all the months he'd been gone that she would've abandoned the mourning clothes she'd donned after his brother, Sam's, death in the first month of the war.

Her dark hair streaked with gray was pulled back into a tight bun. "And my—" She took a step back to admire Will. "—you surely do make a handsome soldier."

"Thank you, Mother, but I know how you feel about the army."

His mother gestured with the fan. "War is nasty business. I don't see why civilized men have to fight." She laughed. "But then, I forget, the Yankees aren't civilized."

Will smiled. "Jenny tells me there's to be a welcome home dinner. May I ask who's attending?"

She cleared her throat, fanning herself. "Only Miss Courtland. She's such a lovely young lady."

And she's from a respectable, wealthy family. He kept the smile frozen on his lips. "I do hope you're not playing matchmaker again, Mother."

She gasped. "It's been two years since poor Anne left us. Your daughter needs a mother. And your father wouldn't mind having a grandson."

"Jenny isn't yet married."

His mother pursed her thin lips. "He wants a grandson who will bear the Montgomery name."

The clip clop of a horse's hooves and the clatter of wagon wheels outside interrupted the conversation.

"It's your father." She peered out the window. "We'd best go greet him."

Will hesitated. His father was the last person he wanted to see. His mother waved her fan toward the door and frowned her disapproval when he didn't move.

Knowing he had little choice, he gestured at the entry. "After you, Mother."

He escorted his mother to the short granite walkway beside the garden, swinging the wrought iron gate open as Zachary Montgomery alighted from the carriage. As always, his father was impeccably dressed in a brown wool suit and black stove-pipe hat.

Approaching his wife and son, he nodded with obvious approval at Will's full dress uniform. He didn't smile but wore his usual stern expression.

"Hello, Father," Will said.

"Heard you were wounded at Gettysburg," he drawled. "I'm happy to see you're not too bad off. How long will you be with us?"

"I have a medical furlough for the winter to allow me to fully recover."

His father nodded. Reaching inside his coat, he patted his vest pocket and extracted a cigar. "Would you care for one?"

"No, thank you, sir."

He nodded again and looked at his wife. "What time will we be dining, my dear?"

"Tillie will have it ready by seven."

"Very well." He motioned to Will. "Come with me to the study, I'd like you to regale me with stories of your heroics at Gettysburg." Without waiting for an answer, he entered the house.

Will glanced at his mother but said nothing. After escorting her inside, he followed his father into the study.

His father's large, mahogany desk, where he conducted business when away from the bank, was the centerpiece of the room. Two upholstered chairs, where guests could sit and enjoy Zachary's stash of fine cigars, flanked the desk. A large portrait of the first Zachary Montgomery hung on the wall behind his father's chair. His grandfather gazed at him with the same stern expression his son now wore. Will paced across the plush oriental carpet.

Zachary, puffing on his cigar, took his seat behind

the desk. He motioned for Will to sit across from him, then eyed him speculatively. "Word is, the war's taken a downturn since Gettysburg."

"It seems that way."

"No matter." He blew out a stream of aromatic smoke. "Our side will prevail."

Will knew better than to argue with his father. "Yes, sir."

"I'm glad to see you've not been wounded gravely."

"Thank you." He waited, wondering where the conversation headed.

"Mother and I have been speculating as to when you'll take a new wife."

Will said nothing.

"You've been a widower for two years now. It's time you resume courting."

He stared at his father but didn't reply.

Zachary leaned back in his chair. "There are a number of eligible young women in town."

"Like Miss Courtland?" Will said.

Zachary sighed. "Your mother told you...or was it Jenny?" He waved his cigar. "It doesn't matter. She's a lovely young lady from a very fine family."

"Sir," Will said, "After my furlough, I'll be going back to war. I could be killed. Nearly was at Gettysburg. I can't think about getting married now."

"That's all the more reason," Zachary replied. "Amanda needs a mother."

"She has you and Mother."

"We're too old to be parents to a young girl."

"Jenny, then—"

"Jenny will be marrying and starting a family of her own. You can't expect her to take on the burden of her brother's child."

"You can't expect me to marry just any woman so Amanda can have a mother."

"Miss Courtland is not just any woman."

Will sighed. "I can't make any promises. I'm a

captain in the Confederate Army, and I have an obligation to that post." He stood. "A post *you* pushed me into taking."

"I understand, son. But you also have to take personal responsibility for your family before you go off to battle."

"I'll think on what you said, sir." Wanting to escape this interview, he stood and walked out before his father could utter another word.

Will paused at the base of the stairs. A feminine giggle from above drew his attention. His gaze rose to two figures at the top of the staircase.

Jenny, in a rose-colored gown, held the arm of Erin O'Connell. Will stared at her. He couldn't believe this was the same woman he'd brought from camp. The deep blue of the gown she wore brought out the sapphire color of her eyes. The wide skirt hung like a bell emphasizing her small waist. A white lace triangle covering the front of her bodice adorned her rounded bosom.

As the two women slowly descended the stairs, Mrs. O'Connell locked eyes with him. The desire he'd had for her back in camp, intensified. He was unable to look away.

Chapter Fourteen

Erin swallowed, unable to look away. Will looked dashing in his gray captain's uniform, and she detected admiration in his eyes. So focused on him was she that when she reached the base of the stairs, she nearly stumbled over her crinoline. Only his firm grip on her arm kept her from tripping. A pleasant warmth spread over her when he escorted her into the foyer.

"Well." He turned to Jenny, "My dear sister, you surely do work wonders."

She flashed him an "I-told-you-so" smile. "I had excellent material to work with." She smiled at Erin.

Heat crept up Erin's face. She *had* to be blushing.

"I would have to agree with you," Will said. He took Erin's hand and lifted it to his lips.

A delightful shiver ran down her spine. They locked eyes again, and she couldn't seem to catch her breath. Was it the kiss, the intensity in his eyes or...the damn corset? Jenny had insisted on lacing it tightly. How the hell was she supposed to eat anything or even breathe with this on? "I need to sit down."

Will escorted her to a velvet, straight back chair at the base of the stairs. "I'll get you some brandy."

"No, water will be fine."

Will and Jenny exchanged glances.

"If it's too much trouble—"

"Oh, no," Jenny said. "Tillie should have drawn some water for tonight's meal. I'll go to the kitchen and get some." She ran down the hall.

"I didn't mean to be so much of a bother," Erin apologized.

"It's quite all right," Will said. "After all, you are

our guest."

Oh, my. No wonder Southern belles needed those hand fans.

"That gown looks lovely on you."

"Thank you, but I have to give your sister the credit for that." She glanced around the room to avoid looking into those eyes. Maybe then she could regain her breath. "Your home is beautiful."

He shrugged. "This is my parents' home. Unfortunately, my station as the son of a well-off banker carries with it responsibilities I don't wish to contemplate."

Erin digested his statement, wondering what he was trying to tell her. "You're not happy to be home?"

He sighed. "I must say, I'll be happy to leave this house for the duration of the war."

She didn't know what to say. Why was he suddenly confiding in her? He'd never discussed his family when they were in camp.

An uncomfortable silence followed. She wished Jenny would hurry with the water. Will cleared his throat but said nothing. She breathed a sigh of relief when Jenny appeared holding a ceramic mug.

"I must apologize for taking so long." She handed the mug to Erin. Aside to Will, she said, "You know how talkative Tillie can be."

"I do indeed."

After Erin felt a bit better, Jenny left her in Will's care.

"Allow me to show you the rose garden." Will lifted his arm.

Erin reached for his elbow, nestling her fingers in the warmth of his coat sleeve.

He escorted her to the front door, then along the side of the house toward the back. As they strolled the cobbled path along the flowerbeds, Will said, "My mother takes great pride in her roses."

Erin surveyed the large roses in full bloom,

varying in colors of red, pink and white.

"Seems to me Tillie should be the one to take pride." She glared at Will. "She does all the work."

Will smirked. "While you are likely right, don't allow my mother to hear you say that."

"To avoid being thrown bodily from your house, I'll be sure to keep my opinions to myself."

Will stooped and plucked a red rose.

"Be careful," Erin advised.

He picked a few thorns from the stem, then presented the flower to Erin.

"A rose for a beautiful rose."

Erin flushed. *Is it getting hot out here or what?*

She accepted the flower, holding it under her nose, but her gaze rested on the handsome man at her side.

Afterward, he escorted her to the property line behind the house where a clear creek ran beyond the small outbuilding that housed his father's horse and carriage. The soothing sound of running water drew her.

If only she could cross that stream and find herself back in the twenty-first century. As visions of what might be happening in her own time drifted through her thoughts, she had to wonder if she'd regret leaving Will, if she could go back.

****

After completing the tour of the garden, Will ushered Mrs. O'Connell onto the front stoop. The sound of horses' hooves approaching drew his attention from the lavender scent of her skin and hair.

A carriage stopped before the house on the cobbled street. He knew just who it was and sighed.

"Is something wrong?" Mrs. O'Connell asked.

His gaze focused on the carriage. "No, nothing's wrong. Go inside and find Jenny. I'll be in shortly."

She glanced at the carriage before entering the house.

Will waited on the stoop while the driver pulled to

a stop. Emily Courtland sat alone, behind the driver. She wore a green gown with an ivory bonnet perched over her blond curls. He stepped toward her.

She smiled when he reached for her hand.

"Miss Courtland, welcome."

"Why, Will," she drawled, "we don't need to be so formal. You know you can call me Emily."

"Don't allow my mother to hear you say that. She'd consider it forward and wouldn't stand for it."

Emily covered her mouth with a gloved hand and giggled. "We won't be so familiar in front of your parents, but in private..."

He smiled but said nothing when he helped her down and escorted her inside. Mrs. O'Connell and Jenny stood in the foyer. Apparently, they'd been deep in conversation. From the guilty looks on their faces, their talk must have been about him.

Damn. This is going to be one trying evening.

Nodding at Emily, he said formally, "Miss Courtland, allow me to introduce Mrs. O'Connell."

Emily eyed Mrs. O'Connell with interest. She arched an eyebrow and pursed her lips.

Will's mother entered the foyer. Her thin lips broke into a tight smile. "I see our guest has arrived. Welcome, Miss Courtland."

"Thank you for having me, Mrs. Montgomery," Emily said. Glancing at Will, she added, "When I heard our war hero was home, I was just aching to pay him a visit."

His mother's gray eyes hardened and raked over Mrs. O'Connell. "William," she scolded, "you've neglected to introduce me to our houseguest."

Will stiffened. "Mother, this is Mrs. O'Connell. Mrs. O'Connell, my mother, Mrs. Montgomery."

Frowning, his mother eyed Mrs. O'Connell's gown. "Jenny, dear, I do believe you have a dress similar to this." She gestured vaguely toward her daughter.

Jenny scowled. "It's mine, Momma. Mrs. O'Connell

is just borrowing it."

His mother's eyebrows rose. "Oh, I see." She fixed Will with a withering gaze.

He wasn't about to go into an explanation now of just what Mrs. O'Connell was doing here. All he wanted was to survive this evening.

Fortunately, Amanda took that moment to bounce down the stairs and distract his mother.

"Grandmama. Tillie needs to ask you if she can take me with her to the grocers." She watched Madeline and bit her lip.

Will smiled at the serious expression on Amanda's small face. "That sounds like fun, darlin'."

Amanda rewarded him with a smile.

"Bring Tillie here, and we'll see," his mother said.

Seeing his chance to escape, Will quickly excused himself and exited the house.

****

After Will left, Erin felt the urge to do the same. She should have stayed in camp. Will's mother obviously didn't like her, and Miss Courtland apparently had designs on Will. Erin was simply in the way. She wished she could go back to camp, better yet, wished she could vanish back into the twenty-first century. Where's the time machine when you need it?

Jenny came to the rescue, excusing them both. She dragged Erin to her room so they could have some privacy until dinner. Jenny told her Emily Courtland had been trying to catch Will's attention for the past year, whenever he was home on leave. Since their parents approved of her, they'd been conspiring to get the two married, but he resisted.

"He feels the same about Emily as I do," Jenny folded her arms across her chest. "I despise her. But my parents think she'd make the perfect wife for him."

Erin smiled. She recalled seeing Jenny with the young soldier in camp. "I suspect they've been doing the same thing to you."

"Of course. They've already picked out several young men from here in town and as far away as Baltimore and Washington City, who would make *proper* husbands for me. But I love Kevin."

"And they won't allow you to marry him," Erin guessed.

"He's Irish, Catholic, and poor." Jenny sighed. "They won't even allow me to see him."

"Then what will you do?"

"I'll run away. I'll become an army nurse."

"What about Will? He won't tell your parents?"

Jenny hesitated. "He'd likely side with them and forbid me to do any such thing."

"It would be a hard life for you," Erin agreed.

"But I have to get away from them. If I stay here, Kevin will be gone, and they'll marry me off to one of their choosing."

Erin felt sorry for Jenny. Her wealth, instead of freeing her, made her a prisoner in her home. She had to find a way to help her. "Aren't all the men in the army now?" she reasoned. "That should buy you some time."

"Buy me time?" Jenny seemed mystified by the expression.

"I mean they can't force suitors on you when they're all off to war."

Jenny smiled. "I wish you could stay here with me when Will goes back. What will you do? Will you travel with the army?"

Erin hadn't thought about that. Her choices of where she could stay were limited. "I suppose, when he leaves, I'll have to go with him. I have nowhere else to go."

"Then, stay here," Jenny said.

Erin shook her head. "Your parents wouldn't like it. I know you mother wouldn't."

"You're right. I wish I could go with you."

While Erin wouldn't mind having a companion

like Jenny in camp, she hardly thought Will's sister would last more than a few days with the army.

****

Will stood inside the carriage house stroking the muzzle of his father's, gray dappled stallion. He fed the horse, named Snicker, an apple he'd picked from the tree growing beside the house. As Snicker munched the fruit, Will continued to pet him. He was able, for the first time since coming home, to relax and forget his problems, if only for a few minutes.

Longing for freedom, he had none. His marriage to Anne had been arranged by his parents. Even though he could have dissented, he'd never considered doing so, because of his family's expectations. He'd also taken the post of captain after his father had used his political pull to get him the commission. Now, they were trying to arrange a second marriage for the sake of Amanda. At least the army provided a temporary escape from his parents' meddling.

At the sound of Amanda's voice, Will looked toward the house.

"Tillie says dinner's almost done," she called.

"I'll be right there, darlin'."

He turned back to pat Snicker's flank before heading up the path. The comforts of home didn't outweigh his family obligations. Like a weight around his neck, they threatened to drag him down and choke the life out of him. Although he had obligations to the army, he felt freer there. Even though he had superiors to answer to, he commanded other men. Here, he felt thoroughly controlled by his family's expectations. And one of them waited inside at the dinner table. Emily Courtland was a lovely woman, but she wasn't what he wanted.

****

Dinner lasted forever. Although he'd been hungry and the meal Tillie had prepared smelled appetizing, Will found it hard to digest any of the ham, cornbread, potatoes, and corn, followed by the Negro woman's specialty, apple pie.

The family sat at the long dining table, his father at the head, his mother opposite. Emily had been placed between Will and his father. Jenny, Amanda, and Mrs. O'Connell sat across.

Normally Amanda dined in the kitchen with the servants, but his mother had made this concession. Amanda, however, showed impeccable manners for a five-year-old. No doubt his mother's doing.

Mrs. O'Connell seemed amused by his daughter. "My, what a little lady you are."

Amanda looked up at her, glanced at her grandmother, then looked down at her plate, saying nothing.

His mother eyed Mrs. O'Connell. "The child is not permitted to speak at the table."

Mrs. O'Connell shot a glance at Will. He caught it, then cast his gaze down to the food on his plate.

"I can't quite place your accent," his mother said to Mrs. O'Connell. "I take it you're not native to Virginia."

Jenny shot their mother a glare.

"I've lost my memory," Mrs. O'Connell answered.

"Ah, yes, the accident with the horse." His mother looked at Will. "Jenny tells me you came to this young lady's rescue."

He cleared his throat, aware Emily studied him intently. "I was there when the horse reared up and injured Mrs. O'Connell. Of course, I took her to the surgeon. She appeared to be badly hurt."

"How horrible." His mother sighed. "I do hope your memory returns, dear."

"Thank you, Mrs. Montgomery. I hope so, too." She raised her gaze to Will as if pleading for rescue.

"Miss Courtland, have you told Will about the dinner at the Peterson's this Saturday?" his mother asked.

"Why no, ma'am. I haven't had the chance." Emily gazed at Will.

He cleared his throat. "My apologies, Miss Courtland, but I'm afraid I'll be occupied on Saturday."

Zachary frowned. "May I ask what is so important, son?"

"It's personal." He stared at his plate to escape the perplexed glances of his parents, as well as Emily.

His face heated, knowing his parents expected him to compliment and shower attention on her, but he'd spent the entire meal watching Mrs. O'Connell.

Shoving a forkful of pie into his mouth, he nearly gagged. He couldn't wait to escape from the dining room but didn't dare excuse himself until his father left to smoke his after dinner cigar.

Although, up until now, his father had said nothing, Will felt his father's eyes upon him all through dinner. When the meal finally ended, he suggested Will join him for a cigar in the study to discuss the war. He declined and escaped the house, leaving Emily behind.

He retreated to the, now empty, carriage house. Isaac must have taken Snicker out for some exercise. He glanced through the window toward the creek and found Mrs. O'Connell had left the house, too. She stood a few yards from him, gazing out at the rushing water. In the borrowed gown with her hair elegantly styled and confined in a matching blue ribbon net, she made an enchanting picture.

Drawn to her, he left the carriage house and approached from behind. When he was a few feet away, she turned, sensing his presence. The corners of her lips curved into a smile.

"I'm sorry," she apologized, "but I felt awkward around your parents."

"I'm afraid they can be quite intimidating."

She laughed. "Jenny would agree with that. I'm surprised she isn't out here, too."

"I see you've been talking with my sister."

She nodded.

"My parents are not the easiest people to get along with," he said. "They have certain...expectations."

"I understand." She glanced up at the house. "I hope Jenny and Amanda will be okay when you leave."

Will sighed. "I hope so, too, since I have no choice in the matter."

"I suppose there's no way you could take them with you."

He shook his head. "Army life wouldn't suit those two."

"From what I've seen, I would have to agree."

His pulse raced when she gazed at him. She displayed both strength and vulnerability. He edged closer, catching the scent of lavender. "When I return to the army, will you be going with me?"

"I have nowhere else to go."

The fear and sorrow in her voice made him long to take her hand and comfort her. He restrained himself. "Doc could use your help in the medical tent, I'm sure."

She eyed him with obvious suspicion. "And what about you? Do you want me to come?"

"It makes no matter either way to me," he lied.

Her gaze dropped.

What he wanted to do was take her in his arms, kiss her senseless, and carry her to his room for a night of lovemaking. Now that he had her under his roof, he had to control his feelings, so as not to bring scandal on his family.

But he doubted he'd catch a wink of sleep tonight.

Chapter Fifteen

From a window, Will watched Emily saunter up the walkway. He turned to escape when his mother entered the parlor.

"And where do you think you are going?" She blocked his exit.

"Anywhere, but here."

"It would be impolite for you to leave with your guest arriving."

"I don't recall inviting her."

Will overheard voices in the hallway. Tillie escorted Emily to the parlor.

"Welcome, Miss Courtland. Will and I were just talking about you."

"I hope it was all good." Emily flashed him an innocent smile and batted her eyelids.

"Have a seat, Emily. I'll find Tillie and have her bring some refreshments for you two." Madeline eased out of the room.

Will sat opposite her but hoped he could have left as his mother had. For a brief moment, he was relieved when Tillie served tea and molasses cookies. If it hadn't been improper, he would have asked the servant to join them.

After being served, Emily took a sip of the tea and gazed candidly at Will. "I had hoped to spend more time with you while you're still home on furlough. The last few times you were home, your visits were so brief." She placed a gloved hand on his arm.

Will glanced down. He needed to be honest but didn't wish to hurt her feelings. He removed her hand. "Emily, I—"

"Is there something wrong, Will? Is your wound still plaguing you?" Concern shown in her eyes.

"I'm recovering just fine. It's just that..." He hesitated. "My feelings for you are not as strong as yours are for me."

"It's that Yankee woman you've brought home with you—you're in love with her."

Will glared at Emily. "She's not a Yankee."

"Well, whatever she is—" Emily sat down the cup and waved her hand. "I can tell you have feelings for her."

He couldn't deny her accusation. "I'm sorry, Emily," was all he managed to say.

Her eyes flashed. "But why? What can a woman like that offer you?"

Before he could utter a word, she shook her head. "Oh, no, I'm not that naïve. I do realize what that type of woman can give a man."

"Mrs. O'Connell is not *that* type of woman. She's had a hard set of circumstances. We're friends."

"Friends?" Emily's mouth gaped. "I do not understand you at all, Will Montgomery."

"I never intended to hurt you."

She pulled out an embroidered hanky and sniffed daintily. "Well, you have. I'll be taking my leave now."

He escorted her to the door and watched her depart through the iron gate. Although Will felt a bit guilty for the way he'd handled things, Emily's departure brought relief, until his mother appeared and joined him in the parlor.

"Where has Emily gone?"

"She had to leave." Will didn't want to explain any more than that to his mother.

"I declare, William. It must have been something you said. I've watched your actions with Miss Courtland over the past weeks. How dare you treat that poor young woman like that!"

"I'm sorry, Mother. I don't have any interest in

Emily, and it's cruel to keep her hopes up." He glared at his mother.

Her eyelids narrowed to slits. "Nonsense. She's the perfect match for you."

"Perfect! In whose eyes, may I ask."

"Why, anyone's."

"I'm the one who would have to marry her. It should be my decision alone." Will dropped onto the settee.

"You've upset Miss Courtland," Madeline sputtered, "and her parents will be outraged by your behavior as well. I demand you apologize."

"I will not." He caught her gaze and held it. Madeline huffed and left the room.

****

Aside from the debacle with Emily, Will savored the months spent recovering at home with Amanda and Jenny. The days preparing for Christmas were a comfort to him.

Mrs. O'Connell proved to be a total distraction. Away from the camp wearing the refined clothes Jenny had loaned her, he couldn't imagine the past she'd led. She no longer resembled the rough-edged Irish woman who'd entered camp six months ago. The fall from the horse had changed her. His judgments about her character could have been wrong.

Over the past few months, his initial attraction for her had grown. Since the dinner where he'd spurned Emily, his parents had been reserved toward Mrs. O'Connell but hadn't been unkind, although they'd questioned his motives for bringing her here. He'd told them she possessed excellent nursing skills and had been in a bad situation. He helped her as she helped him. He then refused to discuss the matter further. Although his parents were far from pleased with the situation, they'd wisely remained genteel hosts to his guest, while he healed.

Christmas Day had been a joy, watching the

bright, blue eyes of Amanda when she unwrapped the porcelain doll Mrs. O'Connell helped him choose and wrap. The year prior, he'd been at Fredericksburg and unable to get a furlough to be with her on the holiday. Mrs. O'Connell bought his daughter a rag ball with the bit of money she'd made doing laundry in camp. Delighted with both gifts, Amanda gave him and Mrs. O'Connell a sweet kiss on the cheek.

Today, the morning after Christmas, he brought a pine wreath, adorned with red ribbons and pine cones, to place on Anne's grave. Since she'd died, he'd had a few furloughs to pay a visit, but since the war had escalated, he'd had fewer chances to return home.

After placing the wreath on the thin crust of snow at the base of her headstone, he paused to read the inscription. *Anne Eugenia Montgomery, Beloved Wife and Mother.* His mind drifted back to that Christmas, the second one they'd celebrated as man and wife, when she'd told him he was to be a father.

****

Will had entered the house, arms loaded with packages wrapped in brown paper. Anne's sweet voice echoed from the parlor, the strains of "Deck the Halls" sounded loud and clear. She sang like an angel.

Carefully, he deposited his parcels on the mahogany table in the entry, brushed snow off his greatcoat, then slipped the coat off, hanging it on a peg by the door.

As he stood in the parlor doorway watching Anne's trim form, he couldn't keep the smile from his lips. Her tiny waist was accented by her burgundy hoopskirt. Her back was to him as she worked the twine of popcorn onto the spruce he'd brought home the night before, her auburn hair shining in the candlelight. She'd twisted her locks into an elaborate braided style adorned with velvet ribbons. When she turned to find him in the doorway, she gasped in delight.

"Will, I didn't expect you home so soon." She raced

into his arms. The scent of lilac, vanilla, and bread greeted him.

"You've been baking," he said.

She flashed a smile. "Of course, silly. It's Christmas Eve."

He gazed a moment into her clear hazel eyes. "I've got a surprise for you."

Grinning, she patted her stomach. "And I've got one for you." When his eyebrows rose in question, she added, "It's what you've wanted since our wedding day."

Comprehension dawned on him. Since they'd married over two years ago, they'd talked about having a child, but so far, it hadn't happened.

"Darlin', are you telling me..." He didn't finish.

She nodded eagerly. "We're going to have a baby."

He'd never been happier since the day they'd wed.

****

Kneeling by the stone, Will pressed his lips against it. The taste of cold granite brought the pain back anew. All he had left of her now was Amanda. Their stillborn son rested by Anne's side.

He left the small, church cemetery and strolled home as his thoughts filled with Anne and Mrs. O'Connell. Each woman was so different. Anne had been refined and well-mannered. He hardly recalled a complaint coming from her lips. She'd been the perfect wife, mother, and hostess.

Mrs. O'Connell, on the other hand, could be bold and sometimes brash. She often asked direct questions of a personal nature, causing his father's eyebrows to rise and his mother to shake her head. She was curious about everything, and he'd often catch her scribbling in a journal Jenny had given her to pass the time.

He found her unpredictable, but at the same time, she intrigued him. Anne had been gone two and a half years. And Mrs. O'Connell *was* a lovely distraction. He caught the glances Jenny gave the two of them. She, no doubt, had matchmaking on her mind.

When he arrived home and entered the parlor, the scent of fresh pine and wood burning in the fireplace greeted him.

Jenny, wearing a forest green frock, stood by the tree lighting candles set in the branches. She wore her hair in a braided ring around her head with a black ribbon hairnet for adornment.

"Lighting the candles so early?" he asked.

She gasped and turned to face him. "You scared me, Will. Don't sneak up on me like that."

He grinned and slid onto the settee.

Her hoop-lined skirt spun about as she turned her attention back to the tree set atop a side table. "The lights are so lovely. I just want to sit here and stare at them all day."

"I would have thought Mrs. O'Connell would be here with you. I haven't seen her since early this morning."

"She took Amanda for a walk." She turned from the tree and took a seat beside him. "They came back all covered with snow. They had a snowball fight."

Will smiled as a picture formed in his mind of Mrs. O'Connell and Amanda throwing snowballs at each other.

"Now she's helping Tillie prepare the meal."

He raised his eyebrows.

"Says she can't stand sitting around all day. Seems she's bored."

"Well, she's used to working hard. After being pampered for so long, I suppose she wants to get back to the life she knows."

Jenny smoothed her skirt, then crossed her hands over her lap. "I've been talking to Miss Erin about what it's like in camp..."

"And?"

"It just got me to thinking. It sounds so exciting.

The soldiers marching off. The battles... She told me she assisted the surgeons at Gettysburg."

"That she did."

"Well, I thought—" She glanced toward the window and rubbed her hands together.

"Thought what?" he prompted.

"That I could be a nurse." Her eyes met his.

"In a hospital?"

She licked her lips. "No...on the battlefield."

He laughed. "Jenny, you don't know what you're saying." The very idea of his pampered sister on a dirty, bloody battlefield appalled him.

"I want to go with you when you return to your regiment," she rushed on.

"Absolutely not."

"But Miss Erin does it."

"Erin O'Connell is an exceptional woman."

"And I'm not?" Her eyes misted over. "You think I'm too weak."

"You're refined. The battlefield is no place for a lady. Besides, Father would never permit it."

"You, Mama, and Papa—all of you want to keep me away from Kevin." She dabbed at her eyes with her lace-trimmed hanky and stormed from the room.

****

Erin wiped her hands on her apron. After her jaunt in the snow with Amanda, the heat of the hearth and cookstove felt heavenly, warming her to her core.

"Miss Erin," Tillie said, "after all the time you spent with Miss Amanda, I'm sure surprised you have the energy to help me out."

"You do it all the time," Erin protested. "I see how hard you work, and after all that, when they call you in to serve them, you're there with a smile on your face. Besides, I've spent five months in an army camp. Living here is like a vacation."

The Negro servant eyed her. "A what?"

"Umm..." What did they call vacations? It was

likely this woman had never had one. "I just meant it's very comfortable here."

"Compared to an army camp."

Erin nodded, laughing. Not only had she befriended Jenny, but she'd grown close to Tillie. And she absolutely adored Amanda.

But she still felt unsure of her feelings for Will. After the kiss in camp last summer, she wanted more, but he'd avoided her. Not until he was wounded, did she realize she was not only attracted to him but had fallen in love with him.

When he'd asked her to come here, she'd been wary but at the same time thrilled. An indication he cared for her would be a help.

"You'd best get dressed for dinner, Miss Erin," Tillie said, pulling her from her thoughts.

"But I want to help you."

The woman shook her head. "Mr. Montgomery won't like that none. You're a guest here."

Erin sighed. The thought of changing clothes again exhausted her. And the last thing she wanted was to get into that damned corset. "Oh, I guess I'll have to go change, then."

Tillie shot her an exasperated glance.

Erin was sure the woman would change places with her in a second if she could.

She left the kitchen and headed to the second floor. On the way to the guest room, she halted when Jenny emerged from her room wearing the rose-colored gown and hoops.

Jenny smiled. "My brother has been asking for you."

"When?" The thought of Will asking about her set her heart racing.

"When you were out with Amanda earlier." She studied Erin. "I do hope you're changing for dinner."

Erin ran a hand over the skirt of her plain, unhooped dress. "That's my plan."

100

"I'll be happy to help if you want me to."

"That would be very nice. Thank you." Maybe she could learn more of what Will said before they went down to dinner.

****

An hour later, Erin was corseted and hooped with every hair in place. Although she didn't look forward to returning to camp, she had to admit, she wouldn't miss this nightly ritual.

They entered the dining room. Will, dressed in a silk cravat and dinner jacket, was already seated and in conversation with his father. Her breath caught at the sight of his handsome face.

He raised his gaze toward her, and his eyes widened in apparent approval. He and his father rose and ushered the women to their seats.

When Will seated her, his masculine scent and close proximity made her breath catch. She decided the ordeal of the past hour had been worth it, after all.

"Jenny, Miss Erin, you both look lovely tonight." His gaze fastened on her.

He called me by my first name! She found it hard to draw a breath.

She glanced toward Will's father, noting the rise of his bushy eyebrows. That was the first time Will had called her Erin, instead of Mrs. O'Connell or ma'am.

Catching the smug smile on Jenny's face, she suspected Will's sister had matchmaking on her mind all along. But had Will purposely called her Erin or had he slipped?

Mrs. Montgomery entered last and explained Amanda had already been fed by the servants in the kitchen. "The child was exhausted. Tillie had Isaac carry her off to bed."

Jenny grinned. Erin knew she'd heard about the snowball fight but obviously hadn't told her mother.

"I hope she's all right," Erin said. "We had a great time this afternoon."

"Why, I thought Tillie was caring for her today." Madeline Montgomery lifted her napkin, shaking it out.

"I thought Tillie could use a break."

Madeline frowned.

"Break what?" her husband asked, perplexed.

"I mean, help with handling all she had to do."

"Why, that's her job, my dear," Zachary Montgomery said.

"I like doing things with Amanda. We had a lot of fun."

Madeline pursed her thin lips in obvious disapproval, but Will came to her rescue.

"I believe Miss Erin is good for Amanda." He gazed at her. "She needs someone like you."

A thrill raced through her as Will's parents both shot glares his way. Jenny wore a look of absolute triumph.

Chapter Sixteen

March, 1864

Will cleaned his pistol in preparation for his return to the army. Tillie laundered his uniform, while Isaac polished his brogans. Will had purchased several new shirts and undergarments.

Through his long recovery and the months he'd spent here at his home, he'd finally come to a decision about Erin. In caring for him, she'd shown how much she cared. The touch of her hand, her smile, her scent had all helped him heal from the wounds he'd suffered at Gettysburg. She also brought joy into a part of his life he'd believed dead. A glimpse of her or the sound of her voice set his heart racing and his body responding.

She was wonderful with Amanda and seemed to really care for his daughter.

Since Anne's death, he'd dismissed the thought of remarrying, afraid of being hurt again. But maybe it was time to reconsider.

Just after Christmas, he'd cut off a lock of his hair and taken it to a hair jeweler. The woman had woven the lock into an engraved-edged brooch. He planned to present it to Erin tonight. Should he fall in battle, she was the woman with whom he wanted to leave a piece of himself.

He watched her all through dinner. Her hair, confined in a braided coil, was adorned with one of Jenny's blue velvet ribbon hairnets. Her eyes seemed brighter, her complexion pink and cream. The time spent here had agreed with her. The gray and pink striped gown she wore complemented her coloring.

And the bodice accentuated her lush bosom.

He watched her generous lips as she bit into and chewed every morsel of food. Or curved into a smile at something he or Jenny said. Under her smooth jawline, the creamy skin at her throat fascinated him, making it difficult to swallow his meal or converse politely.

Erin's gaze lifted to him as she sipped her tea. The tip of her tongue darted out to lick her lips. Swallowing, he found himself unable to look away. He longed to hear those lips form his name, tell him she felt for him as he did for her.

No longer able to concentrate on what his father was saying, he cleared his throat and stood.

"Pardon me," he said, his gaze sweeping the table, "I need some air." With measured steps, he walked from the dining room into the foyer. Opening the door, he stepped into the frigid air and let the chill wash over him and bring his erratic breathing under control. One thought monopolized his mind. He wanted to see her before she went to bed. He feared he wouldn't get any sleep with his need for her so strong.

After everyone retired, he moved quietly to Erin's door. Light flickered beneath the crack at the bottom. He'd hoped to catch her before she retired. Raising his hand, he lightly rapped.

The door opened a crack, and a vivid blue eye regarded him.

"Captain?"

"Please, call me Will."

The door opened a few more inches. She'd changed into her nightclothes, and her hair flowed loosely about her shoulders. Her brows rose in question.

"Forgive me, ma'am. I have something I want to give you."

She opened the door further, inviting him in.

He glanced over his shoulder, before awkwardly stepping into the room.

She closed the door behind him, tilting her chin as her lips curved into a smile.

****

What is going on here? Erin's heart skipped a beat as she anticipated finally being alone with Will Montgomery. He'd been her hero from the start, since the dreams that had begun this whole adventure. He was the one bright spot in an otherwise nightmarish experience.

He reached into the pocket of his coat, pulling out a small item wrapped in brown paper and presented it to her.

"What's this?" She accepted the small parcel turning it over in her hands.

"Open it, ma'am."

"Just a minute," she said. "If I'm supposed to call you Will, I'd appreciate it if you'd stop calling me ma'am...or Mrs. O'Connell. Call me Erin."

"Yes, ma—, Erin." His dark eyes gentled when he spoke her name.

The sound of her name on his lips made her skin tingle. She tore the paper off the package. At the sight of the brooch, her breath caught.

"Do you like it?" he asked anxiously. "I had it made just for you."

Eyeing him, she had a hard time finding her voice. This was Erin O'Connell's brooch, the very one that had sent her back in time. It shone in her hands, new and unworn from time and wear.

What did this mean? She must be following Erin O'Connell's footsteps. As far as she knew her being here hadn't changed anything. Will was still destined to die this year.

"I didn't mean to upset you, Erin. If you don't want the brooch—"

"No." She clasped the pin against her chest as the meaning of his gift sank in. "It just means so much to me."

His look of concern softened into a lopsided grin. "I'm happy you feel that way."

"Thank you, Will." She slipped the brooch into the pocket of her wrapper, then stood on her toes, lifting her arms to circle his neck. She kissed his cheek, inhaling his musky scent.

His mouth was on hers, hot and urgent. The softness of his moustache and chin beard tickled her lips. She opened to him, her tongue slipping inside to taste him thoroughly. He groaned, pressing the length of his body against her. Through her thin wrapper and nightgown, she felt his hardened need against her belly. Her heart fluttered in overdrive when he turned her and backed her into the wall. Cupping one of her breasts in his hand, he gently kneaded it and thumbed the hardened nipple through the fabric. Her breath caught, and she moaned deep in her throat as waves of pleasure raced through her core. He growled in response. Her insides heated as moisture pooled between her legs. She didn't know how long she could last. Although she denied it, she'd secretly dreamed of this moment for months. Reaching between them, she attempted to undo the buttons traveling down the length of her wrapper. He obliged by helping her until, together, they slipped the garment off her shoulders, leaving her wearing only her nightgown.

Pulling at the buttons of his shirt, she loosened the first few, exposing dark curls covering hardened muscle. His hands covered hers, and together they undid the remaining buttons. She pushed the shirt over his broad shoulders down to his elbows, and ran her hands over his taut chest. When she brushed one of his brown nipples, his breath hitched.

"You're just as I dreamed you'd be," she whispered. She planted soft kisses along his exposed skin, inhaling his musky scent.

He groaned again, reaching to loosen the tiny buttons at the neck of her nightgown. He slid the gown up over her hips. In seconds the garment dropped to the floor, leaving her naked. Watching his eyes, she shivered in anticipation, wondering if he approved of what he saw.

In the soft glow of the oil lamp, his eyes burned with desire. He bent his head to suckle one of her breasts.

"Oh, Will, please..." She moaned softly as his hot tongue teased her nipple. Pure sensation took her back to the sensual dreams she'd had of him. He was her love, her only love.

Lifting her into his arms, he carried her across the room and laid her on the quilt covering the bed. He gazed down at her. She kicked off her slippers, then leaned up to reach for the buttons at the crotch of his trousers. There were no buttons. When she cast him a perplexed look, he grinned, guiding her hand. The buttons were inside. He quickly undid them and slid his pants to the floor. His drawers followed.

She stared in admiration, as he stood naked before her. He was definitely ready for her.

Once he joined her on the bed, she draped herself over his body, inhaling the delicious scent of sandalwood and maleness. Raining kisses over his warm, slightly damp skin, she worked her way from his face, to his neck, shoulders, and chest, all the way down to his hard shaft.

"Heavens, woman!" He rolled her onto her back. He suckled each nipple, in turn, pushing himself up and bestowing soft kisses on her forehead, eyelids, and cheeks.

"I never believed this would happen again, but I'm afraid I've fallen hopelessly in love with you, Erin," he said before taking her mouth.

After pulling away to take a breath, she said, "I loved you before I ever met you."

"Mmmmn," he murmured, "I feel as if I've know you always, too, darlin'." He parted her legs gently stroking the sensitive folds between them with his fingers until she cried out. If he stopped now, she'd surely die, her need was so great.

"Please," she said. "It's been so long. I can't take much more."

He lowered himself over her, taking her mouth again, moving his hot lips against her neck. His hot breath and the heat of his hard body tormented her. By the time he reached her breast, taking each nipple in turn into his mouth, her insides had turned to liquid fire. She writhed beneath him.

"Will, please."

His kisses continued down over her stomach. When his teeth gently squeezed her flesh at the inside of her thigh, she nearly jumped out of her skin.

"Will, please, I'm ready."

"And I'm more than ready for you, darlin'."

Nestling his hips between her thighs, he thrust into her, filling her. She wrapped her legs around his waist, and he moved within her tightening her need into a hot coil in her belly. His rhythm matched her own, until they dissolved into waves of ecstasy as they found their long sought release together.

****

Will hadn't been with a woman since Anne, except for the comforts of an occasional prostitute. All through the night, they made love, then they dozed, only to wake and make love again. After his heartbreak at losing his wife, he thought he'd never love anyone that way again.

But Erin had put a spark back into his life. He felt as if they had always been meant to be together. Through the months, they'd grown to be a part of each other. No one else's thoughts, including his parents, mattered. He loved her more than his own life.

She murmured sleepily as he ran his hand along her silky thigh. What would his parents think if they caught them like this? He grinned wickedly. They'd likely banish them both from the house. Well, he'd be sure no one caught them.

He reached for her again, cupping one of her lush breasts in his hand. She gasped in delight, turning toward him.

"You're really here," she whispered. "I thought it was all a dream."

"It's no dream, darlin'," he said.

She reached up, circling his neck, and pulled his head down to her lips.

He obliged by taking her mouth and felt himself grow hard yet again.

They made love once more as the first rosy rays of sunrise lit the sky.

Chapter Seventeen

Will woke with a start, then settled back when he felt Erin's warm body beside him. It had been so long since he'd awakened beside a woman. Not since Anne. Reaching beneath the quilt, he caressed Erin's silky thigh. She answered with a low purring sound deep in her throat.

His body responded. As much as he wanted to stay beside her and make love again, he had to get out of here and back to his own room. If they were caught in this compromising position in his parents' house, there would be hell to pay.

"Darlin'," he whispered, running his thumb along her cheek and lips, "I'm sorry, but I have to leave."

She stirred, opened her eyes, and stared at him. He rose and drew back the curtain so he could locate his tossed clothing. Sitting up, she clutched the quilt against her body as she took in the situation.

"Darlin'." He handed her the nightgown. "You may want to put this on."

She took the gown, lifting it over her head as he retrieved her wrapper.

After he pulled on his trousers, he buttoned his shirt and glanced up to find her studying him.

"Will," she said, "before you leave, there's something I have to tell you."

****

Ever since he'd given her the brooch and declared his love for her, Erin decided she had to tell him. She didn't want to conceal the truth from him any longer.

His dark gaze narrowed as he fastened the final button on his shirt. "Can it wait until later?"

"No." She shook her head. "I've been keeping this from you, and now I've got to tell you the truth."

He sighed, his eyes taking on a haunted look. What did he think she was about to tell him?

"Go ahead if you must." He paced the length of the bed.

She drew a steadying breath and exhaled slowly. "I don't know how I can expect you to believe this, but here goes..."

He watched her expectantly.

"I've come from a distant place."

"Yes, I know you came from Ireland."

"No. That's not it...the place I've come from doesn't yet exist." She rose from the bed and pulled on her wrapper. After pacing back and forth, she turned to face him. "I've come from the future."

He frowned. "The future? What future?"

"The twenty-first century." His eyes widened. She was crazy to have thought he'd ever believe her. "Until the accident when I was told I fell off a horse, I'd been living more than one-hundred and forty years in the future."

His dark eyes hardened. Why had she said anything?

Now that she'd gone this far, she had to tell him all of it. "I had a life there and a fiancé. We broke it off because I couldn't stop dreaming about you."

"This is utter nonsense." He raked his hand through his hair.

She held up her hand, desperately needing him to understand. "It didn't make sense to me at first, either."

"If what you say it true, how and why are you here now?"

"I'm not sure how, but I do know why." She reached her hand out to him. "I've come back in time for you, Will."

****

Will stared at her. His pulse thundered, and he feared he'd collapse. He'd expected her to tell him she was a Yankee spy or a whore, but this...how could she expect him to believe this preposterous story? She had to be daft. He groaned inwardly. After two long years, he'd given his heart to a woman who was insane.

"I've got to get back to my room," he said.

Her face fell.

He walked down the hall, his fury building. She actually expected him to believe her crazed story.

Of all the women I could have fallen in love with, why did I have to choose a raving lunatic? He'd actually planned to propose. Thank God, he hadn't.

****

Will dressed and went down to the empty dining room. He needed time alone to think. What a mess this had turned out to be. And now, he had no choice but to take her back to camp with him. After they returned, he'd distance himself from her. And now that he'd told her he'd fallen in love with her, that was going to be difficult.

As he considered his options, Jenny appeared at the door, startling him.

"Will, I'm so glad to see you up," she said. "I need to speak with you before you leave."

"What is it?" he asked.

She took the seat across from him. "You have to take me with you."

Will gritted his teeth. "We've already been over this. I can't take you."

"But you can take Miss Erin."

"That's different."

"How is it different? She's a woman, too."

"But she's used to hard work. You're not."

She drew her mouth into a pout. "Please, Will, you can't leave me here with them."

"Jenny—"

"I'll just die if you leave me here."

"You're being dramatic." His gaze drilled over her. She wore her morning gown, her hair covered with a white cap. "You would not even last one day in a grungy, smelly army camp."

"I've been to camp." She eyed him with scorn.

"As a visitor. It's not the same as living there."

"I can do it."

He shook his head, folding his arms across his chest. "You can take lice, rats, men covered in blood, amputations, enemy shelling, constant rain, mud...you'll set eyes on the most horrible sights you can imagine. No, my dear sister, I do not believe you are ready to do that."

She stood, anger flashing in her gray eyes. "You won't even give me the chance to prove myself."

"Because I know how it will turn out. I'll be shipping you back home before the second day dawns."

"That's not true!"

"Mother and Father will never permit it, anyway."

"You could persuade them." She clasped her hands.

"No, I cannot. And furthermore, I won't."

"I hate you!" She stormed from the room.

He sighed. Women were turning out to plague him right and left. If it weren't for Erin, he'd almost look forward to returning to the army.

****

Erin folded her clothes and packed them in the satchel she'd brought with her.

She'd absolutely blown any chance she had with Will. The look on his face when she'd told him she'd come from the future would torment her forever.

But she should've known. She couldn't expect anyone to believe her crazy story. She still had a hard time believing it herself. It wouldn't surprise her if he refused to take her with him. Then what would she do? She had nowhere else to go. She'd have to beg in the streets.

This is all going wrong. All she could hope was that he'd take her to camp, so she could have a second chance with him. If he even spoke to her again.

A knock at the door drew her from her anxious thoughts.

"Come in."

Jenny burst in, dabbing her eyes with an embroidered hanky.

"Will's being so stubborn," she said.

"About what?"

"I asked him to take me to camp so I can be a nurse like you."

Erin stared at her. "You'd want to do that?" She couldn't imagine this pampered woman nursing soldiers.

"Yes. I'd be good at it. I swear."

Erin hesitated. She wondered why Jenny was telling her. "You said Will won't let you go."

"No, he says I won't last a day in camp."

"Well." She had to suppress the urge to laugh. "I guess that's that."

"You could persuade him for me, couldn't you?"

"Your brother's a bit unhappy with me right now. I'll be surprised if he takes *me* back with him."

"Oh, no," Jenny whined. "Why does he have to be so difficult?"

Why, indeed.

****

In the end, Erin had been no help to Jenny. Will ordered his sister to stay home.

He assisted Erin into the carriage for the ride back to camp. Since she'd told him the truth, he'd been aloof—the air between them strained. Before he could climb in beside her, Amanda raced from the house followed by Tillie.

"Papa!" she called.

Will's expression turned to stone. Amanda had created a scene early this morning, begging him not to go. His jaw tensed as his daughter neared him. He was obviously having a hard time keeping his emotions under control.

"I'm so sorry, Mr. Will," Tillie apologized. "But she says she had something to give you."

Will swallowed as he gazed down at his daughter. Tears welled in her eyes, as she watched him keep himself under complete control amidst such a heart-wrenching scene.

Amanda extended her small hand. In her palm, an auburn curl tied with a powder-blue ribbon rested. He lifted the lock.

"Amanda, who cut your hair?"

"I did it for her, Mr. Will," the Negro woman said.

Erin's eyes burned.

He lifted the lock and stared at it.

"You have to carry it with you always," Amanda said.

"I sure will, darlin'." He opened his coat, inserting the curl into an inside pocket. "I'll keep it right here, next to my heart."

The girl raised her delicate brows. "Even when you go to the battle?"

"Especially then," Will assured her.

Tillie dabbed at her eyes.

Tears trickled down Erin's cheeks. Her thoughts went to the brooch he'd given her. She must have meant something for him to give her such an intimate token.

And she'd ruined everything.

She averted her face when he climbed into the carriage, taking his place beside her. She longed to bury her face in his coat and hold him but was sure he'd never permit it. He obviously noticed her tears but hadn't reached for her. He sat stiffly beside her, the tension mounting between them.

Although he was just a touch away, right now she felt miles and a universe apart.

Chapter Eighteen

Confederate camp outside Mason, Virginia
March 1864

Jake watched Captain Montgomery as he assisted Erin from his carriage. After so long, Jake had wondered if he'd ever see the bitch again. Her tent, along with the belongings she'd left, had been disassembled and packed away after she'd gone and kept in a small shed built to house extra supplies when the men moved into winter quarters.

After Montgomery left, Jake continued to observe her while she inspected her tent that had been erected when the company knew they were returning. Once she disappeared inside, he strode over and yanked back the flap of canvas. From where she stood leaning over her trunk, she half turned and gasped.

A red leather-covered book sat on top of her clothing. "A new journal?" he asked.

"If you must know, it was a gift from Will's sister, since I lost my other one."

"Will, is it now?" When she didn't answer, he continued, "Reckon you'd like to know what happened to it."

"I'm sure I know who took it."

He took a step towards her. "I have your book, and I know all about how you just *tolerate* my presence for the information I hand you, you whore. I also know about you and the captain."

She licked her lips. "What about him?"

"You spent over six months with him, and I assume you did more than tolerate *his* presence."

"Get out of my tent," she ordered. "I no longer have need of your services."

"Is that right?" He grinned, enjoying the feel of power he held. "If you have any notion of turning me in, I'll have you up on charges of spying for the Yankees quick as greased lightning. And I have it in your own handwriting."

A look of panic crossed her eyes. "I haven't said anything to Captain Montgomery."

"But he knows about us."

"All he knows is you appointed me laundress. I told him we were cousins."

Just like a woman to move on when she found someone who could give her more. And he suspected the captain had given her much more than he'd ever been allowed. He raised a finger. "If anyone learns of my part in this, I'll drag you down with me, missy. You'll likely be sent to a Confederate prison."

Her eyes widened as she chewed her lower lip. She moved closer to him. "I only went with him to get information." She traced her finger over his collar. "He trusts me now. We can use him."

What's this Yankee whore up to now? He grasped her wrist and pushed her away.

****

Erin had to think fast. She needed to get that book back. She wouldn't let him complicate things by calling her out as a spy. Although he made her skin crawl, she'd have to entice him into giving it back.

"Jake, I'm not lying. He's a captain, and I can get him to tell me anything." She reached for his hand. He didn't pull away.

"You just said you don't need me." His eyes narrowed. "I don't reckon I should trust you."

She kept hold of his hand and reached her other one behind his head. Pulling him close, she hoped she could gain his confidence. The stench of whiskey and tobacco juice on his breath nearly gagged her, but she couldn't have him holding the journal against her. Without the book, she didn't believe he had any proof of her great-aunt's activities. And since she'd told Will her story of time travel, he'd been nothing but cool and polite toward her. He didn't believe her, so she had no ally in this time period. No one she could confide in.

When Jake bent his head toward hers, she didn't flinch. She concentrated on her goal. If Grandma's great-aunt Erin could do this, so could she. But when he forced his tongue into her mouth, she pushed both palms against his chest, forcing him away. She couldn't do this.

Jake scowled. "You don't seem all that enthusiastic."

"I'm just tired, is all. We're in this together. I have no interest in Captain Montgomery. I used him for the information I could gather."

He sneered. "Like you've been using me."

"No. We're partners."

"Have you forgotten I read your book? And I know that's what you're after now, bitch!" Abruptly, he turned and left the tent.

She followed, grasping his arm, the book uppermost in her mind. He tried to shrug her off, but she tightened her grip, refusing to allow him to leave. Twisting around, he shoved her with his other hand and knocked her to the ground.

****

Will couldn't believe the scene before him. Wagner stepped from Erin's tent, while she clung to his arm trying to pull him back inside. After all these months, he'd believed her story that the sergeant was a controlling relative who demanded a percentage of her pay, but nothing more. Will's face heated, and he prepared to turn away. She was a liar after all. Her time travel story had been pure invention. He'd cared for her and thought she cared for him, but he'd been wrong.

Wagner shoved her, knocking her to the ground. Blood pounded through Will's temples. No man, no matter who he was, should do that to a woman. He approached the couple, ready for a fight.

Wagner turned, his eyes widening.

"Sergeant," Will said, "I thought I ordered you to stay away from her."

"I came for my payment, *sir*."

Will glanced at Erin. She gathered her skirts, preparing to rise. He extended a hand. She took it but didn't look at him directly.

"Be on your way, Wagner," he ordered.

Without another word, the sergeant strode off.

"Would you care to tell me what that was all about?" Will asked.

Erin shook her head.

He clenched his fists. "It looked like you were trying to pull him back inside."

"He has something that belongs to me." She dropped her gaze, wiping her hands on her apron.

"What is it?" He scowled.

"I—I can't tell you."

Releasing a long sigh, he realized he'd been right about her and Wagner all along. "I can't help you if you won't be truthful with me."

She looked directly into his eyes. "I don't need your help in this matter."

He swallowed. "Well then, good morning, ma'am." Tipping his cap, he turned his back and left. He'd known from the start this woman was going to be trouble. And damned if he hadn't been right.

Chapter Nineteen

That afternoon Will noticed a well-dressed, young woman strolling through camp chatting with a soldier. His rage bubbled to the surface when he realized the woman was his sister. What the hell was she doing here? He moved toward her. She calmly lifted her lace-trimmed parasol and tilted her chin defiantly.

He hadn't received any word of her visit. His parents surely wouldn't have allowed her to travel alone.

Kevin Donnelly stood behind her. He whispered in her ear. She smiled. Donnelly also smiled, but when he raised his gaze to Will, the Irishman's smile disappeared, and he stood at attention.

"I'll be getting back to me duties, sir." Donnelly saluted, waiting for a return salute before leaving.

Jenny flinched when Will moved within inches of her, but the smile plastered on her heart-shaped face didn't waver.

"No one wrote me you were coming," he said.

"No one knew but me."

"Mother and Father don't know you're here?"

"They would never have allowed me to come. I left without telling anyone."

He clenched his teeth. How could she be so foolish? "You can't just go running off like that. The country's at war. It isn't safe for a woman alone—"

"I don't need to be lectured." She backed off, closed her parasol, and pointed it at his chest.

"I'm your brother. I have a responsibility for your safety."

Her eyes flashed. "You think I'm just a helpless

female."

"Mother and Father will be frantic. And what about Amanda?"

"Tillie can take care of her." She dismissed his concerns with a wave of her gloved hand. "And Momma and Papa are being impossible."

"How?" Although he asked the question, he knew just how impossible his parents could be.

"Papa was trying to marry me to a stranger from South Carolina."

"Surely not!" Will crossed his arms over his chest.

"Well, the man was looking for a wife and..."

"And your heart belongs to someone else."

Her cheeks colored. "I've tried to keep it hidden, but I do believe you've known all along." She locked her gaze with his.

"Yes, I know about Donnelly."

"And you don't approve."

He sighed. "You know what Mother and Father will say."

"I've had it drilled into me since I was small that I was to make a socially acceptable marriage." She removed her gloves and slapped them against her skirt. "Isn't love more important than social status?"

"They're only thinking of your future."

"But it's different for you, because you're a man."

"I'm still expected to choose an acceptable wife. Anne came from a well-respected family."

"I don't want to be controlled. I want to live my life and do important things."

"Like marry a poor Irish lad. Wash his clothes, cook his meals, bear his children?" He shook his head. She wasn't thinking straight.

"You make it sound like a life of drudgery."

"It is, my dear sister."

"Please, Will, don't tell them I'm here. It could be my only chance to have an adventure before I'm forced into a loveless, acceptable marriage."

"You don't know what you're asking."

"Please, I'd do it for you. I'd never tell if you had a secret sweetheart."

Erin's face came unbidden into his mind. But she wasn't his sweetheart. He had to stop thinking about the laundress. She wasn't his responsibility. But Jenny was. He had to decide what he'd do if his parents contacted him about her.

He'd have to find a place for her to stay tonight, but first thing tomorrow, he'd make arrangements to send his headstrong sister home.

****

Up to her elbows in hot, sudsy water scrubbing soldier's dirty laundry, Erin realized the workload hadn't taken long to shift back to her. She thought about Will again and how she could regain his confidence. Should she even try? She'd bared her soul only to have him drop her like a hot potato.

She wanted more than anything to talk to him, convince him she wasn't insane or a liar. The scene with Jake had made things worse. Damn that man. He always showed up at the worst possible time.

She had to convince Will she was telling the truth. But she couldn't prove she'd traveled over one-hundred and forty years from the future. If she'd met a man who'd claimed to have come from the twenty-second century, what would she have done?

Suppressing a laugh, she never would have believed him unless he'd landed in a spaceship. So, she couldn't expect Will to believe her.

She wrung out the last of the shirts. Arms aching, she carried the heavy wet pile to the clothesline. Automatically, she reached for the wooden clothes pins and started to drape the shirts over the line.

Her mind focused on Will and her dilemma. She wouldn't give up on him. She loved him and had come here to be with him.

She had to find a way to prove she wasn't a liar.

Chapter Twenty

The next morning Erin woke to the sound of Jenny's soft breathing on the cot across from her. Erin had offered to share space in her tent, and although Will seemed reluctant, she'd insisted Jenny stay. They'd had a long talk before falling asleep, catching up on events since Erin and Will had left.

Jenny related the story of her parent's expectations, and Erin agreed she needed a chance to experience life before settling down. She advised her to speak to Doc about staying on as a nurse.

After a quick breakfast of leftover corn muffins and strawberry jam, Erin brought her to Doc's tent. Jenny had met the doctor on her visit last summer but commented aside to Erin that he appeared thinner and older than she remembered.

"Jenny wants to stay on as a nurse," Erin told him.

Doc wiped his hands on a towel, then ran a long finger over his thick mustache. "Reckon we could use more help." He looked Jenny over. "You *have* cared for family members."

Jenny fidgeted under his gaze. It had been a statement rather than a question. "I've read to Papa and Amanda when they were ill with the croup."

"I suppose that will be some help."

"I can write letters for the soldiers, too," she offered. When he hesitated, she blurted, "I'll do anything you need me to do if you just allow me to stay."

"What does your brother have to say about all this?"

"He's just fine with it," she lied. She glanced at Erin, who kept silent.

He tapped his chin. "As long as Will approves, you can stay. But if you're not able to do the work or become ill, we'll have to send you on home."

"Thank you, Doc. You surely won't regret allowing me to stay."

"The first thing I suggest you do, young lady, is find a suitable dress. Fancy clothing and hoops have no place in an army camp."

"I'm sure we'll find her something appropriate," Erin said.

When they left, Jenny breathed a sigh of relief. "Thank you so much, Miss Erin."

"You still have to convince your brother."

"I know," Jenny said. "But I'll show him...and everybody, that there's more to me than a pampered female who needs to be protected and controlled by a man. Women should be allowed to do whatever they want."

Erin smiled. "In the future that will certainly be true."

"The future? How can you be sure?"

"Women will fight for their rights and win them. But it will be a long time before we're considered men's equals."

"Men's equals," Jenny repeated.

Erin detected awe in the young woman's voice.

****

That afternoon, Will arrived at Doc's tent to check on two of his men who were recovering from measles. He caught sight of a familiar, dark-haired woman dispensing water to the patients.

Damn his sister. He'd planned to send her home this morning, but duties had prevented him from making the arrangements.

Jenny turned his way. Her startled glance softened into a wavering smile. She wore a plain brown wrapper, covered with an apron. No hoop. What in blazes was she up to now?

"Doc said I could stay to help," she said.

"He said what?"

"He told me he needs women volunteers with nursing skills."

Will rubbed his chin. "You're going to nurse ill and wounded soldiers."

"That's right." Her eyes flashed.

He chuckled at the thought of his spoiled sister assisting at an amputation or wiping up vomit or other unmentionable duties. She wouldn't last the day.

"You can stay, for now," he said. "But at the first complaint out of your pretty little mouth, I'm shipping you home. Is that understood?"

"Oh, Will." She rushed to him and kissed his cheek. "You won't regret allowing me to stay."

"I fear I will."

Her gaze narrowed. "Why? What's wrong?"

"I received a dispatch today from Father. He's written me that you've run off. If I see you, I'm to immediately send you home."

She shook her head. "You won't tell him I'm here, will you?"

"What you're asking..." He sighed. How could she place him in such a position?

"Please, Will. Tell them you haven't seen me. They'll never know."

"But it's wrong to worry them like this."

"William Montgomery! I know how glad you are to be out of that house with their impossible demands. Once the war is over, you can take Amanda and start a new life elsewhere. I only ask that you give me the same chance."

"But I fear for your welfare here."

"Just as we all feared for you and Sam when you went off to war."

"That's different—"

"If you say because you're a man—" Jenny raised her palm toward him, "—I fear I shall have to scream."

"I can't protect you here," he protested.

"I don't need your or any man's protection. Miss Erin says that in the future men and women will be equals." Her chin lifted.

"Is that right?" Apparently, she hadn't told his sister her fantastic story of her travel through time. But after seeing how Erin dealt with Wagner, he began to think she could show a man a thing or two.

"In the future, she says, I can do anything I want, and no man can stop me."

"All right," he relented. "I'll send word that I haven't seen you, but I warn you—"

"I know. One complaint..." She rolled her eyes. "You won't hear a single one from my lips."

He nodded. But he doubted Jenny would adjust to the harshness of camp life. In a few days time, he was certain he'd be sending his parents word of his sister's arrival home.

****

After rubbing his hands briskly together, Jake blew on them to ease the chill. A crusty layer of snow covered the camp, and the sun hadn't yet made an appearance today, if it ever would.

Charlie lumbered toward him, his thick hands wrapped around a steaming mug.

"Is that coffee?" Jake couldn't recall what real coffee tasted like.

"Coffee?" Charlie wheezed. "Where in the hell would I get a thing like that?"

"Then what is it?" Jake's patience was on edge.

The big man grimaced. "It's that damnable chicory blend. Tastes kinda like seasoned dishwater if you ask me, but it's hot. Like some?"

"Reckon so."

"C'mere. I've got a pot brewing. Maybe the flavor will seep into the next cup." He motioned Jake to his grate, where a small fire flickered.

Jake crouched and held his hands close to the flame. Charlie grabbed a towel and lifted the pot. Jake reached to untie his mug from his belt and lifted it for the other man to fill. He took a quick gulp, savoring the warmth, if not the flavor.

Charlie motioned to a couple of stools. They both sat.

"Reckon now that spring's comin', the fightin' will start up again." Charlie looked off into the distance.

Jake frowned. "Reckon the Yankees are gonna win this thing anyway."

"Then we might as well all go home."

Jake shook his head. "It's a lost cause. Never should have gotten into this thing. Should have gone up north and joined up with those Yankee boys."

"We have to fight for our homes and families," Charlie protested.

"I got none of those. Got nuthin' at all."

Charlie shrugged. "Why don't you just desert, then?"

"And be shot?"

"Reckon you're stuck here, like the rest of us. Until the bitter end."

Jake dumped his grounds into the fire pit and rose. "Reckon so. I've got to clean my rifle before inspection."

After Jake returned to his tent, he considered what Charlie had said. Why not desert? Since Erin had come back, she'd completely cut him off in every way. The captain seemed to be watching him constantly, always ready to pounce. And Montgomery seemed to find fault with everything he did. He'd been put on report three times since that high and mighty bastard had returned.

Since he'd taken her journal, Erin had tried to sweet talk him into giving it back, but he refused to give it up. He needed that book to insure she wouldn't betray him now that she'd cozied up to the captain.

She had Montgomery's sister staying with her. She was a sweet little thing, too, but he couldn't go near her without bringing down more of the captain's wrath.

He couldn't talk to Erin without someone overhearing. He'd a mind to leave the journal for the colonel to find, then desert. He could head north. Make a new life for himself now that his extra income had been cut off.

But he wasn't quite ready to do that.

Yet.

****

For days, Will watched Wagner skirt around Erin's tent, like a dog waiting for leavings. Jenny's presence obviously kept him away. But now he had to worry the man would harm his sister. He'd never believed Erin's story that he was a relative. What were they to each other?

After the crazy time travel story, he'd started to wonder about the papers he'd found near her tent the night—nearly nine months ago—when she'd fallen from the mare. He suspected she may have dropped them, but he'd never suggested that to the colonel. Blinded by a beautiful woman, he found himself unwilling to believe she could be in any way responsible for traitorous activity.

If she could tell him an outrageous story about time travel, how easy would it have been for her to lie about everything—her relationship with Wagner, where she'd come from. He wondered if anything she'd told him had been true.

What about Wagner? Will had no trouble believing him capable of treachery.

He needed to know the truth about those two.

Erin talked to Doc. If she were a Yankee spy, she wouldn't reveal it to the doctor, but she could have let something slip, or said something that may have aroused suspicions.

He decided to pay Doc a visit and found him sitting down to a meal of salt pork and cornbread.

"Join me?" Doc asked.

Will shook his head. "I just need to ask you something."

"Ask me what?" Doc motioned at the seat across from him, then took a bite of his bread and chewed while he waited for Will's question.

"I know you've grown fond of Mrs. O'Connell." Will pulled out the chair and sat.

"Erin's been helpful and good for my patients."

"You call her Erin? That seems a bit familiar."

Doc reddened. "She insisted. She doesn't like being called Mrs. O'Connell or ma'am." When Will didn't reply, he blanched. "Just what, sir, are you insinuating? I'm a married man."

"Who hasn't seen his wife in over a year."

"Erin and I are friends." Doc rose and glared at Will. "She's very intelligent and not squeamish in the least. I do believe she'd make an excellent doctor."

"She's a laundress," Will stated.

"You've spent a great deal of time with her." Doc took his seat but leaned forward over the table. "You must have noticed how different she is from other women in camp."

Will slid his finger over his lower lip. Since he'd known Doc from before the war, he could trust this man with his life. "I found pages torn from a journal last summer outside her tent."

"What was on them?" Doc's brow furrowed.

"Handwritten notes on troop movements—ours."

"What are you saying?"

"That someone in camp is or was spying for the Yankees."

"No." Doc shook his head. "You're not saying Erin—"

"I found the pages in the spot where she fell."

"Did you question her about it?"

"No."

"Why not?"

"She'd hit her head. Didn't remember anything," he replied in way of explanation.

"And afterward? Didn't you report this to anyone else?"

"Of course. I gave the pages to the colonel. But nothing was ever proved. I had no reason to suspect her of espionage."

Doc brushed a finger over his mustache. "She's never given me any indication that she may be a spy."

"If she's good at her job, I don't suppose she would."

"Just what do you plan to do?" Doc locked his gaze with Will.

Will shrugged. "I've been keeping an eye on her." In truth if he found out she was a spy, could he turn her in? She was the first woman since Anne who caused his pulse to race. He'd felt that way since the day he'd first laid eyes on her. But the time travel story had alerted his defenses. Could she have used that tale to cover the real truth?

Doc studied him a moment, then nodded, saying nothing more.

Will rose from the table and turned to leave.

"Take care, Will," Doc called after him.

Will inclined his head in acknowledgment, then walked away. Doc could most likely read his thoughts concerning Erin. But he had to guard his heart. The loss of Anne had wounded it almost beyond repair. He'd given Erin the brooch as well as his heart, body, and soul only to have everything ripped from him again.

****

Light rain pattered against the canvas over Erin's head. Lying awake, she listened to Jenny's steady breathing on the bunk across from her. Erin truly liked the young woman and felt a connection to her plight. If anyone had tried to force *her* to marry a man she didn't love, she'd bolt, too. Luckily, in her time, things like that didn't happen. Her mother had seemed almost relieved when she'd announced her marriage to Rick had been called off. To her credit, Mom had kept her opinions of Rick to herself and supported Erin through the many wedding cancellations.

She sighed, pulled her quilt around her and rose. Sleep wasn't possible right now. She kept reliving the night she'd spent with Will.

Trying not to wake Jenny, she eased her way out of the tent. Soft rain continued to patter overhead on the tarp that shielded the entrance. After she'd told Will who she really was, she'd felt such a rush of relief.

But he hadn't believed her. Now he thought she was crazy.

Erin sank onto a wooden chair she'd set out to do mending that day. Tracing a finger over her lips, she recalled his kiss, the feel of his hard naked body as they'd made love, and the thrill when he'd caressed and held her close.

He'd come to her rescue three times already and had declared his love. She'd made a serious mistake by being truthful. She never should have expected him to believe her tale.

Right now she could use those strong masculine arms around her, telling her everything would be all right.

She may have destroyed everything she'd been sent here to do.

Chapter Twenty-one

Erin stood at the threshold of the funeral parlor room where Grandma Rose had been laid for viewing. The cloying scent of so many flowers crammed into the small space had sent her out to get some air, while her mother and other relatives held court before the oak coffin.

As she stepped back inside, mourners offered their sympathy. After accepting their condolences, she approached the body. Grandma looked small and frail as she had just before her death. Erin laid a hand on the smooth edge of the coffin. A jolt shot through her, turning her knees to jelly. Grandma's blue eyes opened wide.

Erin gasped. No one around her seemed to notice. Her gaze locked with Grandma's. Her pale lips parted. "You are Erin O'Connell," she said.

"What?"

Erin sat bolt upright. A dream.

Jenny's steady breathing brought her back to reality. She remained in the past. But Grandma had said she *was* Erin O'Connell.

She perched on the edge of her cot. Before coming here, she'd speculated about the dreams being memories of a past life. Was *she* the Yankee spy Grandma had told her stories about?

If that were true, it would explain a lot, except for why she was here now. If she'd lived this life before, why had she no memory of what was to happen? Could she be lying in a coma reliving her past life, while she still retained memories of her life in the twenty-first century?

Trembling, she gathered the quilt about her, rose, and left the tent. She paced the length of the overhead tarp, forcing herself to remember. If she *had* lived this life before, she had to know how the story ended.

Erin slowed her pacing as she started to feel separated from her body. She was on a ship, feeling the pitch of the waves beneath her feet. Halting, she concentrated on the vision forcing its way into her mind.

****

She'd been seasick for days as the ship continued to heave and roll. Some of the passengers were ill, but not all from the sea—they were starving. That's why they'd left their home. The English had made life in Ireland unbearable.

She'd hated leaving her parents, but they'd urged their offspring to go to America. They wanted their children to have a chance at a better life. At the dock of Killarney, her parents stood huddled, frail, sunken, and defeated, sending their children—their future— away forever. That was the last she'd seen her ma and da.

Days later, after the sea finally calmed, she made her way on deck, raising her face and closing her eyes to absorb the warmth of the sun.

"Here, lass." A male voice startled her. "You look like you could use this."

She looked into the eyes of an auburn-haired man, holding out a crust of brown bread.

Eyeing him suspiciously, she took in his shabby state of dress. But his hazel eyes were kind. "Thank you, sir." She accepted the bread. "Where did you get this?"

He winked. "I have me ways. Stick with me, and yer passage will be easier."

She stared at him in awe. "You're not a crew member. Who are you?"

"Rory O'Connell." He removed his cap with a

flourish. "I'm goin' to America to start a new life."

"I'm Erin Coyne," she replied while chewing.

Many days had passed since she'd eaten anything to stop her stomach from complaining. The small bit of food her parents had managed to scrounge up had to be divided among her six siblings. She'd had little more than a morsel each day since they'd left Ireland. A knot formed in her stomach as she recalled her brothers and sister languishing below deck. She was a horrible sister, but she couldn't resist easing the terrible gnawing in her stomach.

"Pleased to meet you, Miss Coyne."

"And you as well, Mr. O'Connell."

He winked again, produced a flask and handed it to her. Without a thought, she raised it to her lips, gasping in delight after the liquid burned its way down her throat.

"Irish whiskey!"

"Only the finest for such a lovely lass."

She smiled, warming to the comely man. "What do you plan to do in America?"

"Oh, I have me plans. Once we make port in New York, I have contacts that will set me up just fine."

"Is that so?" She suspected this man was full of blarney.

"Stick with me, Miss Coyne. I'll help you get on yer feet in the New World."

"And why would you be doing that? You don't even know me?" Her suspicions rose at his familiarity.

"I have a feeling about you, lass."

****

Erin gasped. How had she remembered that? It had felt so real, as if she had been the Irish emigrant aboard that ship. She'd felt the nauseating seasickness, experienced gnawing hunger. Somehow, she seemed to be remembering Erin O'Connell's thoughts. The man she'd spoken with must have been Erin O'Connell's husband. She wondered why she remembered this now.

A shiver ran down her spine. Never before had she experienced anything so mystic. In her own time, she could have visited someone who did past life regressions to shed light on the situation. Did people in this time believe reincarnation possible? Was she seeing through her great-great-great aunt's eyes, or had she *been* Erin O'Connell?

Left with nothing but questions, she resumed pacing before the tent in the inky darkness.

Chapter Twenty-two

October 1864
Cedar Creek, Virginia

Will paced before the troops assembled in the chilly evening air. The generals planned to attack the Federal soldiers while they slept and rouse them from their tents. The Confederate soldiers had to start marching now, to make Federal camp before dawn. In the darkness, he could barely make out the faces of his men.

"Ow!" a gruff voice bellowed. "What'd you do that for?"

"I can't see but a few inches in front of me. How was I to know your big foot was there?" a voice whined in defense.

"Quiet in the ranks," Will ordered. Peering through the mist, he tried to distinguish the source of the disruption. Jake Wagner's sullen face glared at him as the sergeant lifted his rifle to his shoulder.

I should have known. His jaw tightened when he pictured Wagner manhandling Erin.

"Is there a problem, Sergeant?" Will asked.

"Yes, sir, there is," Wagner replied. "How are we supposed to attack the Yankees when we can't see where we're goin'?"

A few of the men grumbled assent.

"We are going to take the Yankees by surprise. They won't expect an attack while it's still dark."

"Sounds foolhardy to me," Wagner griped.

Will spun toward the sergeant. "When I want your opinion, Sergeant, I'll ask for it. Until then, you do as you're ordered."

"Yes, sir."

While the men settled down to await further orders, Will worried about Wagner. He didn't trust the man. He'd best keep him in sight to be sure the plan wasn't thwarted from the start.

And if he found any evidence of espionage, he'd be only too happy to bring him up on charges.

****

Once Montgomery was out of earshot, Charlie Ross muttered, "Reckon you're goin' on report again."

"The hell I am," Jake said, seething.

"There's no doubt the captain's got it in for you," Charlie continued.

Jake peered through the moonlight at the big man beside him. "Like I don't know that already."

"It's that washer woman, isn't it? Montgomery's sweet on her."

"Shut your—"

"Wagner!" the lieutenant reprimanded.

"Sir?"

"Keep order in the ranks, Sergeant."

"Yes, sir." Jake saluted, then sent Charlie a reproachful glance.

"Reckon we'll surprise the hell out of the Yankees," the big man said when the lieutenant moved away.

When the captain gave the order to form up, Jake clenched his jaw. He shouldn't be here. If he had deserted after Erin and Montgomery had returned, he'd be safely up north. Instead, he had to go into battle, again. Another chance for the Yankees to kill or maim him. He wasn't about to die for these accursed Southerners. He'd never been one of them.

****

Will surveyed the men before him as best he could in the darkness. Many looked bone weary, as if they hadn't fully awakened, while others were keyed up,

137

anticipating the coming battle. Hopefully, the element of surprise when they attacked the Yankees, would help turn the tide of the war. Since Gettysburg, things had not been going well. They needed this victory to invigorate the men. If things didn't go their way, he didn't have much hope the Confederacy could hold out.

Will ordered his company, arranged in three columns, to start the march, lighted only by the moon. He could barely make out the faces of the young privates. His gaze alighted on Kevin Donnelly. Although Jenny had tried her best to hide it, he knew she'd been visiting the Irishman last summer on the pretext of bringing Amanda to see him. He also knew her motive in becoming an army nurse was to be near Donnelly.

The thought of Jenny's grief if he didn't bring the young private back to camp, gave him pause.

He gazed at the stars while his men made their way along a pig path, wondering, as he always did before a battle, if he'd ever see the light of day again.

****

Jake was dog-tired as the troops continued to march through the night. Fear kept him from dropping out of rank from sheer exhaustion. Devised by the generals, this foolhardy plan, a desperate attempt by a defeated Confederacy, just couldn't work. He shouldn't have stayed. As they made their way to the Yankee camp, his teeth clenched, causing his jaw to ache, and he longed to take out his rage on anyone he could. It didn't matter what side they were on. And if he survived this battle, Erin O'Connell and Captain Montgomery would be perfect targets.

The fog was thick and cloying just before dawn when the orders came to strike. Bayonets drawn, Jake and the other men roused the sleeping Yankees from their tents.

He briefly fought hand-to-hand with a wide-eyed soldier who tried to wrestle his rifle from him.

Plunging the bayonet into the man, he recoiled from the sickening wet thud, then went to the next tent.

Chaos erupted as the half-clad Yankees tried to fend off the Confederates. Federals who weren't killed or taken prisoner broke and ran, still in their bedclothes.

"Let's get what those Yanks left behind," Charlie said.

Rifling through the deserted packs in the tents, they pulled out sugar, coffee beans, and other rations they hadn't seen in their camp for months.

"Whooee!" Charlie called. "We're gonna have a feast for our trouble tonight."

****

When General Early arrived and called a halt to the attack, declaring it a Confederate victory, Will thought about bringing his men to order, but they were fully occupied in pillaging Union stores. The men were hungry. They hadn't had any sleep. How could he deny them?

By afternoon, after having eaten his fill of Yankee supplies, Will stretched out under a wide oak and gazed up at the leaves that had started to change color. He fell into a fitful sleep.

Someone hummed—a female voice, low and soothing. Will lay in an open meadow on a clear, sunny day. He shielded his eyes, turning his head toward a large oak. Erin sat on a low branch, holding Amanda, while she hummed a lullaby.

Will smiled at the pair. They smiled back, then Amanda's eyes opened wide. "Papa, wake up!"

Will woke with a jolt. One of his lieutenants stood beside him.

"Sir," he said, "the Federals are attacking."

Will lurched to his feet. Officers scuttled about preparing the men to repulse the coming onslaught.

The battle Early had thought was over, was just beginning.

****

Jake swore when the Yankees fired into the assembled troops. He was not going to die here. Not at the hands of the Yankees he'd been aiding. But if he broke rank and ran, the Confederates had every right to shoot him.

Union cavalry broke the Confederate line. When the captain gave the order to retreat, Jake was all too ready to comply. He and Charlie raced toward the bridge they'd crossed last night. If they could outrun the Union soldiers, they might achieve safety.

Being one of the last companies to arrive last night, they were the first to make it over the bridge. Once they'd crossed, a group of Union cavalry arrived, surrounding them.

"Men," the Yankee captain ordered, "destroy the bridge so no more Rebs can get across."

When Jake glanced back at Captain Montgomery and the others who'd followed him, the captain signaled to his men to lower their arms.

"The hell I'll surrender to these bastards!" Charlie called.

Before Jake could stop him, the big man barreled into the nearest Yankee soldier, knocking him to the ground. Another soldier raised his rifle and shot Charlie in the back.

"Yankee bastard!" Jake yelled. Another shot sent a stinging shaft of pain into his thigh. He fell heavily to the ground.

In the chaos that followed, someone tried to lift him. Blinding pain caused him to lose consciousness.

****

Feeling trapped, Will gave the order to surrender, but the actions of the men ahead of him had changed the plan. A group of privates raced forward and were cut down by Yankee cavalry. To his dismay, he watched Kevin Donnelly fall.

In an attempt to organize the remaining soldiers,

Will stumbled and nearly tripped over a body. Glancing down, he saw the red hair of Sergeant Wagner. Was the man dead?

He lifted him by the collar, then noticed blood coated his thigh and spread beneath him on the marshy ground. Will stepped over him. Nothing could be done for the sergeant now. He glimpsed movement in the woods, and his breath caught at the sight of a Yankee cavalryman angling toward him with revolver raised.

"Drop your weapon, Reb!" the man shouted.

Will clenched his jaw. He gingerly held up his revolver.

"Put in on the ground," the Yankee yelled.

He crouched, placing the gun beside him. His heart raced. He didn't want to pass the rest of the war in a Yankee prison camp, but saw no other way out.

Recalling the dream, he wondered if he'd ever see Erin or Amanda again? Raising his arms in surrender, Will prepared to move to the left of the Yankee's stallion. The man sat with his revolver outstretched. A blast sounded, and Will flinched when the Yankee slipped from his mount and crumpled to the ground. The horse whinnied and trotted off. Glancing behind him, he stared in disbelief. Wagner sat clutching Will's smoking revolver.

"I thought you were dead," Will said.

"Not yet, sir." Wagner scowled at the fallen Yankee. "He shot me and killed Charlie."

Will followed his gaze to the prone figure of Charlie Ross sprawled several feet away. Turning to look behind the sergeant, he noted the rest of his men were chasing Yankee cavalry toward the bridge. The Yankees raced across, then turned and fired on the Confederates.

"Retreat!" Will called. His men would only get themselves killed.

His men aimed covering fire in the direction of the

Yankees, then darted toward Will. He glanced down at Wagner, his feelings about the man mixed. "You need that leg wrapped."

"Yes, sir."

Will and the other soldiers checked the fallen men. Donnelly was alive, but blood oozed from his side. Stuffing a neckerchief inside his coat, Will tried to staunch the flow.

"Hold on, Donnelly."

"Aye, sir," the Irishman wheezed.

"We'll get you back to camp," Will assured him. "My sister would never forgive me if I didn't."

Donnelly grimaced.

He moved on to see how many wounded they had to take back while his men rounded up cavalry horses that had lost their riders.

A loud blast drew Will's attention to the bridge. The Yankees had destroyed it, preventing any more Confederates from escaping.

He approached Wagner, whose leg was now wrapped in a muslin bandage. "We'd best get out of here quick," Will said. "The Yanks will likely start firing on us any minute."

Wagner sullenly studied his leg. "Don't reckon I can walk."

Will glanced toward the group of Yankee cavalry horses. "You'll be riding back to camp, Sergeant."

With the Yankees now occupied on the opposite side of the bridge, he gestured to one of the corporals to see to Wagner while he moved to organize his men.

****

When the men returned to camp at sunset, Erin breathed a sigh of relief when she caught sight of Will leading the company. Jenny clasped her hands as her gaze settled on Kevin. While other soldiers helped him to dismount, she fussed over him. Jake Wagner brought up the rear, astride a dark brown stallion, his left thigh wrapped in a blood soaked strip of muslin.

Although she'd never wish death on anyone, Erin bristled at his return. She'd hoped the Yankees had captured the bastard. At least then, he'd be out of her hair.

Kevin told them of the Confederate loss and that many had been captured.

Although Erin knew their defeat was inevitable, she couldn't help feeling sorry for these people, who'd had their hopes dashed today. She restrained herself from running into Will's arms and hoped he would be the one to make amends.

If there were no way to win him back, then why was she still in this time period? If only she could go back to the future and forget about him for good.

Chapter Twenty-three

Jake reclined on one of the cots in the hospital tent, with his injured leg propped on a rolled-up blanket. The night before last, Doc had dug out a bullet and told him it wasn't too bad. He just had to keep off his leg for the next few days.

The tent was crammed with other wounded men who'd made it back after the battle. He recalled Charlie's death, missing him already. The big man had been a constant companion, since Jake had joined up.

Sounds of spoons scraping against bowls drew his attention to a pleasant sight. Two lovely nurses made rounds angling themselves between the bunks in the confined space. He grinned when his gaze alighted on Erin. And the other dark-haired beauty he'd seen around camp. Although they hadn't been introduced, he knew she was Montgomery's sister.

Such a lovely way to start the day. Bored after lying around for two days, he decided it was time to have some fun.

The dark-haired woman approached him with a bowl and spoon. He gave her his most charming smile. "Well now, who might you be?"

She pursed her luscious pink lips, then held the bowl and spoon out for him to take. "I'm Miss Montgomery," she said.

"Any relation to our brave Captain Montgomery?" He eyed her speculatively.

"I'm his sister."

"Well then, permit me to introduce myself, ma'am. I'm Sergeant Wagner serving under your brother."

She nodded. "Pleased to meet you, Sergeant."

"I saved your brother's life, you know. Did he tell you about that?"

Her eyes widened, and she shook her head.

"Shot a Yankee who was aiming to shoot the captain."

"Will was nearly shot?" Her hand rose to cover her mouth.

"Surely would've if I hadn't been there."

"Jenny," a woman called, interrupting the conversation.

Jake looked over to find Erin glaring at him.

"I need to see to the other patients," Jenny apologized.

"That's quite all right, ma'am. I'm just fine now." He smiled and lifted a spoonful of porridge to his lips. When she moved away, he whispered, "Jenny."

****

Erin waited until Jenny went to attend Kevin. Once she was out of harm's way, Erin sidled up to Jake.

"Just what are you trying to pull here?"

His eyebrows rose. "Pardon me?"

"You stay away from Jenny Montgomery." She tried to bore a hole through him with her glare.

"Playin' the mother hen for the captain's sister, are you?"

"I'm serious," she grated out. "You want something, you ask *me*."

He grinned. "Why, I didn't think you cared."

She lowered her voice. "Once your leg's healed and Doc sends you back to your tent, I don't want to see you anywhere near here."

He took a mouthful of porridge, then swallowed slowly before replying. "You would deny me access to the doctor?"

"I have no problem with you seeing Doc. Just stay away from Jenny."

"Or what?" he taunted.

She clenched her jaw and came, oh so close, to smashing that bowl of porridge into his smug face. "You don't want to know what I'll do to you, plus she's the captain's sister. You want to make more trouble for yourself?"

"I don't reckon the captain will be giving me any more grief," he said.

"Oh, and why is that?"

"He didn't tell you?"

"Tell me what?" She crossed her arms over her chest.

He grinned. "I saved your captain's life."

"What are you talking about?"

"Ask him, sweetheart."

Another man called for water, and Erin moved toward him.

"When you're finished there," Jake said, drawing her gaze back to him, "bring me some, too. I'm mighty thirsty."

She turned, wanting more than anything to wipe that grin off his face. What the hell did he mean he'd saved Will's life?

****

One month later, Erin sat outside her tent. Caring for the wounded from this latest battle had exhausted her. *I need a vacation.* But then, so did everyone around her. She'd caught a glimpse of Will when he'd marched out with the troops this morning, looking magnificent in his uniform. Just the sight of him set her heart racing.

Because 1863 was drawing to an end, the fear he wouldn't return gripped her every time he marched off. She tried to recall the exact date on his headstone. Fighting to survive day to day in this century had caused her to lose track of why she was here. Was she supposed to change history? She didn't think that possible.

Jake had proved to be a real pain in the ass while

his wound healed. He expected her to wait on him hand and foot. When she balked or tried to have another nurse care for him, he caused an embarrassing scene. Finally, Doc had intervened and set the bastard straight. She also warned Jenny to avoid the man.

And now that he was healed, Erin had to contend with him sneaking around her again. The man gave her the willies. The worst part was others had verified he *had* saved Will's life. And Will had seen to it he made it back.

An unholy alliance if she ever saw one. But she knew Will would never leave one of his men behind, no matter what he thought of him. For that she respected him.

A woman with honey-colored hair approached and disrupted her thoughts. She wore a maroon calico dress covered with a blue-checkered shawl, and her head was topped with a brown bonnet. The woman carried a basket on her arm. Likely, she was one of the locals come to hawk her wares.

"Pardon me, ma'am," the woman said. "I'm looking for Mrs. O'Connell."

Erin looked her over, trying to decide how to answer. "And you are?"

"My name's Miss Rachel. I was sent here to find Mrs. O'Connell."

Her reporter's instincts kicked in. "Who sent you?"

Rachel's fine brows drew into a frown. "That would be Mrs. O'Connell's business, ma'am."

Erin sighed. If she wanted to learn anything from this woman, she had to reveal herself. "All right, you got me. I'm Erin O'Connell."

The woman seemed puzzled. "You're the Irish laundress?"

"That I am," Erin replied.

Glancing around, Rachel licked her lips. "I'm to tell you to come to the barn over yonder. The one just outside camp."

"And who am I to meet there?"

"I can't tell you that. You'll know. Go behind the barn just after sunset tomorrow." She turned to leave.

"Wait," Erin called. "That's all you can tell me?"

Rachel turned back, her eyebrows raised. "There's nothin' more to tell. Just be at the barn, and all will be explained."

As the woman strolled away, Erin bit her lip. What should she do? She thought it best to just ignore her and stay put. But she itched to sneak out to meet this contact to satisfy her curiosity.

She only had until sunset tomorrow to decide.

****

Jake held his breath as he crouched behind a wide oak a stone's throw from Erin's tent. Luckily, he'd seen and heard the blond-haired woman. He'd hightailed it to this spot, where he wouldn't be seen but had a chance to overhear at least some of the conversation.

Knowing Erin wouldn't confide in him, he'd meet the contact and convince the Yankee to pay him directly. Hell, he'd even defect to the North if the pay was good. But for now, since the woman hadn't told Erin who her contact was, he'd have to find out for himself.

Discreetly, he followed her until she approached the pickets. She produced a pass and allowed them to inspect her basket, leaving them happily munching on a couple of blueberry muffins.

Once she was out of earshot, Jake sauntered up to the pickets. He didn't have a pass to town, but one of the men standing guard owed him a favor, and he was about to collect on it.

Following the trail to town, he crept into the woods bordering the road. He trailed the woman without her being aware. After making sure no one else was around, he sprinted to the road and grabbed her from behind. When he clamped a hand over her mouth, her basket dropped to the ground.

"Come with me. I won't hurt you," he whispered.

She trembled in his grasp. He took a deep breath, inhaling her sweet perfume. She was a fine looking woman. Longing coursed through him. If he had the chance, maybe he could satisfy his lust with her, since Erin had denied him.

He dragged her into the woods deep enough so they couldn't be seen. "If you promise not to scream, you won't be hurt," he purred against her ear. At her nod, he cautiously released the hand covering her mouth and kept his other arm clamped around her upper chest to prevent flight.

She turned her face toward him, beads of sweat covered her face, and her eyes were as wide as an owl's. "What do you want with me?"

"Just need you to answer some questions. That's all."

"What questions?" Her heart thudded against his arm.

"Who's your Yankee contact?"

She tensed in his grasp. "I don't know no Yankees."

"Now, I know for a fact that's not true."

"Please, sir, I'm telling you the truth."

Spinning her around to face him, he grasped both her upper arms. "You're lying. I saw you talking to Mrs. O'Connell."

"I was sellin' muffins."

He squeezed, his fingers biting into her flesh. He'd wring her neck if that would get him the name.

She gasped.

"Tell me the name of the contact."

"I don't know no Yankees."

Enraged, he swung at her face, knocking her to the ground. She fell hard, and a sickening crack sounded. Her eyes gazed up into the trees while blood splattered over the rock where her head lay tilted at an odd angle.

Pulse thudding, Jake stared at the woman. That wouldn't have been necessary if she'd just told him what he wanted to know. It served her right. But he wasn't about to be brought up on murder charges. He had to get back to camp before anyone found her.

Chapter Twenty-four

"Captain?"

Will poked his head out of his tent. One of his men stood outside.

"Yes, Corporal. What is it?"

"Sir. We were on patrol this morning and found something you should see."

Will eased from the tent. The portly, auburn-haired corporal scratched at his beard, and Will raised his brows in a silent question.

"Sir, we found a dead woman."

"Where?" Will's pulse raced.

"Just outside camp. In the woods."

"One of the women from camp?" He feared the answer.

"No, sir. It was a local woman. There was one here yesterday selling muffins."

Will relaxed a bit as he tried to remember if he'd seen the woman. "You'd best take me to her, Corporal.

****

Twenty minutes later, the corporal led Will and two privates, brought along as litter bearers, to a spot a few yards off the road. Hidden among the brush, a blond-haired woman lay spread-eagle. Splattered blood surrounded her head where it rested on a large rock. A brown bonnet lay a foot behind her.

"How did you find her?" Will asked.

"We noticed an empty basket laying in the road, then saw scavengers back in the woods. We investigated, shooing them off. Then we found her."

Although Will bent to check for a pulse, he was certain he wouldn't find one. Her skin had already grown cold. He closed her eyes, then pulled a handkerchief from his pocket to cover her face. Something about her seemed familiar. Maybe he'd seen her yesterday.

Will motioned to the litter bearers. "Let's get her back to camp."

They lifted her onto the stretcher. He asked the corporal, "How far away was the basket?"

"A few yards that way, sir." The man motioned toward the road. "Do you reckon animals could have dragged her back here?"

Will stroked his beard, considering. "I suspect a two-legged animal."

"Sir?"

"Never mind. Let's take her back to Doc."

****

Erin stood over the washtub rotating the dolly to push slivers of soap through the heated water. Although she'd gotten used to doing laundry this way, she still pined for her modern life.

"Oh, Miss Erin, wait'll you hear." Brigid raced up. She wrung her plump hands in her apron, her normally ruddy face deathly pale. She looked as if she'd seen a ghost.

"What's wrong?" Erin asked.

"Found a woman dead, they did."

Erin's heart rate sped up. "Who found a woman? Where?"

"A woman from town. A patrol found her in the woods beside the road."

Rachel? It couldn't be. "What happened to her?"

"They say she fell and hit her head on a rock," Brigid said. "But why would she be all alone in the woods?" Her eyes widened. "I'd say someone dragged her there."

"Are you saying someone killed her?"

"Aye."

Erin struggled to make sense of this. "Did they

bring her back to camp?"

Brigid nodded. "She's in Doc's tent."

"I've got to see her." Erin abandoned the laundry, drying her hands on her apron as she sprinted to the medical tent, leaving the cook behind.

****

Erin burst into Doc's tent, trying to control her erratic breathing. "Where is she?"

Doc spun toward her, his eyes wide. She'd apparently startled him.

"I need to see the woman they brought in. The one they found in the woods."

Wordlessly, he motioned toward a cot up against the far wall of the tent beyond the bunks of the wounded men.

Following Doc, Erin moved through the tent to the back where a shrouded form lay.

Glancing at Doc's face, she sucked nervously on her lower lip. "I have to see her."

He nodded, stepped to the head of the cot, and pulled back the blanket covering her face.

She swallowed hard. The hazel eyes were closed, but it was Rachel. Blood matted in her hair, and her slender neck was bent at an odd angle. He let the blanket fall back into place.

"Rachel," she stated.

"You knew her?"

"I spoke to her yesterday." She met his gaze. "She was in camp selling muffins."

He didn't speak.

"How could this have happened?" she asked.

Doc folded his arms across his chest. "Either she wandered into the woods, slipped and hit her head...an animal frightened her, or..."

When he hesitated, Erin searched his eyes. "Or what?"

"Or someone dragged her into the woods and killed her."

****

Jake kept his silence while the camp buzzed with speculation about the death of the local woman. Since the pickets had allowed him out of camp without a pass, he didn't have to worry about them talking. They'd only get themselves into trouble, and nothing else would link him to her death.

That night, he seethed with anger. He kept watch on Erin, expecting she'd steal away to meet her contact. He planned to follow her as he'd done with the blond woman, but this time he'd tail her until she led him to the contact. But she never left camp. Had the woman's death frightened her off? He should've gone to the barn to see who showed up. But it was too late now. He'd have to get the name from her.

A candle illuminated her tent. He could make out her form through the canvas, where she sat brushing her hair. His groin tightened as he watched her. That bitch was going to tell him what he wanted to know.

****

Erin brushed her hair, then parted the strands for braiding. Exhausted, she longed to just lay her head down but dreaded waking to a tangled mass in the morning.

"Just leave it loose," a voice at the entrance of her tent said. "I like it loose."

She gulped when Jake eased his way inside. "What are you doing here? I was going to bed."

"We need to have a conversation first." He pulled out a stool and sat facing her.

"I'm too tired to talk tonight." Her pulse raced. Could he have killed Rachel? "Come back in the morning."

"No, ma'am. We'll talk right now."

"About what?"

He leaned forward and fingered a strand of her hair. She wanted to recoil but was afraid to move, afraid he'd suspect she feared him.

"I've decided," he said still groping her hair, "that I no longer want to be associated with you."

She inwardly breathed a sigh of relief. Maybe now he'd leave her alone.

"But I need to have the name of your Yankee contact, so that I can deal with him directly."

Her blood turned to ice. Rachel hadn't given her a name. And even if she had, she didn't want to give anything to Jake. There was no telling what he'd do with the information. He might even kill her to keep her from revealing his activities.

"I don't have the name," she told him.

He yanked on her hair, pulling her face to within an inch of his. "Don't lie to me."

Pain shot through her scalp. His rancid breath gagged her.

"I'm not lying," she grated out.

He clucked his tongue. "If you don't tell me, I'll have to do to you what I did to your little friend."

She gasped. He *had* killed her.

He rubbed his callused lips over her cheek, and she tried to pull away.

"I don't have the name. I was supposed to meet him tonight but didn't go."

"If you won't give me the name," he murmured against her throat, "you *will* give me something else."

He yanked on her chemise, ripping out the seam, exposing her breast. Enraged, she pushed and kicked at him, knocking him off the stool.

He rose and came at her again. She screamed at the top of her lungs.

"Shut up, you bitch," he growled.

He hit her face sending bright sparks shooting through her head. She felt herself fall, followed by a flash of excruciating pain when her head hit the edge of the table...then all went black.

Chapter Twenty-five

Jake stared down at Erin, sprawled on the cot. Her jaw, where he'd struck her, had turned an angry red. He roughly grasped her shoulder and shook her.

"Wake up," he ordered.

She responded with a low moan.

"You're going to tell me what I want to know." He lifted her arm, then let it drop. It fell limply, her fingers brushing the ground.

What was he going to do now? Montgomery would skin him alive when he found out. High time he left and went north. Make a new life in Pennsylvania. Since he'd been supplying Erin with information to aid the Yankees, he should be welcomed there. But he might need her to support his claim. He didn't want to end up in a Yankee prison camp.

Yes. He'd take her along. Once they were safely within the Pennsylvania border, he'd dispose of the bitch. But until then, he needed to keep her alive.

A rustling sound alerted Jake either a person or animal crept outside the tent. He stilled and watched the tent flap draw back. He made out the dark outline of a small, rounded woman and realized it was the cook. He yanked her in. Her startled gasp snuffed out her candle, which fell to the ground at her feet.

The Irish busybody was not going to wreck his plans. He clamped his hand over her mouth before she could shriek. Her heart hammered in her ample bosom as he held her prisoner against his chest.

"Now, now," he crooned against her ear, "I can't have you blabbing this all over camp."

Her wide eyes stared at Erin's prone form. No

doubt she thought he'd killed her. He grinned, enjoying the heady sense of power. If he killed Brigid, he'd ensure she wouldn't say anything, but any noise could bring others.

The leather cord he'd found in Erin's trunk would serve his purpose. He pushed the Irish cook to the floor face down, then wrapped a length of cord around her neck. She struggled, gagging, then went slack. When he released the cord, she didn't appear to be breathing.

He needed to skedaddle out of here before any more witnesses appeared. Using the same cord he used to strangle Brigid, he bound Erin hand and foot, then gagged her with his neckerchief. He threw her limp body over his shoulder, covering her with the quilt from her cot. Under cover of darkness, he made for the brush and trees on the west end of camp. Hopefully, he could stay out of the sight of the pickets. He stashed her among brush while he rounded up a horse, a small supply wagon, and whatever supplies he could scrounge up for the journey.

An hour later, he drove the wagon down a wooded path, with Erin hog-tied in the wagon bed, covered head to toe in blankets. He'd removed the stripes from his brown sack coat, hoping to pass as a civilian. If anyone stopped him, he'd claim to be a grieving relative, taking his brother's corpse home for burial.

He planned to get as far away from camp as he could before dawn.

****

After a breakfast of oatmeal and a stale slice of bread, Will nursed his lukewarm chicory coffee and contemplated the mess he'd made of his life. This war couldn't last forever. What would he do when it ended?

With the exception of Amanda, he had nothing at home. The only woman who interested him was Erin, but since her crazy time travel story, he'd avoided her. He didn't want to get involved with someone who'd lost her mind, or worse yet, lied. Even though the papers he'd found all those months before had never been traced to her, he still had his doubts.

He was better off, no matter what anyone said, to keep his heart to himself. Less pain.

"Will," a male voice called.

Doc strode in his direction. He was in shirtsleeves and a vest he'd left unbuttoned. The garment flapped open as he walked. A look of grave concern pulled his thin face into a frown.

"I can't find Erin." He stopped in front of Will. "She didn't report for duty. Have you seen her?"

"No, I haven't. Jenny shares a tent with her. Doesn't she know where she is?"

"Your sister spent the night in the hospital tent tending to Donnelly. He took a turn for the worse. I'm not sure if he'll make it."

While Will digested this, Doc went on. "When she went to wake Erin this morning, she said she wasn't there, and her quilt was missing."

"Anything else gone?" Will asked.

"Your sister said, no. Nothing that she could see, but she's concerned something's happened to Erin. She found a table upturned."

"I'm sure Erin's around here somewhere. If I see her, I'll be sure to let you know." But when Doc turned away uneasiness settled over Will.

A young, red-haired soldier approached.

"Corporal," Will called.

"Yes, sir."

"Fetch me Sergeant Wagner."

"Yes, sir." The corporal scurried away.

Twenty minutes later the corporal returned alone. "Sir, Sergeant Wagner's not in camp."

"Did he have a pass to town?"

"No, sir."

"Did anyone see him leave?"

"No, sir...and something else."

"Well?" Will's patience was wearing thin.

158

"All of his equipment is gone, too."

He sat up straighter. Erin and Wagner both gone?

"Corporal, I want this camp searched for Sergeant Wagner and Mrs. O'Connell. I want to speak with anyone who's seen either of them in the past day."

The corporal's eyes widened. "Yes, sir."

The young man raced off. Will contemplated what this meant.

Erin and Wagner had run off together. She'd been lying to him all along. The two were lovers and spies. If he got hold of either of them, he'd be sure they hanged.

****

Will strode into Doc's tent.

Doc turned from where he stood cleaning his medical instruments. He studied Will's face. "What the devil is wrong now? Have you found Erin?"

"No, but I can tell you who she left with."

"What in blazes are you talking about? Erin wouldn't run off without telling anybody."

"She would if she were a Yankee spy afraid of being caught."

Doc shook his head. "She is not a spy. I'd stake my life on it."

"I do hope you are not serious." Will's bile rose. "She and Sergeant Wagner left together."

"Jake Wagner? How do you know this?"

"Because both of them are missing. Along with all of his gear."

"That doesn't mean—"

"He appointed her as laundress."

Doc sat on the edge of his bunk. "I just don't believe Erin could have been lying to us all this time."

"She has. While on furlough at my home she told me an insane story."

Before Doc could question him further, Sergeant Malone appeared at the tent entrance. The big Irishman saluted, then ushered his wife inside.

"Begging yer pardon, sirs, but me wife urgently needs to speak with you. She's been attacked, and there's been an incident."

Her husband supported Brigid Malone's weight. He led her to a chair and eased her into it. The Irish cook was deathly pale and her left eye blackened. Trembling, she worried her hands in the skirt of her wrapper.

Doc rose to examine the woman. "Look here, Will," he said.

Will drew near and looked where Doc pointed. A bluish discoloration wound around her pale throat.

"Who did this, ma'am?" Will asked.

"Sergeant..." she whispered hoarsely, "Wagner."

Will straightened, glancing at her husband. "Wagner tried to choke you?"

Brigid nodded. Her hazel eyes misted over.

"When did this happen?" Doc asked while he applied a compress to her eye.

"Late last night," she whispered. Her husband nodded.

"I was out on picket," the sergeant said. "She was in the tent alone."

"I couldn't sleep," she went on, "I heard a scream and went to check."

"Who was screaming?" Will asked.

"It must've been Miss Erin, sir. I went to her tent, and Sergeant Wagner pulled me inside. He'd done something to her. She may have been dead."

Will caught Doc's worried glance. What if Wagner had killed her? And he'd allowed it to happen.

"Go on, ma'am," Doc prodded after she hesitated.

"The brute pushed me onto the floor and choked me. When I came to me senses, it was just before dawn, and they were both gone. I got meself up and went in search of me husband."

Malone nodded. "I didn't find her when I returned from picket and thought she was already up and about. She'd thought me to be still on duty, and it took awhile for us to find each other. When she told me what happened, I thought you should know right away, sir."

Doc glanced at Will. "Then if Erin is alive, she couldn't have left under her own power."

Brigid shook her head, then burst into tears. Her husband rushed forward to comfort her.

Doc moved close to Will. "If Erin *is* still alive," he said softly, "I reckon Wagner took her."

Will's heart sank. If anything happened to Erin, it was his fault.

****

Will saddled his horse, then rechecked the contents of his pack.

Doc paced beside him. "I know you have to do this, but if you leave without permission, you'll be charged with desertion."

"I know that."

"What about your family?"

Will grimaced. He didn't want to hurt and humiliate his family, but he had no choice. "If I don't find her, he'll kill her."

Doc nodded, saying no more.

Will hadn't really thought Doc would try to talk him out of it. Will had felt powerless when Anne and then Sam had died. He couldn't help but feel responsible for Erin's situation. By rejecting her, he'd allowed Wagner the opportunity to take her.

He'd also made sure the sergeant had made it back after the battle at Cedar Creek. He could have left him behind in the field for the Yankees. But Wagner had saved his life, even though he did it for revenge of his wound and for the death of his friend. Will couldn't have left any of his men behind.

But...he hadn't protected Erin.

If Wagner hurt or killed her, he'd never be able to forgive himself.

Chapter Twenty-six

Emerging from a haze, Erin slowly focused on her surroundings. At first, only the pain registered. Her jaw and head throbbed. Tasting cotton, she realized she was gagged. She tried to spit out the rag, but it was too tightly laced.

Rolling over, she found herself in a barn lying on a pile of straw with light filtering through the wall. Her wrists were bound, as well as her ankles, the leather cord cutting into her skin.

Every time she'd awake on that hellish ride that seemed to last an eternity, dizziness and pain caused her to black out. During one of her moments of consciousness, she managed to tear off a square of her quilt and conceal it in her clenched hand. She then pleaded with Jake to allow her to care for her personal needs. He untied her and let her partially conceal herself behind shrubs. As she climbed back into the wagon, he momentarily turned his back to retrieve the cords he'd used to bind her. She glanced around for any kind of weapon, but seeing nothing she could use, she dropped the square by the side of the road. Though she didn't believe anyone would come after her, anyway.

Jake had told her he'd taken her to get him through the Yankee lines. Little did he know she'd be useless to him. If she told him where she'd really come from, he wouldn't believe her any more than Will had. An image of Will's face as he made love to her and later, when she'd told him she'd come from the twenty-first century, flashed through her mind.

She couldn't expect him to come to her rescue this

time. Even if he could find her, he probably figured she and Jake deserved each other.

But if Jake found out she wasn't who he thought she was and couldn't help him, he'd probably kill her as he had that poor woman, Rachel.

Where was he, anyway? She glanced around the interior of the barn. She didn't see him or any of his gear. The bastard hadn't left her anything to eat or drink, she was sure. Maybe he'd left her here to die.

She pulled up her legs to examine the bonds on her ankles. He'd used the same leather cord that bound her wrists. If she could get her legs free, it would be easier to find something she could use to cut the cord binding her hands.

Her fingers were numb and her head threatened to explode, but she had to focus on freeing herself if she wanted to live.

****

Will had ridden all day not daring to stop for fear the trail he followed would grow cold. After Brigid's statement, he'd investigated and found a mare had been stolen, along with a supply wagon and other gear. He followed the north-bound trail all day and hoped they'd stopped somewhere along the way to rest.

He couldn't keep his thoughts from Erin. The night they'd made love, she'd looked so beautiful with her red-gold tresses hanging loosely around her ivory shoulders. She'd gazed lovingly at him with her beautiful sapphire eyes.

He didn't want to think about what he'd do if he found her dead or didn't find her at all. He couldn't allow himself to think about that possibility. He'd deserted his post—a position he'd sworn to honor—to find her. He couldn't live with himself if he didn't at least try. But if he failed, he had nothing. He'd be charged as a deserter, arrested and likely shot. His family would be disgraced, and Amanda would grow up hating him.

He followed the trail through wooded country roads and something red at the base of a barren oak caught his eye. He stopped, alighting from his gelding, and crouched to retrieve the object. He lifted a square of material, a piece of a patchwork quilt. Jenny had told him Erin's quilt had been missing when she'd returned to the tent. If this were a piece of her quilt, they'd passed this way. Tucking the square into the pocket of his coat, he mounted his horse and continued.

****

Hours later, Will topped a rise in the trail, and a farm came into view. If it were a working farm, the fields would already have been harvested. But when he neared the house, no smoke rose from the chimneys. He saw no sign of life. He drew closer and saw the charred interior of the house along with a gaping hole in the roof. The Yankees had likely torched the structure when they'd passed through.

Guiding his mount into a canter, he rode along the side of the house to the back and found a barn. The red and gray building didn't seem to have been burned as the house had, but again, he saw no signs of life.

He patted his gelding. "Maybe we can find you a drink." The horse nodded as if in agreement. He dismounted, grasped the reins, and led the horse around the side of the barn in search of a water trough.

The walls of the barn badly needed a fresh coat of paint. Quite a few planks were so worn he could see into the interior. He froze when he sighted a wagon a few feet away from the barn door. A torn quilt lay in the bed.

He drew his revolver. Quickly he tied his horse alongside the wagon. He approached the barn door, his pulse racing.

****

Once Erin had loosened the knot in the cord tying

164

her feet, she searched the barn and used the sharp edge of a shovel to slice through her bonds. She threw away the cotton gag and looked around for anything useful she could take with her. She didn't plan to be here if and when he returned. Since her arms and legs cramped from being bound so long, she stretched to work out the kinks.

What if he hadn't left but was right outside?

A pack half-buried in the hay caught her attention. Rifling through it, she found one of her dresses, a petticoat, a pair of stockings and her shoes. When Jake had taken her, she'd only been wearing her chemise. Apparently, he'd thought to bring her something to wear. She pulled the dress over her head, then headed for the door. Pressing one ear against the wood, she listened for any sound, while deciding what to do.

If he were right outside, she had to find a weapon. Searching the barn, she found exactly what she needed—a sharp-tonged pitchfork. This would do the trick. If Jake were anywhere around, she'd surprise him and run him through.

When she again approached the door, this time with weapon in hand, a horse neighed. If the horse were here, he must be, too.

Pointing the pitchfork at the door, she braced herself as it cracked open.

****

Will approached the barn door, revolver drawn. Pressing his ear against the peeling painted surface, he strained to hear any sound. Scuffling noises assured him that, indeed, someone was inside. He couldn't call out. That would give him away if Wagner were in there. Taking a breath, he pulled on the door handle.

The sharp tines of a pitchfork flew toward him, followed by a gasp.

"I almost speared you!" Erin cried.

165

"I almost shot *you*," he replied, his pulse racing.

She lowered the pitchfork, but he kept his revolver leveled. "Where's Wagner?"

"I don't know. I think he left." Her eyes were wide.

What had that bastard done to her?

After holstering his gun, he gently removed the pitchfork from her and propped it against the wall. "You really planned to stab him with this?"

She nodded.

Relieved she was alive, he wrapped her in his arms. Her heart beat reassuringly against his chest. He should have protected her from Wagner while they were still in camp. "Did he hurt you, darlin'?"

Sagging against him, she sighed. "He hit me. I blacked out." She raised her gaze to his. An ugly greenish bruise ran the length of her jaw on the left side of her face.

He traced a finger over the spot, and she flinched. "He did this?"

She nodded.

"I'll kill him."

"Not if I don't first. When I came to, I was bound and gagged in the back of a wagon. He brought me here, then just left. I don't know if he'll be back. That's why, when I heard you outside—"

"You tried to spear me," he finished. Positioning his hand to hold the back of her head, he pressed her face into his coat. As she reached around and clung to his waist, her warmth and scent enveloped him. He'd never loved another woman as much and had feared he'd never see her again. Or worse, he'd find her as he had Anne, already beyond his reach.

"He didn't do anything else, did he?" If Wagner had violated her, he swore he'd kill him.

"No," she answered. "I think he just took me because he thought I'd get him through the Yankee lines, but I can't."

"You told him this?"

She shook her head. "Told him that I've traveled through time? I couldn't. He'd never believe me anyway. You didn't."

Will stiffened. "I've done some thinking on that."

"And?" She raised her chin.

"I believe you."

Her eyes widened. "And what brought this on?"

"I reckon I've fallen in love with you. And I believe you when you said you came here for me. To save me." His lips grazed hers, so lush and satiny smooth. Emboldened by her soft sigh, he took her mouth fully, her sweetness heightening his desire. He hardened when she pressed herself against him.

He pulled back from the kiss and gazed into her eyes. Tears shone on her face. "Darlin'." He brushed the wetness from her petal-soft cheeks. "What is it?"

"I'm so happy," she said.

"Because I found you?"

"Not just that. It's because, after all these months, I don't have to pretend anymore."

****

Erin melted against Will's hard chest. He cradled her face between his hands and kissed the tears coursing down her face. For months, although surrounded by new friends, she'd felt alone. Here, in his strong arms, all the tension dissolved from her body, and a sigh escaped her lips.

He gently brushed his lips over hers, then kissed her thoroughly, without putting undue pressure against her sore jaw. She gave herself over to the kiss, her insides turning to liquid fire. She wanted to forget about Jake and all the horrors of the past year. To be here with Will like this made it all worth it.

She pulled back, studying his face. His eyes held a weary, sunken look. Stubble covered both cheeks. He looked as grungy as she felt.

Grasping the soft curls at the nape of his neck, she said, "I love you, Will. I always have and always will."

He sighed. "I'm sorry."

She stiffened.

"I should have believed your story." He smiled, and her heart melted. "When I found he'd taken you, I knew then that I'd made a mistake. I should have listened to what you were telling me—"

"Oh, no," Erin said. "I should never have expected you to believe—"

"I should've," he interrupted, "because a man should always have faith in the woman he loves."

A thrill ran through her. He *did* love her. This hadn't all been for nothing.

He gathered her close, and they simply held on to each other.

****

Jake circled the side of the barn, reining his mount in sharply. A rust-colored gelding stood beside the wagon he'd used to carry Erin. Someone was in the barn with her.

He'd gone into town for a few needed supplies believing she'd be unable to break free and escape. Had the owner of the farm returned and found her?

After tying up his mare, he pulled his pistol and cautiously approached. The dilapidated wooden door creaked outward. He tensed, his finger on the trigger. Captain Montgomery stood wide-eyed in the open doorway. Glancing down at the captain's hands, Jake noted he wasn't armed.

My lucky day. A grin spread across his face. He glanced over Montgomery's shoulder to where Erin stood behind him. "Hello, sweetheart." He kept his pistol aimed at the captain's chest.

She gasped. "Jake, you bastard!"

"Now, now. After all I've done for you, missy." He caught Montgomery's gaze, enjoying the fact he now had the captain right where he wanted him. He'd twist the man into submission, just as he'd been repeatedly reprimanded and punished, first by his father, then by haughty officers like Montgomery since he'd joined the army.

"Reckon you haven't figured it out yet, Captain." He gestured toward Erin. "This whore's a Yankee spy."

Montgomery scowled but didn't speak.

"That's right, Captain. She used you to get information for the Yankees. I helped her too, for money...and other things she promised."

"Jake!" Erin shrieked. "Just let us go."

"But sweetheart, you promised me you'd get me over the lines. They know I helped you. If they catch me, I'll be shot or hanged. I've got to get into Yankee territory."

"We can all go together," she pleaded.

"Not likely." Jake's finger tightened on the trigger. He was going to enjoy this.

****

Erin's thoughts flew into overdrive. He meant to kill Will. The moment she'd been sent here for had arrived. She had to stop Jake.

Flinging herself at Will, she pushed him out of the way at the moment Jake's pistol fired. Sharp pain drove into her chest knocking her off her feet. She slumped to the floor. Will's strong arms were beneath her, supporting her. She gazed up into his agonized face.

"You shouldn't have done that, darlin'," he said.

Numbness overtook her. She could barely feel his arms around her. "I had to," she whispered. "This is what I came here for. To save you."

He shook his head. "If I lose you, nothing will save me."

I've made a big mistake, she thought before darkness descended.

Chapter Twenty-seven

Will held Erin and prayed for any sign of life. All color had drained from her face, and blood coated his sleeve. Lowering her body to the floor, he cupped the back of her head with one hand and ran the fingers of his other hand gently over her hair, straightening loosened strands.

Numbness settled over him. He raised his gaze to Wagner, who stood over him with a smoking pistol. Will's jaw clenched. "You killed her, you son of a bitch!"

Wagner shrugged. "Didn't mean to." He smiled. "Dumb whore just got in the way, is all. That bullet was meant for you, Captain." He leveled the gun at Will.

Gazing down at Erin, Will gently pressed her eyes closed. He didn't care what Wagner did to him, now. At the sound of the pistol cock, he flinched. Nothing happened.

He looked up at Wagner. "Get it over with. You've already killed me."

Wagner shook his head. "Don't reckon I will. I'll let the army kill you when they catch you."

"You're in the same boat as me," Will growled.

"I have connections up north," Wagner said. "I'll find a way to get through the lines, then I'll be home free." He grinned. "But you, Captain, are another story. You'll end up in a Yankee prison camp, or be shot by your own people." He shook his head.

"Reckon I'll be on my way." He glanced at Erin. "You can take care of the body." Turning his back on Will, he headed for his mare.

Will's urge to kill the man was overshadowed by the grief that paralyzed him. He'd again lost the woman he loved and had also lost his home and family. He couldn't go back. Couldn't go forward.

He was lost.

****

Bright. Too bright. Erin tried to raise a hand to shield her eyes, but her arm wouldn't cooperate.

Where am I? Where's Will?

She slowly opened her eyes, blinking against the glare. She squeezed them shut again at the sight of an electric lamp hanging over her bed.

"Erin?"

Opening her eyes again, she focused on a strange woman with short dark hair standing over her. She wore blue hospital scrubs. In a panic, Erin tried to move, but her muscles wouldn't obey. She was hindered by tubes attached all over her body.

"Erin, can you understand what I'm saying?"

She strained to answer, but nothing but a strangled whisper hissed from her parched throat.

"No, no," the woman said, "Don't try to speak. Just blink twice if you understand."

Erin blinked twice.

The woman squeezed her hand. Turning toward the open doorway, she called to someone out of Erin's sight. "Get the doctor. She's awake."

****

Will lovingly wrapped Erin's body in burlap he'd found in the barn and tied it around her with cording to keep it in place. He placed her in the wagon Wagner had left behind. After watering his gelding, he hitched the horse to the wagon. Erin had told him she'd lived in Philadelphia, and her grandmother lived north of Gettysburg.

The Yankees could do to him whatever they wanted, but he would see to it she went home.

****

171

Two weeks later, Erin had been removed from the ICU and placed in a regular hospital bed. She was undergoing intensive physical therapy to help regain her strength and muscle tone.

During visiting hours, her mother sat beside her bed knitting, while Erin caught up with current events on the television hanging on an arm alongside her bed. When the evening news anchor signed off, she turned to her mother.

"How can it have only been six weeks since the accident?"

"It's true," her mother said. "You've been in a coma for a month. I was afraid you'd never wake again."

Erin shook her head. The year she'd lived through couldn't have been a coma-induced dream. Could it? She refused to believe that. It had been real. *He* had been real.

"Mom. There's something I've got to tell you."

Her mother listened attentively while she related the story of her incredible journey.

"I saved him, Mom, just like Grandma Rose wanted. But I must've died instead. And now I'm back here." She'd made a mistake that had changed history but not the way it was supposed to be.

"There, there, dear." Her mother patted her hand. "It was all a dream. Your grandmother's stories before she died must have brought this on."

Erin pushed her fingers through her hair. It was short again, although a bit longer than she normally wore it. Maybe her mother was right. It *had* been a dream.

But she couldn't get Will's face out of her head. Biting her lower lip to hold back her tears, she turned back to the TV where a rerun of *Seinfeld* was playing.

She'd been home all along. She felt like Dorothy in *The Wizard of Oz*. But was Will lying in a graveyard in Virginia, nothing but bones?

It had been so real.

172

A few months later, Erin moved to a rehab center and underwent intense therapy every day to rebuild her weakened muscles. She needed to recover and get out of here. To get back to her life.

A life without Will.

Why couldn't she get the man out of her mind? He wasn't real. At least not to her. He was from the past. A ghost. She couldn't love a ghost. But she did.

****

Days later, one of the nurses, a young black man named Raymond, appeared at the door of her room. The tall, thin man's head was shaved, and he wore gold stud earrings in both ears, as well as one under his lower lip.

Erin liked the man. He always had a witty comment to brighten her day. "Hey, Raymond," she said.

"You have a visitor."

Expecting her mother, Erin felt shocked when Rick entered the room. He clutched a bouquet of roses.

"Thanks," Erin called to the nurse when he retreated.

Fully dressed in a Phillies tee-shirt, shorts, and sneakers, she sat on the edge of her bed where her therapist had left her after their last session.

When Rick didn't speak, she finally asked, "To what do I owe this visit?"

After pushing his blond hair off his forehead, he handed her the flowers. "Your mother told me about the accident. And that you were in a coma."

Erin nodded. She motioned for him to take a seat and set the roses on her nightstand.

"I felt bad," he continued. "Even though it was over between us, I felt I at least should see you one more time. Be sure you're all right."

"I'm just dandy." She gestured to the wooden cane propped beside her bed. "I'm up and walking with a little assistance. They tell me I'll soon be as good as new."

Rick smiled. "That's great."

"And how are things going with you?"

"I'm still with the firm in Philadelphia. I've had a full case load, otherwise, I'd have been here sooner."

"I understand," she said. "After all, we're not together anymore."

"I've done some thinking about that." He stared at his manicured fingers. "Maybe I've been too hard on you. I pushed you, and that's why you called off the wedding."

Erin sighed. Same old Rick. Only thinking of what's best for him and his career. "I think I made the right decision. For both of us."

"But we could take our time. Start over."

"No, Rick. The truth is, I'm in love with someone else."

His brows knitted. "We haven't been apart that long. At least not before the accident." He pointed a finger at her. "Don't tell me you've fallen for your doctor."

"No. He's not a doctor."

"Then one of your therapists?"

"No—it doesn't matter who it is anyway. It's over between us."

"If that's what you want..." He stood.

"Yes, that's what I want." She sagged as if all the air had gone out of her. She and Rick weren't meant to be together.

He nodded and walked out of her life.

****

Late in January, Erin sat before the fireplace in her late grandmother's house, sipping a cup of hot chocolate. She'd been staying here with her mother, until she finished with her outpatient therapy.

She'd also been going to a local firing range learning how to shoot an 1860s black-powder revolver. While her instructor, a middle-aged Civil War buff, found her interest admirable, her mother didn't understand this compulsion.

"You need to forget all this nonsense if you want to get back to a normal life," Mom had complained.

"It's something I need to do," Erin had insisted.

"But what sense is there in learning to fire an antique gun?"

Erin really couldn't explain it herself. Shrugging, she'd said, "It will come in handy some day."

Taking her mug with her, she rose and parted the chenille curtain covering the window. Lake-effect snow had coated the ground outside making for a picture postcard view during daylight hours. Now that darkness had fallen, she had wrapped an afghan around herself while she rocked in Grandma Rose's favorite chair. Her mother had long since gone to bed.

Now with her therapy finished, she felt ready to go back to her job in Philadelphia, find a place of her own, and get on with life. Although she looked forward to seeing friends and colleagues, she didn't know if she wanted to start over.

A log popped in the fireplace sending red sparks against the screen. The scent brought her back to the camp in Virginia where she'd spent all those months, while only weeks had passed in real-time.

How could it all have been a dream? A coma-induced dream as her mother had insisted. Before she returned to Philadelphia, there was one more thing she had to do.

****

Cemetery in Candor

Snow coated the ground blanketing the graves, giving the cemetery a magical glow. Erin looked for the newly erected stone her mother had had placed on Grandma Rose's gravesite. Clutching the bouquet of assorted flowers she'd purchased at the grocery, she scanned the row of stones until she saw her Grandma's name: *Rose Mary Magilly*.

After placing the flowers against the headstone, she circled behind to check the earlier gravesites dating back to the 1800s. Before she resumed her old life, she had to know.

She found the weathered granite stone bearing the name of Erin Coyne O'Connell—born February 22, 1837; died November 23, 1864.

Erin tightened her wool coat around her. Chilling numbness sliced through her. *This wasn't right.* Erin O'Connell had lived into her eighties. She'd told Grandma Rose stories of her life when Grandma was a young girl.

The movie *Back to the Future* flashed into her mind. If the dates on the headstone had changed, that meant only one thing. She'd really been in the past. And she'd changed history. But had she made anything better, or had she made things worse.

Chapter Twenty-eight

Mason, Virginia

Erin approached the old church cemetery with trepidation. If Jake had killed her that day in November of 1864, what had happened to Will? She had no choice but to find out. She couldn't go on with her life without learning the truth.

She found his grave in the family plot nestled between his wife, Anne, and Amanda. Her eyes blurred when she read his name, then she sharply refocused when she read his death date. Instead of 1864 when he'd originally died, the engraving read 1904.

Her knees nearly buckled beneath her. Jake hadn't killed Will, but he'd killed *her* that day. She'd saved Will's life, but they hadn't lived the life they were meant to live together.

Disheartened, she drove back to the hotel where she was staying. *It had all been real.* She collapsed on the bed. *It hadn't been a dream.* She'd really gone back in time, but she'd failed. Nothing for her to do now, but go back to Candor, pack her bags, and head for Philadelphia.

****

Candor, Pennsylvania

Erin closed her suitcase. She planned to spend one final night with her mother, then hit the road in the morning. Her brother in California would be flying out in a few days to help Mom put the house up for sale. He wanted her to come live with him. She would miss her mother but was glad she'd be well taken care of.

This was the last night she'd ever spend in this house. She undressed, slipped into her two-piece cotton pajama set, and settled down to sleep.

****

She stood in the cemetery. Snow coated the ground. Although she was barefoot and wearing only her light cotton pajamas, she didn't feel cold. A woman with flowing, vibrant red hair seemed to glide toward her.

"Erin, child," the woman said.

She stared and realization hit her. This was Grandma Rose as she'd looked in her youth.

"Grandma?"

"You must go back," Grandma said.

"Back? Back where?"

"Back to William. You belong with him. It was destined to be."

"But I can't go back. It's impossible."

"You must find the brooch," Grandma said. "Find it, then take it to your grave."

"My grave? What do you mean?"

"Go to him, or you'll never know happiness," Grandma said.

****

Erin sat up with a jolt. *What a crazy dream.* She pushed her hand through her newly cropped hair, then rose, and paced in front of the window. The full moon reflected off the snow casting an eerie glow over the landscape beyond the house.

Brooch, Grandma had said. She must mean the brooch containing Will's hair. She'd been wearing it when she'd had the accident. Its connection to him had to have been the catalyst that sent her through time.

Maybe her mother would know where the brooch was. She'd ask her in the morning. If her mother didn't know, what would she do? She'd planned to leave tomorrow.

Nothing she could to until morning. She climbed

back into bed but doubted she'd get any more sleep.

In the morning after a restless night, Erin sat across from her mother at the oval pine table in Grandma's country kitchen. Her mother had gotten up early to make Erin a breakfast of pancakes and bacon to fortify her for her long drive.

She sipped her orange juice, trying to figure out a way to ask her mother about the brooch. Finally, she said, "After my accident, did the hospital give you anything I'd had with me in the car?"

Her mother frowned. "Just your purse, cell phone, and of course, your suitcase."

"What about the clothes I was wearing?"

"Oh, yes." Her mother rose and started collecting the plates and silverware. "I took them home and had what was salvageable cleaned."

"Where are they now?"

"In your grandmother's closet. In her bedroom."

"Was there a brooch attached to the jacket?"

"Brooch?"

"An antique brooch Grandma had given me. It dated back to the Civil War. It's really important to me."

"I do seem to recall something like that. I may have put it in your grandmother's jewelry box."

"Is the box still here?"

"Of course. I planned to take it with me to California after the house is sold. But if your grandmother gave you the brooch, you're welcome to take it with you."

"Actually, Mom. I've decided to stay on a few more days. There's something I have to take care of before I leave."

****

After dinner, Erin sat before the fireplace fingering the brooch. She ran her hand over the curved glass covering Will's hair. Lifting it to her lips, she recalled his scent, the feel of his kiss, his hands and hard body pressed against hers. She closed her eyes and could swear he held her. Grandma had been right. She had no life here without him. If it meant she had to give up all her modern conveniences, then so be it. This might be her one shot at happiness. She had to take the chance. But was it even possible?

Her mother entered the room, setting two steaming mugs of hot chocolate on the coffee table. She sat across from Erin on the upholstered sofa.

"That's a lovely piece of jewelry." Her mother eyed the brooch.

"It belonged to Grandma's great-aunt Erin O'Connell."

"Oh, is that so?"

"Mom." She bit her lip, not knowing how to start. "Grandma came to me in a dream last night."

Her mother reached over and patted her hand. "Of course, dear. I know how close you were to her and how you miss her."

"No, Mom." She stood. "It wasn't that type of dream. It was more like...a vision. Grandma came to give me a message."

Her mother stared at her. "I don't understand."

Erin rose and paced a few steps trying to decide what to say. She sat again and reached for her mother's hand. "She told me I had to go back."

"Back? To Philadelphia?"

Erin shook her head. "Back to 1864."

"You're talking about that again? But it was just a dream!"

"No. It was real. And I've got proof." After she explained about the dates on the gravestones changing, the lines in her mother's face deepened into a frown.

"That can't be true," her mother insisted. "You're remembering it wrong, that's all."

"No. You've got to believe me." Erin had to convince her. "I was really in the past. I met a man, and I fell in love with him. I love him more than my own life."

Her mother shook her head. "It was a dream. No one can travel through time."

"I did. I made things change. And now, I have to go back. I know how to fix it. Make it right."

"What are you talking about?" Her mother's hazel eyes widened. "I'm calling your doctor."

"Please. I need you to believe me. When I go, you'll have Rob to take care of you. You'll be in California." She cringed at the look of panic on her mother's face. "I don't want to leave you, but I have to go back and make things right. I'm not sure how it will affect my present life, but I hope it will work out for all of us."

Her mother's mouth went slack, while her eyes brimmed with unshed tears. "*How* can you go back?"

"I'm not sure how it works, but this," she held up the brooch containing Will's hair, "will somehow take me back there."

"But what about your job at the paper?"

"I have to take care of my past life, only then will the present fall into place."

****

Erin approached the cemetery gate. If this didn't work, how could she go back and face her mother?

If that happened, she'd deal with it then. Right now, she had to concentrate on why she was here.

Darkness had fallen early on this late winter night. Although she'd bundled up, the tip of her nose felt numb as well as her fingers, even through her gloves.

Once she located the grave of Erin O'Connell, she brushed snow away from the base of the stone. Grandma had told her to seek *her* grave. Erin assumed this was what she meant.

"Grandma," she whispered, "are you here?"

A light breeze rustling through the barren oaks was her only answer. She pulled the brooch from her pocket and clasped it between her gloved hands.

"I need you, Will. I'm only a shell here. I need the life I had back there with you."

A vibration ran up her arms, weakening her knees. She sank onto the grave into the snow. Wetness seeped through her jeans, but she didn't care. All she could see was his face the night he'd first made love to her. "I can't go on without you."

The buzz increased, thrumming in her ears. She collapsed on top of the grave.

"Darlin'," she heard from somewhere far off, "Don't go. Come back to me."

"Will," she called. "Where are you?"

A howling sensation overtook her. She felt herself being yanked from her body. She must be dying.

****

Erin opened her eyes. The cemetery was gone. She sat on a bale of hay in a barn.

She was back! Will, his back to her, approached the barn door. She had to stop him.

"Will," she called. "Don't open that door!"

He pushed the door open, then half-turned toward her, a puzzled expression on his face. She stood, already knowing who was on the other side.

"Hello, sweetheart," Jake said.

He stood just beyond Will with a pistol aimed at Will's chest. If she had to play this scene out again, she'd be sure to do it right this time.

"Jake, you bastard!" she called.

He looked over Will's shoulder. "Now, now. After all I've done for you, missy." Facing Will, he continued, "Reckon you haven't figured it out yet, Captain." He gestured toward Erin. "This whore's a Yankee spy."

Will didn't move or speak.

"That's right, Captain. She used you to get information for the Yankees. I helped her too, for money...and other things she promised."

"Jake!" Erin shrieked, determined to play her part.

"Just let us go."

"But sweetheart, you promised me you'd get me over the lines. They know I helped you. If they catch me, I'll be shot or hanged. I've got to get into Yankee territory."

She had to distract him. Keep him from killing Will...or her. "We can all go together," she said.

"Not likely."

This was her cue. She had to move now.

Racing toward Will, she pushed him to the floor landing on top of him. Jake's gun discharged. A stinging pain tore through her right upper arm. She slumped to the floor. Supporting her, Will's strong arms were beneath her. She gazed up into his agonized face.

"You shouldn't have done that, darlin'," he said.

"It worked," she whispered. "I'm still here."

He cradled her close. "What kind of crazy, fool thing was that to do? I thought I'd lost you."

She flinched as a sharp wave of pain knifed through her arm.

"My, my, what a touching scene."

Erin looked up at Jake, who stood over them.

"You son of a bitch," she said. "You shot me!"

"I do believe you got in the way. It's *him* I want." He waved his pistol at them, then leveled the barrel at Will's face.

****

Jake grinned. He had them right where he wanted them. He'd finish off Montgomery first, then deal with Erin. If she cooperated, maybe he'd keep her around.

Until he got tired of her.

"This will atone for all the punishments you dealt out, *Captain*," he said. "I joined the army to escape my father, but you were no better than the bastard that raised me."

"I was always fair with you, Wagner. If you were punished, it was because you did something to deserve it."

Jake scowled. "All you officers are alike. You order us about and send us out to be blown to bits by Yankees."

"I was right there with you," the captain ground out.

Enjoying the heady feel of power, Jake smiled. "I saved your life at Cedar Creek, but now, I'll just take it back." He waved his pistol in front of the captain's face.

"Jake, please," Erin said. "Just leave us. You go ahead and find that life for yourself wherever you want."

His hand wavered. "No. You...and him, you both caused me to suffer. You're both going to pay." He leveled the barrel at the captain.

"Damn you, Wagner." Montgomery pushed Erin aside, then dove into Jake's legs, throwing him off balance.

They fell to the floor, the captain's full weight on top of him. Montgomery knocked the gun from his hand just out of his reach.

****

Will growled in anger. This man had hurt and nearly killed Erin. He'd never allow him to harm her again. He pummeled Wagner with both fists until he slumped beneath him.

Erin was hurt, and he needed to get back to her. He started to rise. The sergeant's body heaved. He knocked Will onto his back and rolled on top. Will tried to push him off but froze when he felt the cold metal of a gun barrel pressed against his cheek. "Got you now, Captain," the sergeant whispered.

Will thought with regret of Erin. How could he save her now?

Chapter Twenty-nine

After Will pushed her aside, Erin watched him wrestle with Jake. She had to do something fast. Jake's pistol lay on the other side of the scrabbling men. She'd never reach it in time.

The packs! Cradling her right arm in her left to give it support, she raced to the bags and found Will's revolver. Now she knew why she'd learned to shoot. She could save his life.

She grasped the gun with her good arm. A shaft of pain radiated from her wounded arm up through her shoulder and threatened to bring her to her knees. She couldn't fail. That would mean death for both of them. Cocking the gun, she leveled it at Jake as he pressed his pistol against Will's face.

"Jake!" she screamed.

He half-rose and smirked. "Put that down before you hurt somebody."

"Oh, I fully intend to hurt you, unless you get up right now."

He rose slowly, one hand out, the other still clutching his pistol.

"Give the gun to Will," she said.

Jake glanced down at Will, who pushed up onto his elbows. Instead of handing the pistol to him, Jake pointed it at his face.

"No!" Erin screamed. She pulled the trigger. The recoil sent a shaft of white-hot pain up her arm into her shoulder, and she collapsed onto a pile of hay, but she held onto the smoking gun.

Jake flew backward, his pistol falling to the ground.

Erin carefully placed Will's revolver beside her. The pain in her arm and shoulder burned. She bore down as best she could and made it to Will's side where she sank into his arms.

Glancing over her shoulder, she asked, "Is he...?"

"I don't reckon he'll be getting up."

Erin turned her face into his wool coat, inhaling his comforting masculine scent. After being away from him for so long, she felt safe.

"I'd best check on Wagner," Will murmured against her hair.

She nodded. He rose and gently positioned her so as not to hurt her arm.

"Stay here." He moved cautiously toward Jake, scooping up the sergeant's pistol. After inspecting the body, he turned back to her. "He's dead."

"Oh, God!" Erin gasped. She'd never aimed a gun at anyone before. Knowing she'd killed a man, even one as dastardly as Jake, chilled her to the bone. She'd done what she had to do to save Will, but, damn it, this was such a horrible feeling to know she'd taken a man's life.

Will sank to her side and gathered her into his arms. "You did what you had to do, darlin'. If you hadn't fired, I'd be the one lying there."

Erin nodded. He turned her away from Jake's body.

"He'd have killed us both. You know that," he said.

"I know. I had to. He wouldn't put the gun down. But, damn it, why did he make me do that?"

"It's all right, darlin'." He brushed his lips against hers.

His touch lit a fire in her. She opened to him, allowing the kiss to erase all the lonely months of her recovery, when she'd thought he had been just a lovely dream. She melted against his strong hard body. "I love you," she murmured between kisses.

He pulled away, gazing into her eyes. "I love you,

too. I just didn't realize it until I thought I'd lost you for the second time."

Erin searched his eyes. He made her feel like she was the most beautiful woman on Earth. "I thought I'd lost you, too. I've been gone for six months."

"Pardon me?"

"I went back to the twenty-first century." She ran her fingers through the thick hair at the nape of his neck. "And the whole time I was there, all I could think of was how I could get back to you."

"But you *did* come back." He kissed her again and drew her lower lip into his mouth, sending a delightful shiver through her.

When he released her, she asked, "Do you believe me?"

"Of course I do."

"You do?"

"You're an amazing woman. I should have known from the start that you didn't belong here."

"But my story sounded so far-fetched. It's no wonder you didn't buy it."

"Buy it?"

"It's just an expression from my time. It means you didn't believe what I'd told you." She shifted in his arms. A white-hot shaft of pain shot through her arm and shoulder, making her wince.

"I think I'd best take a look at that arm."

He left her sitting amidst the hay while he went through his pack. As she waited, she couldn't help but glance in Jake's direction. Blood coated the hay beneath him. She didn't see any movement and was afraid to examine him closely. She'd take Will's word that the man was dead.

Will returned and gently unhooked her bodice, then slid her dress and chemise off her shoulder to get to the wound. While he worked, she was unable to take her eyes off his face. The face she'd feared to never see again.

After examining her wound, he determined the bullet had gone through soft tissue. "I don't believe it's done any major damage. I'll clean it the best I can, then bind it up until we can get you to a doctor."

Erin loved the way he took charge and cared for her. If she had to stay in this century, she believed she could endure it as long as he was by her side.

After he cleaned the wound with water from Jake's canteen, he stuffed it with lint, then wrapped it in muslin he'd gotten from his pack. Using a larger square of fabric, he fashioned her a sling. He ordered her to sit still while he saw to the horses and prepared their packs for departure. He didn't want to stay any longer than necessary.

"What about Jake?" she asked.

"Reckon we'll have to leave him."

"Just lying there like that?" She found it hard to stomach. No telling how long it might be before someone found him.

"We have no choice. We need to skedaddle before someone finds us."

She nodded. He was right.

"We'll take his mare for now," Will said. "And I'll go through his pack to see if there's anything we can use."

He obviously expected to leave on horseback. "Will," she said, "there's something you need to know."

Turning back to face her, he said, "What is it, darlin'?"

"I can't ride a horse."

"Because of your arm?"

"No. I've *never* ridden a horse before."

He frowned, then nodded. "He brought you in the wagon."

"We could ride back in that."

He shook his head. "Horses would be faster and easier to maneuver around obstacles. We need to keep off the roads."

"I'm too scared to get on a horse," she admitted. "If Jake hadn't taken me in the wagon, I'd have died of fright."

"My poor darlin'." Will glanced at Jake's inert form. "The man deserved what he got."

"Damn straight," Erin agreed.

Will shook his head. "Should I even ask what that means?"

"It means, I agree with you."

His lips curved up at the corners. "Reckon that's more of your future-talk."

"Reckon so."

"You'll have to teach me those words and their meanings."

"I'd love to tell you all about the twenty-first century."

"Well, for now," he said, "you'll have to ride with me. We'll bring Wagner's mount along for our gear and switch when mine gets tired."

"But where will we go? Back to camp?"

He shook his head. "I'm afraid we can't do that. Wagner's cast suspicions on you, and I deserted when I came to look for you."

"But where else...?"

"I thought we'd head north for now."

"But you'll be captured," she protested.

"Right now, we've got to get you to a doctor."

Erin opened her mouth to make another objection, but he shushed her.

"You rest while I get things ready." He busied himself preparing for their departure.

She settled back against the hay and imagined riding with Will. When he'd told her he loved her, she'd thought her heart would melt. Warmth rushed through her when she realized he'd actually deserted the army for her.

What were they going to do now?

Chapter Thirty

They made their way north through the back roads of rural Virginia. Will recounted how relieved he'd been to find Erin alive and unharmed. And now the threat of Wagner was gone.

Since Erin had never ridden before, he'd hoisted her onto his gelding and mounted behind her. This way he could hold onto her and protect her arm and shoulder. The sergeant's mare cantered beside them, carrying their packs.

Every mile or so, they stopped to provide Erin rest. He checked her wound and cleaned it. The last thing he wanted was to lose her to an infection.

Along the way, when she wasn't dozing, she'd been entertaining him with stories about the future.

"People in my time still ride horses, but not as a form of transportation," she told him. "We ride in cars."

"Railcars?"

"No. These cars, called automobiles, are self-propelled. They're powered by gasoline and have a steering wheel and gas pedal, so the driver can control where and how fast the car goes."

He tried to puzzle out what she described. "Are these *cars* like carriages?"

"Sort of. But they have pneumatic rubber tires, and they go much faster than carriages."

"How fast?"

"Fifty or sixty miles an hour."

He whistled. "Why is everyone in such an all-fired hurry in the future?"

She shook her head. "I don't know. It's just the

way we are."

"So, you all travel by car."

"No. We also have trains and planes."

"Planes?"

"Airplanes. They fly in the sky."

"Like birds?" This future world sounded amazing.

"They're machines, like cars. They're powered by fuel, and a pilot controls them."

"Do *you* fly?"

She laughed. "As a pilot? No. But I have flown as a passenger."

"And what's that like?"

"Sometimes it's a hassle, but when you're in the air looking below from so high up, it's all worth it."

Will shook his head. "I think I'd like to see this fantastic world you come from."

She settled back against his chest. "I wish I could take you there."

****

Most of the journey was uneventful. They encountered nothing but wildlife along the way. On the afternoon of the second day, the sound of hoof beats behind them put Will on alert. He couldn't afford to be seen by either Confederate or Yankee patrols. Even the locals could present a problem. They had to get off the road.

"Someone's coming up the road behind us," he told Erin. "I have to find us someplace to hide." He dismounted, then moved both their packs onto his gelding behind her. Slapping Wagner's mare on her rump, he sent her down the road, while he led his gelding with Erin still astride into the woods.

After they'd gone several yards, the hoof beats grew louder. Men's voices echoed around them. Will hurried his gelding along trying to avoid noise that might alert the riders. At the same time, they had to hurry. This last day of November, there wasn't much foliage to hide them. They would certainly be seen from the road when the men passed.

"Look," Erin said.

Will swiveled his head to glance up at her. His gaze followed her outstretched arm. They approached a series of hills. Several openings in the rocky hillside suggested caves.

"Maybe we can hide in there," she said.

He smiled. "You must be an angel from the future, because you've just performed a miracle."

Fortunately, one of the caves was large enough for them and the horse. He couldn't afford to lose their last means of transportation. He just hoped he could keep the animal quiet, until the riders passed.

He used piles of fallen leaves and blankets from his pack to make Erin comfortable, then examined and cleaned her shoulder, using the last of the muslin he carried for a fresh bandage. He had to get her to a doctor. Surrendering to a Yankee patrol might be an option. At least she would get help. A Confederate patrol, however, would spell trouble for both of them. And since they were still in Confederate territory, that was most likely the identity of the men on the road behind them.

After tending to his gelding, he returned to Erin. Although wrapped in several blankets, her teeth chattered. He knelt, enclosing her in his arms, trying to warm her.

"Once that patrol passes, I'll start a fire to keep us warm for a spell."

She nodded. He warmed her ice-cold hands between his.

"You take such good care of me," she murmured against his shoulder.

"You saved my life, darlin'. Just like an avenging angel from the Good Book. What ever did I do to deserve such a guardian angel?"

"You're the man I love," she said.

He felt her eyes on him in the dim light.

"The man I always loved."

Cupping her cold cheeks in his hands, he moved his mouth to her face warming her with kisses. When he reached her lips, she responded, opening to him, sending shivers through his body. If it weren't for the danger of being discovered, he'd likely lie down beside her. But he had to stay on guard. And more importantly, he had to find her a doctor.

****

Erin woke alone in the cave. She patted the still warm blankets beside her where he'd lain during the night. The fire he'd built was now nothing but smoldering embers. Sitting up, she winced. Her arm and shoulder were still sore, but the sharp pain had subsided. She hoped that meant her wound was healing.

Where was Will? She wondered if he'd gone outside to relieve himself. Squinting through the darkness toward the back of the cave, she realized the horse was gone, too.

No way would he have left her alone here. Could something have happened to him? Sunlight flooded the cave entrance. She rose, groaning and favoring her arm. Gathering the blankets around her to ward off the chill of the late fall morning, she approached the entrance to gaze outside.

A clear blue sky greeted her. Barren trees, brown grasses, and brush predicted the change of season. They were about three weeks from the winter solstice.

Cracking brush alerted her that someone approached. She ducked back inside the cave to avoid being seen, until she could make out who was there. Two horses appeared. She breathed a sigh of relief when she recognized Will atop his brown gelding. But who was the other rider? A gray-bearded man wearing glasses and a large black hat rode alongside him.

Will dismounted, and Erin ran to him. He caught her in his arms.

"You're supposed to be resting," he said.

"I just woke up. I didn't know what happened to you." She glanced up, puzzled by the other man's presence.

Following her gaze, Will said, "I told you I'd fetch you a doctor. This is Dr. Hoffman. He's a Quaker from a nearby farm."

Dr. Hoffman removed his hat and smiled down at her. "Good morning, ma'am," he said in a German-accent. "Thy young man explained thy situation. I will be glad to help."

"The doctor's wife and son are just down the road with a wagon. They'll take you back to their farm and tend to your arm."

"All right," Erin said. "Just let me get my things from the cave, then we'll go."

Will averted his gaze. "I'm not going with you."

"What?" She grasped his arm.

"It wouldn't be safe. I'd bring both the Confederates and the Yankees on our backs."

"No." Erin shook her head. "You can't leave me now. I came back for *you*."

Will caught her gaze, then glanced at Dr. Hoffman. "Pardon us a moment, sir." Taking her arm, he ushered her to the cave entrance. "We'd best go inside and get your things."

She got the message he was trying to keep her quiet. But no way would she let him abandon her in this century. If she couldn't be with him, there was no point to her having come back.

Glancing toward the cave entrance to be sure the doctor wasn't listening, she whispered, "You're not leaving me. You can't go back, anyway. They'd arrest you."

"I refuse to risk *your* life. I can't just go north. I have Amanda to think of."

Picturing the sweet little girl, she knew if she had a daughter, she'd feel the same way, but she couldn't let him do this.

"I have to tell you something important about the future," she said.

"You've already told me your future stories."

"Not this one. And this concerns *your* future."

He frowned. "Does it concern my family? Amanda?"

She shook her head. "It's the outcome of the war."

He swallowed but didn't speak.

"Come Spring, Lee will surrender," she said. "The North will win."

****

In the end, what Erin said hadn't mattered. Will left her, sending her with the Quaker couple and their teenage son.

After being taken to their farm in Southern Maryland, she spent the next two weeks being treated like visiting royalty while her arm healed. She'd found the journal Jake had stolen in her pack, but now that he was dead and Will believed she'd come from the future, she didn't think it mattered anymore. The comfort she experienced at the Quaker's farm didn't make up for the fear Will had left her. What if she never saw him again?

Dr. Hoffman told her Captain Montgomery had asked him to get her to Pennsylvania.

"My sister runs a boardinghouse in York," he told her. "Greta will be only too glad to put you up."

"But how will I get there?"

"My sons will escort you."

The Hoffmans had two sons living with them. Karl, who'd been with them the day they'd brought Erin from Virginia, was in his late teens. Another son, Franz, was in his early twenties. Both boys were well-built with tanned skin and work-roughened hands.

"Ya, you'll have no problems with these two strong boys at your side," Dr. Hoffman said.

"But what will I do once I get there?" she asked. "I

have no money."

"My sister will see to your needs until you find employment."

"Employment," she repeated. What could she *do* in this century? She was a journalist but wondered if women did that in this time period. The only other skill she had was washing clothes, but she didn't look forward to making a living doing that.

It *would* be best to stay out of the war zone, at least until the war ended next spring. But without Will, she didn't want to be in this century. She still had the brooch he'd given her and thought maybe she could find a way for it to send her back. Unless it only worked one way.

The next day, she packed her few things in the carpetbag the Hoffman's had given her as a gift. Karl and Franz brought the wagon to the front of the house, while she said her goodbyes to Dr. and Mrs. Hoffman.

She took her seat behind the young men, but all she could think was they were taking her farther away from Will.

****

After two days on the road and one night in a Maryland hotel, Erin reached the Pennsylvania border, exhausted and apprehensive about what awaited her in York.

As the wagon lurched down a rural road, a patrol of soldiers, clad in the blue of the Union Army, pulled up alongside them.

Karl explained they were escorting a friend to their aunt's in York. Erin sat calmly. She had nothing to fear from Federal soldiers, but she still felt uneasy and hoped they didn't question her.

While she waited for the men to allow them to pass, she noted one of the soldiers, a young chestnut-haired, clean-shaven man, kept staring at her. She didn't look directly at him, averting her face, hoping he'd take it for modesty.

Finally, just as the soldiers were about to let them go, he approached her, dipping the brim of his cap.

"Ma'am," he said. "I believe the colonel would like to have a word with you."

"What about?" she asked. This was just what she needed. She wanted to slip quietly into Pennsylvania unnoticed, then try to figure out what she could do to fix the mess she was in.

"Please, if you'd come with me, ma'am," the soldier said.

Erin glanced at the Hoffman boys. They both shrugged.

After chewing on her lower lip a moment, she let the soldier assist her in alighting from the wagon. "I'll be right back," she assured the two young men.

She tried to hide her alarm at being singled out by a Union colonel, sure the soldier escorting her could hear her frantic heartbeat. Why the hell had this man sent for *her*?

He led her to a group of soldiers sunning themselves on a crop of boulders on this cold November day. A man with a dark handlebar mustache, wearing a blue coat with a set of epaulets on his shoulders, a black broad-brimmed hat and knee-high boots, rose to great her.

A broad smile revealed yellowed teeth and a sprinkling of deep wrinkles on his leather-tanned face. "Well, if it isn't Mrs. O'Connell." He reached for her hand. "I'm pleased to see you escaped capture by the Rebs."

Her thoughts raced. This man obviously knew Erin O'Connell. She smiled, allowing the colonel to take her hand. He bowed over it touching his lips to her fingers.

Since he knew her, she pretended to know him. She also thought it wise to affect an Irish brogue so as not to arouse suspicions.

"Ah, me dear colonel, sure and I hope ye've been

well."

"Quite well, ma'am. But how has it been going with you? I feared for your safety when we received no word from you for so long. Thought the Rebs had captured you and sent you to one of their godforsaken prisons."

"Ah, no. They never caught on to me," she said.

"Good, good." He nodded. "My aide tells me you've been heading north with two lads."

"Aye." She inclined her head toward the Hoffman boys. "A family friend has taken ill. I'm goin' to spend some time with her. These lads are her nephews. They're takin' me to her."

"Sorry to hear about your friend. But I'm pleased to see you well. What's your destination?"

"York."

"I'll have one of my men escort you there."

Erin shook her head. "No, 'tis not necessary."

"I insist. There is a war on, after all. You'll be safer with a military escort."

This guy wasn't going to take no for an answer. "Thank you, colonel. We need to be gettin' on our way." She wanted to end this conversation before she slipped up or someone else recognized her.

While they waited for the lieutenant who'd been assigned to escort them to saddle his horse, Erin settled back into the wagon with the Hoffman boys. She just wanted this journey to end so she could figure out her next move.

Chapter Thirty-one

Christmas had come and gone. Dr. Hoffman's sister, Greta Wolff, had made Erin comfortable, as comfortable as possible, in a nineteenth century Pennsylvania boardinghouse in January. But she had to admit, it was infinitely better than a canvas tent in an army camp.

Greta took care of all her needs, although Erin insisted on pulling her weight. She helped with cooking and cleaning, washing bed sheets and clothes. Since she'd lost Will and didn't know if she would ever return to the future, she wanted to find a way to earn her own money.

One morning, while helping Greta with the breakfast dishes after the borders left, Erin brought up the subject of a job. "You've been more than kind to me, Mrs. Wolff, but I really need to strike out on my own. I need to find employment."

After wiping her plump hands on her apron, Greta adjusted her glasses and patted her graying bun into place. "I'd be happy to help thee find something here in town," she replied in her guttural German accent. "What skills do thee have?"

"I'm a journalist."

Greta blinked. A puzzled frown creased her round face. "Have thee worked for a magazine or newspaper?"

"A newspaper in Philadelphia. I was a reporter."

"Ya," Greta replied, nodding. "We have a local paper here in town where thee can apply."

"Good. Just give me directions, and I'll check it out."

****

Erin arrived in the office of the *York Weekly Dispatch*, outfitted in clothes she'd borrowed from one of Mrs. Wolff's daughters. The older woman insisted she must make a good impression, and Erin's few articles of clothing hadn't passed muster.

She felt weighed down when she entered the glass-front structure, properly attired in a plaid burgundy day-dress, brown felt bonnet, gloves, and a cloak. Under this, she wore a small hoop, two petticoats, one over and one under the hoop. For modesty, Mrs. Wolff had told her. The woman also insisted she must wear a corset.

"No proper lady would be seen in public without her foundation," Greta told her.

Eyeing the woman's stout form, Erin balked. "You're not wearing one."

Greta laughed. "I'm just an old *Hausfrau*. When I go to market, I'm always sure to conceal my bodice under a cloak or shawl. And no one's the wiser. Thee, however, are seeking outside employment. Not so easy for a woman. Thee must look thy best."

So, Erin had gone along with the woman's advice, even down to the corset. But it didn't make being able to walk or sit any easier. At least, the newspaper office was only a few short blocks from the boarding house. She hadn't had to worry about using a carriage or streetcar to get there.

She stepped inside and found a stout, balding man chomping on a cigar. He raised his brown, bushy brows in question.

"Good morning, sir," Erin said. "I'm here to see the editor."

His brows knitted into a frown. He raked his gaze over her, then stood. "I'm Edmund Radley, editor of the *Dispatch*."

"Oh, good." She extended her hand. "I'm here about a job. My name's Mrs. Erin O'Connell."

He took her hand, but instead of shaking it, he bowed over it. "Please, sit down, Mrs. O'Connell." He motioned to a wooden chair across from his desk. "Do you have poems or perhaps a short story to submit?"

"No. I'm a reporter."

"A reporter, you say?" He tamped out his cigar on the side of a spittoon. "This is most unusual. Where have you worked before?"

"The *Philadelphia Inquirer*," Erin answered truthfully.

"Ah, I suspect you are a ladies' feature writer, society pages, no doubt."

"I have experience on all types of stories and can write anything you need."

"I see." He braced his elbows on his desk, steepling his fingers while he regarded her. "We do have a number of ladies' activities here in town that we need someone to cover."

She leaned forward. Was he giving her the job?

"When would you be available?"

"Right away."

"Very well." Reaching into his desk drawer, he pulled out a bound notebook and a pencil. He laid the pad on his desktop, then scribbled something on the first page before handing the notebook to her.

"Tomorrow afternoon at four, go to this address."

Erin glanced at the top page where he'd written a street address. "What's there?"

"A tea being given by the Ladies' Relief Society. They knit socks, gloves, and scarves for our boys in blue."

"Knit socks...?" She couldn't believe what she was hearing.

"Cover the tea, and write a story about it. I need it to be as sentimental and tear-jerking as you can make it. Bring the finished story back to me, and we'll see about a job here."

Erin smiled, although her first impulse was to

slam the notebook on his desk and walk out. Ladies' Relief...knitting socks? Swallowing a retort, she said, "I'll do my best, sir."

She left the newspaper office and sighed. It *did* beat doing laundry. And who knows, with her knowledge of twenty-first century journalism, once she got her foot in the door, she could push her way to a better position.

****

Will spent a miserable Christmas in a cold, drafty guardhouse. The worst part of his ordeal was being away from Amanda for the holidays and not knowing how Erin had fared. She didn't belong in this century, and he'd left her to survive on her own. Although he'd briefly considered going north with her, that just wouldn't have been possible. For one thing, he couldn't abandon Amanda or his obligations to his home.

The worst he could expect to happen was he'd be shot or hanged, and that would put him out of his misery. He never expected to see Erin again.

The young, russet-haired corporal who'd been standing guard tapped on the door of Will's tiny prison. "Captain," he said, "you've got visitors."

Visitors? He rose and moved to the open doorway, peering out. The corporal stood on one side, while on the other stood his father. Since his arrest for desertion, he'd assumed his father would disown him. He'd never expected a visit. Jenny and Kevin Donnelly stood by Zachary's side.

"Son," Zachary said, "I've just been informed of your arrest. What is this all about?"

Will narrowed his gaze. "You didn't know?"

"Your sister told us you'd left camp and had been charged with desertion, but we had no idea you'd been captured. How long have you been here?"

Will counted back as he adjusted his greatcoat around him to ward off the late afternoon chill. "I'd say about two or three weeks. But I wasn't captured. I returned voluntarily."

"Why weren't we informed that you were here?" Zachary was aghast. "I know you, son. You would *never* desert your appointed post without good reason. Jenny said you'd gone off after a woman."

"Erin O'Connell," Will said. "The man who took her would've killed her. I couldn't allow that to happen."

"Is she here with you?"

He shook his head. "I sent her north, for her own safety."

"And the man who took her?"

"He's dead."

"I see." Zachary seemed to mull this over. "So, there's no one to confirm your story."

"No, sir."

"You can't contact Mrs. O'Connell?"

"I don't know where she is."

"Well, I *will* be speaking to your commanding officer, and this will all be sorted out."

Will admired his father's confidence but didn't believe anyone could get him out of this mess.

Zachary went in search of the colonel. Jenny stepped forward to wrap Will in a hug. A lump rose in his throat. The warmth of his sister's embrace and the concern of his father for his welfare had him wishing he *could* get out of this. Then he'd at least have a chance of finding Erin again.

Jenny pulled back, dabbing her eyes with a hanky.

"Oh, Will. I wish I had known you were here." She glanced past him into the shack that stood for a guardhouse. "They kept you locked in there?"

"They wouldn't allow me to contact anyone."

"How awful! And they kept you here over Christmas with none of us the wiser. Even Kevin didn't know you'd come back."

Will glanced at Kevin who stood at his sister's side. "Does Father know you two are...?" He hesitated, not sure what to say.

Jenny clapped a hand over her mouth. Kevin grinned. "I forgot," she said, "that you didn't know."

"Begging your pardon?"

"We've married." Jenny raised her left hand where a gold wedding band circled her ring finger. "And Kevin and I are having a baby."

Will couldn't believe all this had happened in the short time he'd been away. "And Father knows?"

"Yes. He's even called Kevin, *son*."

"Well, I'll be. And what about Mother?"

Jenny sighed. "Momma's still upset about the whole thing, but in time, I'm sure, she'll come around."

"A new baby will be a big help in that department." He hugged his sister. "I'm glad at least one of us has found happiness."

"Oh, Will." Jenny hugged him again. "Papa will see to it that you're released from this awful place." She sniffed daintily into her hanky.

"How's Amanda fairing? Does she know anything?" He cringed at the thought of his daughter suffering over his fate.

"We told her you had to go on a special mission. And that's why she couldn't see you this Christmas. But we told her you'd sent your love."

Guilt washed over him. Even as he'd risked his life to save Erin, he'd regretted leaving his daughter. If he survived this war, he'd spend the rest of his life making it up to her. If he even had the chance to fight again.

Without Erin at his side, however, he couldn't imagine any kind of life worth living.

Chapter Thirty-two

All Erin could concentrate on was how to draw a breath in the damn corset she'd agreed to wear.

"Tea, Mrs. O'Connell?" Erin glanced up at her hostess, a portly gray-haired woman, who stood over her holding an ornately decorated blue and cream ceramic teapot.

"Please," Erin said. Maybe the tea would help her to concentrate on what she'd come here to do. She sure wasn't about to eat anything. The hated corset would probably pop open, and she'd create a scandal. She smiled at the thought.

She had to make an extreme mental effort to forget about the damn undergarment—even though it threatened to pinch the life out of her—and concentrate on her assignment.

I need this job. Reaching for her pencil, she positioned the notebook alongside her place setting. "You ladies darn socks?" she asked.

"Oh, no, dear, we *knit* socks."

"Oh, sorry, *knit* socks." In her own unique shorthand, she wrote: *Knit socks for soldiers.*

Darn...knit...what the hell is the difference? It's all boring.

"We also knit gloves and scarves," a bird-like, silver haired woman, sitting across from her said.

Erin copied *that* down. "And?" she asked. How was she supposed to write a story about this?

"We ship them to our local troops down in Petersburg."

Petersburg, she wrote. The image of soldiers engaged in battle brought Will to mind. Maybe he was in Petersburg, or wasting away in some godforsaken Federal prison. He may even have been executed. How was she to know? A lump rose in her throat as she considered the possibilities.

"You're more than welcome to join our group, Mrs. O'Connell."

Erin glanced up from her writing. "Huh?"

Her hostess frowned. "Is your husband in the army?"

"Husband?" It took her a few seconds to realize the woman meant Mr. O'Connell. "No, he's dead."

"Oh, I'm so sorry."

The other women at the table actually tittered.

"It's fine." Erin brushed off their concern. "He died before the war started. But—" An idea dawned on her. "—why don't you ladies tell me about *your* men in the service of the Union."

"Well," her hostess began, "my dear husband is stationed in Washington City, and my two sons are in Petersburg."

By the time the tea was over, Erin had enough material for at least five heart-wrenching stories. Satisfied, she bid the ladies goodbye, confident this would get her the job.

She returned to the boarding house and intended to retreat to her room to write the story, then return to the newspaper office to deliver it. Greta emerged from the parlor, on her way to the kitchen, carrying a tray of used cups and saucers.

"I just served afternoon tea to the guests," she explained. "Would you care for some?"

"No, thanks. I've had quite enough tea," Erin said.

Greta glanced at the notebook she carried. "Thee got the job?"

"Not yet. I have to write a story first. Then if the editor likes it..."

"How exciting," Greta said. "I wish thee luck."

"Thank you, Mrs. Wolff. I'll be in my room."

206

Erin started up the stairs, her gaze drawn to an auburn-haired, olive skinned woman making her way down.

Greta took a moment to make introductions. "Mrs. O'Connell, meet out newest boarder, Mrs. Driscoll. Madame, this is Mrs. O'Connell."

Erin stared at the striking, green-eyed woman while Greta made her excuses and headed for the kitchen.

"Yer name is not O'Connell," the woman said in a lilting brogue.

The comment stopped Erin in her tracks.

"'Tis Branigan," she continued. "*Miss* Branigan."

A chill swept through Erin. "How do you—"

"Ye've come from a long distance."

"Well, I *was* in Virginia a short time ago."

"No. Farther than that. 'Tis a place beyond our time."

Erin gaped at the woman. "Who *are* you?"

"Who I am is not important. 'Tis you who don't belong here."

Erin found it increasingly hard to breathe. She needed to get to her room and yank off the damned corset. "Why are you telling me this?"

"Because I am the only one who can help you, Miss Branigan."

Chapter Thirty-three

"Damnation!" a soldier declared when a shell burst behind him.

Will shared the sentiment. He crouched in his trench, while the Yankees spewed shell after shell in their direction.

"Captain." A lieutenant raced up to him, trying to catch his breath. "The men are running low on cartridges and powder."

Will nodded. "I'll pass on the word to the supply sergeant."

For weeks he'd been sitting in this hole in the ground trying to avoid Yankee fire. Back in January, his father had contacted friends who owed him favors. They'd used their political influence to have the charges of desertion against Will dropped. He, in turn, had to swear a new loyalty oath and reenlist for the duration of the war. Afterward, he'd been sent to rejoin his company in Petersburg.

Every day he agonized over his choice in sending Erin north. Had he done the right thing? He wished he had a way to know she was all right. He couldn't get her from his mind.

Doc had assured him Erin was tough. She could take care of herself. But Doc didn't know the whole story. How would someone from *his* time survive if they were thrust into the seventeenth century? God forgive him. He should have found another way to keep her safe. A way to keep her with him.

Another blast close on his right diverted his thoughts from Erin.

"Sir," the lieutenant said. "The Yanks are shelling

us again."

"Men," Will called to those around him, "prepare to fire at will."

Gunfire blasted around him. His only regret, he'd die here in this hole and would never have the chance to see Erin again.

****

Intrigued by Mrs. Driscoll's comments, Erin accepted the Irishwoman's invitation to converse in her room. Although the woman had just moved into the boardinghouse, she'd already marked her territory with personal belongings.

The small table set in the center was covered with a gaudy red, orange and brown tablecloth on which sat three large candles. At least the woman didn't have a crystal ball.

Mrs. Driscoll motioned for Erin to take a seat at the table, then sat across, studying her.

"Have you ever had yer cards read?"

"Cards?"

"The tarot."

"I've heard of tarot cards. But no, I'm not familiar with them."

Mrs. Driscoll produced a deck of cards from thin air, but Erin realized they'd probably been hidden in her voluminous sleeves.

"How do you know I'm not Erin O'Connell?"

The woman hesitated. "You are and you aren't."

"What does that mean?"

"You once *were* Erin O'Connell, but ye've moved beyond this life."

"Are you talking about reincarnation?"

"My ancestry is part Romany and part Celtic. The ancient Celts believed everyone's spirit was reborn many times. Ye've stepped through a doorway." The woman shuffled the cards.

"But why did this happen?" Coldness crept up Erin's spine.

"Yer dreams. They guided you here."

"But that doesn't make any sense. Even if I was Erin O'Connell in a past life, why would I be reliving it now?"

Mrs. Driscoll's eyes glazed over. She seemed to draw into herself. "There are many reasons for a soul to return to their former life. Ye've done something that released a terrible tragedy that was never meant to be."

Erin thought about Will's death and the dream she'd had. Had he died at the hands of Jake the first time? "My grandmother gave me a brooch that contained a lock of a man's hair. She told me it had been given to Erin O'Connell."

Mrs. Driscoll nodded. "Yer grandmother was a seer. You recognized that and gave her the brooch knowing she'd know you in yer next incarnation and return it to you so you could accomplish yer task."

"How do you know about my grandmother? She hasn't even been born yet?"

"Time is immaterial in the spirit world. What matters is that you learn from yer past life." She gazed at Erin intently. "You haven't."

"You mean, my relationships with men?" Erin had never had a serious relationship with any man before Rick. She'd always found a reason to dump her past boyfriends, rationalizing that she wanted to concentrate on her career. Was the reason for her failed love affairs set in her past life?

She glanced down at the cards Mrs. Driscoll shuffled. "What are those?"

"Tarot."

"Are you going to tell my fortune?" After all she'd been through, Erin still held an innate skepticism of fortunetellers.

Mrs. Driscoll ignored her and stared at the cards she'd laid out. "Ah..." She tapped the face of one of the cards.

Erin gazed at the picture. A naked man and woman stood side by side before an angel with the sun behind his head. She pointed.

"What's that?"

"This card is 'The Lovers'. It symbolizes a joining of two souls."

"That can't be me and Will. He was married before."

"'Tis true, but the woman was not his soulmate...the one he was destined to travel through time with."

"Erin O'Connell is his soulmate?" Erin asked doubtfully.

"*You* have always been his soulmate."

Erin shook her head. "That can't be true. Where was he in my present day life?"

Mrs. Driscoll set two more cards out. One had a drawing of a skeletal figure. The other, a man hanging upside down from a T-shaped tree.

"What do those mean?" Erin asked.

"'Tis death." She pointed a long finger at the skeletal figure. "The other is the hangman. You are closing the door on one chapter in yer life and opening another. You must give up control and accept what is to be."

"I don't understand," Erin said. "And you didn't answer my question. Where was Will in my present day life?"

Mrs. Driscoll hesitated, drawing into herself. Finally she said, "He was reborn but wasn't drawn into yer circle."

"My circle?"

"The circle of family members and those ye've had past relationships with."

"Why not?"

"You betrayed him in this life."

"Betrayed him? How did I do that?"

"Erin O'Connell lured him to his death."

Erin thought about Jake. Had he shot Will the first time instead of her? The dates of his original death would go with that. But she hadn't lured Will to her, she'd been kidnapped. This was like some weird time warp. And trying to reason it out was giving her a headache.

"I've come back twice," she said. "The first time I prevented Will's death but caused my own premature death. This time it was Jake who died."

"You still haven't completed yer circle."

"What do I have to do now?"

"You and yer soulmate must come together."

"Impossible." Erin shook her head. "He left me. I'll never see him again in this life."

"You must," Madame Driscoll insisted.

"He doesn't want me." If there were a way to get him back, she'd jump at it. But their lives didn't fit together. She couldn't be Will's soulmate.

She was tired. All she wanted now was to go back to her old life.

"Since you know so much about these matters," she asked the woman, "tell me, is it possible to go back to my old life?"

"Yes." Mrs. Driscoll nodded. "But the cost will be great."

Chapter Thirty-four

Will blew his nose, then lifted the tin cup of chicory blend coffee to his chilled lips. After taking a sip, he spat. The brew wasn't hot or even lukewarm, but damned cold.

He felt feverish, achy, and tired. The trenches the army had dug around Petersburg defended the town, but the people within were prisoners. They couldn't get supplies, food, or medical help, except for what little the deteriorating Confederate army could supply them.

If Erin had been telling the truth, and he now suspected she had, this was all for nothing. The Yankees, who surrounded Petersburg, would be victorious. And where did that leave him? If he survived this siege, he'd go home a defeated man. He'd already lost what was most important to him.

Yankee shelling resumed. The men entrenched alongside him returned fire. He was left to wonder when this nightmarish battle would end. Lifting his head above ground level to view the enemy fire, he quickly ducked back down. The trench warfare took away the pageantry and glory of face-to-face battle but may have saved many lives on both sides. It also prolonged the agony. Nearly nine months had gone by, and the Yankees kept coming.

A young corporal scurried along the best he could in the muddied ditch.

"Corporal," Will called. "Do the men have enough caps?"

"No, sir," the corporal replied. "Everyone's low...on rounds, too."

Will sighed. No caps or rounds and not nearly

enough food. How the hell were they supposed to hold out?

His thoughts drifted to Erin. He hoped she was all right. At least, she was away from the war. The army had left Pennsylvania alone after the defeat at Gettysburg.

Once the war ended, if he survived, maybe he'd have the opportunity to travel north to find her. Would she even want him after he'd sent her away?

An explosion drew his attention to his left. The corporal standing beside him flew backward. The man screamed, sending Will scrambling to help him. His right leg was blown clean off.

Will swore and yanked up a muddy rubber mat used for sleeping. Pressing it against the stump, he tried to staunch the flow of blood. "Son," he said, "you'll be all right. I'll send someone for one of the doctors."

"Yes, sir." The young man's teeth chattered, and his lips turned blue. Will did his best to comfort him until the corporal's light blue eye's glazed over. He lay still, with not even the thready beat of a pulse.

"Damn it all to hell!" Will cried. This wasn't fair. He spread the bloodied, mud encrusted sheet over the young corporal's face.

More explosions echoed through the trenches. He stood, raising his revolver. If he died, he intended to take as many Yankees with him as he could. After firing off six shots, he crouched to reload.

A blast knocked him flat on his stomach, and the trench collapsed, burying him beneath a pile of mud. With his last breath, he called out for Erin and Amanda.

****

"What do you mean, the cost will be great?" Erin asked. "What is *that*? Some kind of Celtic mysticism?"

Madame Driscoll studied her. "Ye'll be lost forever, never finding the man you were meant to spend eternity with."

"But if Will's that man, I've already lost him," Erin protested.

The woman shook her head. "He still lives but won't survive long without yer spirit to guide him. Only you can pull him from the brink of death."

"But what can I do? I don't even know where he is."

"He is a long way from here, but if you don't find him in time, yer spirits will never meet again."

Erin sat back considering her options. Will had made it clear he didn't want her. The last thing she needed to do was traipse back into a war zone.

"You said there was a way for me to return to my own time."

The woman pursed her lips. "On May 1st, the feast of Beltaine, you can return. You have the brooch. Since it exists in the time from which you came and was the catalyst that sent you here, you can use it to return."

If what this woman said was true, she could find a way out of this nightmare. She could go back to her old life. Without Will, she had no reason to be here anyway. "You're telling me that in six weeks, I can go back to the future?"

"Aye. But are you prepared for an eternity without love?"

"Love." Erin shrugged. "I think it's highly overrated." Memories of hot showers, indoor plumbing, pizza, electricity, and Internet surfing excited her. She could go back. All she had to do was wait six weeks. That would be a snap.

But when she returned to her room, memories of Will sapped her resolve. She wondered if he'd returned to the army or was sitting out the end of the war in prison. Mrs. Driscoll had told her he was still alive but wouldn't stay that way without her.

She'd be unable to live with herself if she went back only to learn he'd died in the last days of the war.

On the other hand, if she stayed, how would she ever find him?

****

Will woke in a large open field. His torn, mud-encrusted uniform had been replaced by a neat, clean one, even down to the shiny brass buttons. Warm sunlight flooded the field. Where was he?

"*Papa.*"

He glanced in the direction of the child's voice. Amanda raced toward him, her auburn hair loose and flowing behind her.

"*Amanda, where did you—?*" *She ran into his arms. He gathered her close, inhaling her youthful fragrance.*

"*Miss Erin brought me,*" *Amanda said. She giggled. He scanned the horizon.*

"*Erin?*" *he said.*

Erin appeared, beaming. Her hair was also loose and flowing like a cloud around her face, her eyes large and bright. She looked like an angel.

"Will?"

A deep male voice yanked him from the dream. He reluctantly opened his eyes to glare up at Doc.

"How are you feeling?" Doc asked.

"I was feeling very well—until you woke me."

The doctor chuckled. "That good of a dream?"

"I was with Amanda...and Erin."

Doc patted his arm. "You'll see them again."

"There's a chance I'll see Amanda—if this cursed war ever ends—and if I survive. But I don't believe I'll ever see Erin again." A wave of pain traveled down his shattered body. He winced. His right leg was broken. He'd also suffered a concussion and two fractured ribs when the explosion had collapsed the trench. In short, he was a mess.

"You have to have faith that you'll live to see them both again. Just like I know I'll see my Josie and little Nathaniel."

216

"Doctor?" A soft feminine voice interrupted them. "If you're done with this here patient, I'll wash him up."

Doc grinned, turning to the slight blond girl holding a basin of water and a towel. "This is my good friend Captain Montgomery," he told the girl. "You take extra good care of him."

"Sure will, Doc."

Doc had set up a hospital in one of the homes in Petersburg. Will lay on a mat on a hardwood floor on the second floor of a three-story townhouse. Wounded soldiers surrounded him, taking up all available space.

Will studied the girl. She placed the basin on the floor beside him. She appeared to be no more than fifteen or sixteen. During the Yankee siege, the citizens of Petersburg had offered their homes and services to help the wounded.

"What's your name, young lady?" he asked.

"I'm Jenny Claymore."

"I have a sister named Jenny, although I believe she's a bit older than you. Do you live here?"

"Yes, sir. My mama and me live here. My papa and brothers are in the trenches, but they stop by from time to time." She studied him. "Where does your sister live?"

"Up in Northern Virginia, near Winchester. She's married and expecting her first child."

"How wonderful." The girl soaked the towel, preparing to bathe him. "Is her husband a soldier, too?"

"Yes, but he was wounded, and I haven't had the chance to inquire about him."

"I'm sure he's just fine," The girl parted his shirt and started to gently wash him. "He may have been sent home already."

"I do hope so." Will enjoyed the feel of the warm, sudsy water against his skin. Memories of Erin caring for him back in Gettysburg and later in his home flooded back.

"Are you married, Captain?"

"No, ma'am. My Anne died just as the war started."

When the girl's washcloth moved closer to his private area, she averted her gaze, blushing a bright pink.

Trying to cover up the awkward silence, he added, "I do have a daughter named Amanda."

"How old?"

"Let's see." He counted back. "Reckon she's about seven now."

The girl smiled. "Bet you can't wait to go home and see her."

"You're so right, ma'am."

She finished washing him and helped him change into a clean shirt. Will wondered if he'd ever make it home again. And thoughts of home led to thoughts of Erin. He'd sent her away for her own safety. He couldn't protect her. Hell, he couldn't even help himself. He hoped wherever she'd ended up, she was all right.

****

Erin adjusted her shawl, then retied the ribbons on her felt bonnet for the hundredth time. The damn thing just wouldn't stay knotted, and she was ready to chuck it. Of course, if she did, she'd undoubtedly create a public scandal.

Opening the door to the newspaper office, she drew in a sharp breath. She was prepared to do battle with her editor to get what she wanted.

Radley sat at his cluttered desk marking papers. He glanced up when she strode in and adjusted his glasses.

"I need a new assignment," she said.

The editor sat back and studied her, a frown forming. "What kind of assignment?"

"I want to cover the war down south."

His frown curved into a grin. "You want to be a war correspondent?"

"Yes." She'd come looking for a fight, but maybe that hadn't been necessary. Could it be this easy?

Radley chuckled. "You're a fine writer and reporter, but war correspondent? I can't send a woman to report on the war."

"Why not?" Erin smacked her hand on his desk. "If I'm a good reporter, why can't I do a story on the war?"

"The war zone is no place for a woman."

"I've been to the war zone nursing soldiers."

He raised his shaggy brows. "On the battlefield?"

"Yes, sir. At Gettysburg I was on the battlefield while shells were still flying."

The editor steepled his fingers as if he was considering her proposal.

"Maybe this could work. You could bring a woman's perspective to the War of Rebellion."

Erin nodded, a smile forming.

"On one condition," he said.

"Name it."

"I can't send a woman off alone. You'll have to take an escort."

"Who do you have in mind?" The last thing she wanted was someone checking her every move.

"Brody."

"The clerk?" Erin thought about the mousey young man. He seemed harmless enough. But could he survive living in a war zone? She doubted it. But on the other hand, she couldn't imagine him giving her any trouble.

Reading her expression, Radley said, "You go with him or you don't go at all."

"Well, then," Erin said. "I guess I'll have to accept your terms, because I'm going."

Chapter Thirty-five

Will sat on an upholstered lounge with his leg propped up, while Mrs. Claymore, the lady of the house, served him tea.

"You do look fine today, Captain." She fussed over him.

Although he enjoyed the comforts the gracious lady and her daughter provided in their lovely home, he'd grown tired of being an invalid. But he was none too anxious to resume his post in the trenches. Doc told him his splint would be removed soon, but he'd have to use crutches for a while. If Petersburg hadn't been surrounded by Yankees, he would be home right now with his family.

He took a sip of the watery, unsweetened tea and smiled gratefully. This poor woman could do no better. Supplies couldn't get into the town as long as the Yankees surrounded them. The citizens who hadn't fled their homes at the start of the siege nearly a year ago were extremely brave. But Will feared Erin had been right, the Yankees would win in the end. All this suffering will have been for nothing.

Mrs. Claymore returned with Doc in tow. He'd allowed Will to practice walking with the crutches he confiscated from a patient who'd developed an infection and died, but Doc warned him he needed to rest his leg as much as possible.

"You're looking better today," Doc said.

"I'd feel a lot better if I could get this splint off. My leg itches like hell." He grimaced. "Pardon me, ma'am."

The doctor, on the other hand, looked absolutely haggard. "Looks like you could use a furlough yourself,

Doc."

Mrs. Claymore excused herself, leaving the two men alone to talk.

"I could sure enough use one, but there's no way to get past the trenches. Reckon the end of this damn war would be a blessing for everyone."

Will shook his head. "I don't have a good feeling about how things will turn out."

"Are you talking about the war?" Doc seemed puzzled.

"We can't win. Why drag it out any longer?"

Doc grinned. "You and I have no say. It's up to the generals."

Lowering his voice so Mrs. Claymore couldn't overhear, Will said, "Erin told me the South will lose."

Doc lifted a brow. "When did she tell you this?"

"Just before I sent her north. She wanted me to go with her."

"You couldn't desert your post. Or that little girl of yours."

"You know me too well." Will grunted and shifted his leg to a better position. "Reckon I'll never see Erin again."

"Now, don't be thinking that way. The war will end. You'll go up north and find her."

"I don't know. Maybe she's already found her way back."

"Her way back where?"

Will grinned. "You wouldn't believe me if I told you."

Doc leaned his straight-back chair against the window frame. He sat beside the lounge Will occupied that had been moved from Mrs. Claymore's sitting room.

"Well...?" Doc prodded.

"Oh, no." Will shook his head. "I can't tell you this."

"But Erin and I were friends. We worked

together."

"If she'd wanted you to know, she would've told you."

Doc groaned and lifted his lanky frame to stand over Will. "Just rest and give that leg a chance to heal, then you can go traipsing off after Erin."

After Doc left, Will sank back with despair. He felt that same helplessness as when Anne and Sam had died and Wagner had taken Erin.

Why had he let her go?

****

Will spent the next several days drifting in and out of dreams. He dreamed of horseless carriages speeding down glistening black roadways. Winged machines soaring through the skies. Buildings taller than he could ever imagine. As he observed these wonders, Erin stood beside him.

"See," she said, "I told you all this was possible."

He took her into his arms, amazed by the visions around him, but completely captivated by the woman he held. She smiled, and he kissed her, devouring her taste and scent.

He broke from the kiss. "I thought I'd lost you forever."

"You'll never lose me," she said. "I'll see to that."

But even as she said it, she started to dissolve in his arms. He couldn't hold her.

"No, don't go without me." His fingers closed on air.

He woke to thudding pain in his leg, his body bathed in sweat.

"There, there, Captain," Jenny Claymore said. "You're just having a bad dream." She wrung out a towel over her basin, then bathed his face in the cool wetness.

Sighing, he relished the relief the towel brought.

"Was it about the war?" she asked.

"Pardon me, ma'am?" He still felt stunned by

Erin's disappearance.

"Your dream. Was it about the war?"

"No. It was about someone I lost."

"Your wife?"

Will nodded, not wanting to explain any more. While Jenny Claymore continued to wash the sweat from his body, he reflected again on his loss.

If only he had the chance to do things over.

****

After taking the train as far south as they could go, Erin and Nathan Brody hired a carriage to take them to Mason in north-western Virginia. Erin grew impatient at the slow pace of nineteenth century travel. The young clerk, on the other hand, seemed excited to be out of York. Erin wondered why he hadn't joined the Union Army.

"My three older brothers were killed in the war," he told her when she asked. "One at Bull Run, the other two at Antietam. Being the youngest, I had to stay home to care for my widowed mother."

"I'm so sorry," Erin said. She dropped her gaze. And now, Radley had sent this young man into a war zone to protect her. She'd give her editor a severe tongue lashing when she got back.

The trip to Mason was necessary to locate Will. Most of the fighting on the Eastern front centered at Petersburg, a good ways south. But first, she needed to find out if Will was even there. Nathan was polite and solicitous, deferring to her wishes the entire trip. The young, dark-eyed, chestnut-haired, man would make an excellent husband for some lucky young lady.

****

Although Erin didn't think she'd ever find her way home again, she felt closer to being home than she had in a long time. The familiar, welcoming faces of Tillie, Isaac, and Jenny made her feel she belonged. The only one missing was Will.

When Amanda raced in with her braids, tied off

with pink ribbons, swinging over her shoulders, Erin felt near tears. How she'd missed all of them.

"Miss Erin, where have you been?" Jenny said. "We've been so worried."

"Will sent me to Pennsylvania." Remembering the quiet young man beside her, she apologized. "This is Mr. Nathan Brody, a clerk at the *York Dispatch*, where I'm now working." To Brody she said, "This is Miss Jenny Montgomery, Tillie, Isaac, and Miss Amanda Montgomery."

Jenny smiled. "It's Mrs. Kevin Donnelly, now," she corrected. "I forgot you didn't know. I'm married to Kevin."

"Oh, how wonderful." Erin embraced Jenny. She genuinely liked the young Irishman. He was the perfect match for Will's independent-minded sister. "When did this happen?"

"Right after Will left to look for you." She lifted her left hand, proudly displaying the plain gold band adorning her ring finger.

"I'm so happy for the both of you," Erin said.

"You work for a newspaper?" Jenny pulled Erin toward the parlor. "Tell me all about it."

The group settled in the parlor.

Tillie reached for Amanda's hand. "I'll take Miss Amanda to her room for a nap, then put on some tea."

Amanda rubbed her eyes and left without protest.

"Do tell." Jenny eyed Erin. "What do you do at the newspaper?"

"I'm a reporter."

Jenny clapped her hands. "How exciting! But what are you doing here?"

"We're heading south to report on the war." Erin exchanged glances with Brody.

"This is wonderful news," Jenny said, as Tillie set down the tea tray. "You could find Kevin for me."

"Why? Where is he, what's happened?"

"He's been wounded down in Petersburg. I'd go to

him myself but..." She patted her stomach.

Erin's gaze was drawn to Jenny's swelled, rounded abdomen. "You mean...?"

"I'm having Kevin's baby."

"I'm so happy for you, Jenny. When are you due?"

"In August."

"That's wonderful. The war will be over by then. Kevin will be home."

Jenny and Brody stared at her.

"How do you know the war will be over?" the young man asked.

"Ah..." How would she answer this one?

Jenny frowned. "Do you know something you're not telling us?"

"No, I'm just saying...the war *could* be over by then."

"That's not what you said," Brody put in, "you said the war *will* be over."

"It was just an expression, is all. But I surely hope it will be over by the time Jenny's baby arrives."

Fortunately, they let the matter drop.

"I'm worried about Kevin," Jenny said. "What if he dies?"

"Don't say that," Erin insisted. "We'll find Kevin and send word to you. If he's been wounded, maybe he could come home."

"Oh, that would be wonderful."

"But now—the reason we're here—I need to find Will. Do you know where he is?"

"Oh, that's right. You wouldn't know. Papa got the charges of desertion dropped. Will's with Kevin in Petersburg. But we've had no recent word from him."

Relieved he was still alive and not in prison, Erin's thoughts churned. Will *was* in Petersburg. This would work perfectly for her, thanks to Mrs. Driscoll's card reading.

And she *would* find him.

****

Since they couldn't continue their journey that day due to the hour, Erin and Nathan accepted the Montgomery's hospitality for the night. They'd head for Petersburg first thing in the morning.

Erin was escorted to the guest room, while Nathan stayed in Will's room.

After Brody retired, Erin spent the rest of the evening catching up with Jenny. The young, dark-haired woman was like the younger sister Erin had never had.

"How did you get a job on a paper?" Jenny wanted to know.

"My landlady at the boardinghouse where I was staying told me about the position after I'd told her I was a journalist."

"But I thought you'd only ever worked as a laundress." Jenny's brows knit together in confusion.

"I used to be a journalist...in another life."

Jenny continued to frown.

"It's a long story," Erin said. "It really doesn't matter now."

"Well, anyway...how did you get the position?"

"I walked into the editor's office and asked for a job."

"And he hired you, just like that?" Jenny's mouth was agape.

"I had to write a story first."

Jenny leaned forward eagerly. "What'd you write about?"

Erin laughed at the memory. "I was sent to cover a ladies' tea party. I turned the story into a sentimental piece about the boys in blue in the ladies' families they were knitting socks for."

"And now you're going to Petersburg to cover the war?"

"I insisted on the assignment. I have to find your brother."

"Oh, I do hope you find him and the two of you can

be happy. I have a feeling about you and Will. You're perfect for him. Much better than Anne was."

"Why do you say that?"

"Anne was the perfect society wife, as my mother is to Papa. But you have spirit. You're what Will needs. And I've never seen him so frantic and determined to go after you when you'd gone missing." She clasped her hands. "He was like a knight in shining armor, going to rescue his lady. All he could focus on was finding you, no matter what the cost."

Jenny's words chilled Erin to the bone. Mrs. Driscoll had been right. She and Will were meant to be together.

****

Although Doc warned him not to put pressure on his broken leg, Will couldn't resist stretching his limits every chance he got. Managing the crutches got easier each day. He even found he could assist Mrs. Claymore and her daughter. It felt good to be useful again.

The pain in his leg was gone, replaced by a maddening itch. Doc assured him the splint would be coming off soon.

"But you won't be running off anywhere at least until the end of the summer. You'll need the crutches at first, then a cane, and you'll likely have a limp for a while."

Will wasn't discouraged by his own progress, but news from the warfront was another matter. With Petersburg still surrounded, residents ran low on supplies and found it nearly impossible to bring anything into the town. The Yankees were starving them into submission.

His thoughts drifted to Erin's words the last time he'd seen her. *The South will lose.* It seemed that prophesy *would* come true. He saw no way for the Confederacy to win.

****

Will sat in the parlor rolling bandages, his leg

227

propped on a stool when Doc found him hours later.

"I see the ladies put you to work." Doc took a seat in the rocking chair across from Will.

Smiling, Will said, "It was the least I could do."

Doc rocked back and forth.

Will scowled. "Now, when is this damned splint coming off?"

"Tomorrow."

"You're serious?" Hope surged through him.

Doc nodded. "High time it came off."

Sighing in relief, he said, "Thanks, Doc, I'll be looking forward to it."

"Mind what I told you."

"I know, I know. I promise to take it easy. You have my word." He smiled. "I'm not all that anxious to go back to the trenches, anyhow."

Doc's jaw tightened. "The Yankees will break through, and it will be all over for us."

Will said nothing when Doc rose and left the room. There was nothing *to* say.

****

Will woke to Jenny Claymore's voice. She hummed, *Rock of Ages.* His eyelids felt heavy and gummy, and his head throbbed when he tried to focus on the girl.

She carried a towel and basin filled with water. Setting it on the table beside his bunk, she said, "Thought you'd like to wash up before breakfast."

"Breakfast?" he croaked.

"Yes, Momma's making hoecakes. We still have a small reserve of flour left, and I churned up some fresh butter."

The thought of food made him queasy.

"Are you all right, Captain? You look flushed."

"I..." He struggled to sit up but couldn't rise from his prone position. "I don't feel well."

The young woman reached out and placed her hand against his forehead, her palm smooth and cool.

228

Her eyes widened. "You're burning up. I'll get Doc."

Sinking back on the bunk, Will found it impossible to focus. The room faded, he was back in the trenches. Explosions screamed all around him. The corporal lay at his feet. He bent down to tend him, but his face had changed.

His brother's face stared back at him. Glancing around, he realized he wasn't in the ditch, but in a cornfield. This was Antietam. They'd mowed down the Yankees in the cornfield, but Sam...

"Sam, no!" He reached for his younger brother. Will had promised to protect Sam, who'd just turned eighteen when the war started. Now he lay so still with a gaping, bloody hole in his chest.

"Sam," he groaned.

"Will." Doc's voice cut through his dream, or had it been a vision?

"What's happening?" Will asked.

"You've got a fever. We need to cool you down."

"Sam," Will said.

"Who?" Doc asked.

"I couldn't save him. Or Anne."

"He's delirious." Doc's voice sounded far away, like he was speaking from the end of a long corridor.

Cool towels pressed against his face and chest. He couldn't focus on anything. His hearing went in and out.

I'm dying. He'd never have the chance to see Erin again. He had to tell her...what? Doc hovered over him, and Will reached out, clasping his hand. "Be honest with me, Doc. Am I dying?"

"Not if I can help it," Doc answered. "You likely developed an infection."

"The splint..."

"I'll take that off after I get you cooled down some."

"I need you to do something for me."

"What do you need?"

"I want you to find Erin and tell her I'll always love her."

Doc's brow furrowed. "You can do that yourself."

"But if I don't make it..."

"I'm not losing you now. Not like this."

Will tried to say more, needed to, but he couldn't form any words. His vision blurred until all he saw were shapes hovering over him.

His hearing dimmed. His senses shut down.

He was dying.

Chapter Thirty-six

After what had seemed an endless ride over bumpy, rural roads, Erin and Brody arrived near the outskirts of Petersburg. Their press passes got them into a Union camp a few miles north-west of the town. The reverberations of cannon fire shook the ground reminding Erin of her harrowing stay at Gettysburg.

"Ever been to a war zone?" she asked Brody.

"No, ma'am," he answered, distracted by a group of Federal soldiers passing by.

"C'mon." Erin pointed toward a large wall-tent with a Pennsylvania State flag stuck in the ground beside it. "There should be an officer who can help us in there."

They approached the tent entrance where a young yellow-haired soldier stood at attention.

"Who's in this tent?" Erin asked.

"Colonel Thompson, ma'am."

"We need to see him." She glanced over her shoulder at Brody, who fidgeted behind her.

"May I ask what this is in regard to, ma'am?"

Erin pulled out the passes she'd obtained from Mr. Radley. "We're war correspondents. We need to get into Petersburg."

The young soldier blinked. "Never seen a woman war correspondent before."

"Nevertheless, I am one. Our editor from the *York Dispatch* sent us to cover the Petersburg front. Now, can we see the colonel?"

"Ah..." The soldier seemed nonplussed. "I'll ask for you, ma'am." He pulled back the flap and disappeared inside the tent.

She turned to Brody. "He has to let us at least see him."

Brody nodded, eyeing the soldiers milling around them.

The young soldier returned. "The colonel will see you."

"Thank you." Erin motioned for Brody to follow her inside.

Colonel Thompson sat behind a scarred, wooden table with official looking papers scattered across the top. They were ushered before the thin, balding man. He scratched at his sparse brown hair and studied them with clear hazel eyes.

He removed the cigar from his mouth. "And you are...?"

"Mrs. Erin O'Connell." She gestured toward Brody. "And my associate, Mr. Nathan Brody."

Thompson took another puff on his cigar and raked his gaze over her. He glanced at Brody. "You're both reporters?"

"War correspondents."

Thompson sighed. "An unusual pair, to say the least. What can I do for you?"

Erin leaned forward, planting her palms on the table. "We need to get into Petersburg."

"Impossible." Thompson shook his head. "You can't get past the Reb line."

"Why not?" She was not about to be denied.

"In case you haven't noticed, ma'am, there's a war on."

"You don't have to be sarcastic with me, Colonel. The war's the reason we're here."

"We can't get anyone across enemy lines." He scowled. "You can do your reporting from the Federal camps."

"That won't be satisfactory."

"It'll have to be," the colonel said, irritation in his voice. "I can have a military escort take you to the front Federal lines, but that's all I can do. And, frankly, I wouldn't advise even that."

Defeated, she nodded. "I guess we'll have to accept your offer, Colonel."

When they left the colonel's tent, Erin turned to Brody. "This isn't what I'd hoped for, but once we're at the front, maybe we can find a way to get into Petersburg."

The young man nodded but seemed uncertain. No doubt, he wondered why she was so hell-bent on getting inside. Well, he didn't need to know her real reason. As long as he didn't object or try to stop her, she'd take him along. Otherwise, she'd ditch him and get past the Confederate lines by herself.

****

Erin held her hands over her ears to block the noise of cannon blasts as she and Brody approached the front. Federal soldiers had dug trenches that faced Petersburg. Between them and the town, the Confederates had also dug trenches. No wonder the colonel had said it was impossible for anyone to get inside.

But Will was in there. She had to find a way to get to him and, damn it, she would.

The commanding officer's tent sat well back from the trenches to keep him out of the range of enemy cannon fire. A corporal escorted the pair into the tent, but the colonel was out, likely up at the line.

The corporal invited Erin and Brody to have a seat and wait for the officer to return. Once they'd been left alone, she sighed. "I hope this guy can help us."

"Pardon me, ma'am?" Brody seemed puzzled.

"The colonel," she corrected. "I hope he can get us into Petersburg."

He nodded but still seemed uneasy. "I still don't understand why we need to report from the enemy side. This," he said, gesturing around them, "seems to be the ideal location for our story."

Erin didn't have an answer for that. He was right. Her request to get inside Petersburg must seem unreasonable to him. But she'd only come here for one reason—to find Will.

****

A half hour later, Colonel Barnett entered the tent. He removed his dirt-encrusted hat and brushed his dust-coated uniform and auburn beard. His eyes widened in surprise when his gaze rested on Erin. His puzzled glance shifted to Brody.

"Mrs. O'Connell." He reached out his hand taking hers and bowed over it. "I never expected to see you back in Virginia, my dear. At least not until after the war ended."

"Ah..." Erin wasn't sure how to respond. She certainly hadn't expected to find anyone who knew her. This man had known her as an Irish Yankee spy...with a brogue. She couldn't affect a brogue in front of Brody.

She swallowed, and her pulse raced. "Ah..." She enunciated carefully, hoping the colonel would think she was carrying on another mission in disguise as a newswoman. "Colonel, I'd like you to meet my associate, Mr. Brody." She gestured toward the young man, while watching Barnett's eyelids narrow, and wondered if he'd play along. Or would he think Brody was a spy, too? There was no way to tell what would happen next.

She plunged ahead. "We've been sent by the *York Dispatch* in Pennsylvania to cover the battle in Petersburg."

"Reporters for the *York Dispatch*," the colonel repeated. "I see."

Erin smiled. He was going to go along with her story. Now, she just had to hope he didn't say anything about her past to Brody.

"Madam, how can I be of assistance to you?" the colonel asked.

"We have to get into Petersburg."

The colonel's brows knitted together. "Behind the Reb lines?"

"If that's the only way in, then, yes."

"Surely, you're not serious."

"I am." She stood to emphasize her point. "It's urgent."

Barnett shook his head and glanced at Brody, who'd remained quiet through the whole exchange. The colonel studied her, as if trying to read something in her face.

"My men can take you as far as the Union trenches, but beyond that, I'm afraid, you're on your own."

"I understand, sir," she said. She glanced at Brody, who had a questioning look on his face. "It'll have to do."

If she were to get into Petersburg, she'd have to find a way to sneak through the lines herself.

****

"Captain?"

Will cracked an eyelid and found Mrs. Claymore's thin face hovering over him.

"An army chaplain is here to see you."

"Thank you, ma'am," Will whispered. He hadn't asked for a chaplain, had he?

Mrs. Claymore ushered in a large, burly man with a heavy beard wearing a mixed uniform of butternut, gray and pale blue. When he removed his hat, his light brown hair stood out in wiry disarray.

"You don't look much like a preacher," Will said.

The big man laughed. "Nevertheless, I am. I'm Reverend Paulson with the Twenty-third Virginia, but the men serving with me just call me Pappy."

"It fits." Will liked the jovial chaplain. "Who let on that I needed a preacher?"

Pappy glanced toward the door Mrs. Claymore had exited. "The lady of the house ran into me in town and thought I might be of some help to you."

"Reckon she thinks I'm going to die."

"Are you, son?" Pappy's eyes demanded honesty.

"I surely hope not," Will said, "but I have been feeling poorly. Doc says I have an infection."

"Do you have any loved ones waiting for you at home?"

"Yes, I have a daughter, Amanda. She's seven now."

"And her mother?"

"She passed on just after the war started."

"Ah, I see." Pappy nodded in sympathy.

"But there *is* a woman..."

"A woman you love?"

"Yes." Will grimaced at the memory. "But I sent her away."

"And why is that?"

"It was for her safety. You see, she's a Northerner."

"Times of war cause conflicts. Enmity develops between those who would call each other friends in other circumstances." The big man studied Will. "Do you plan to reunite with her after the war is over?"

"I very much hope so, if I make it through to the end—" He broke off in a fit of coughing. Although Doc had told him his ribs had healed, they still ached from time to time.

Pappy drew a dipper of water from the bucket Mrs. Claymore left behind and helped Will drink.

Jenny Claymore burst into the room, tears streaming down her cheeks.

"My dear," the preacher asked, "what's wrong? Is it your momma?"

"It's over!" She lifted her apron to dab her eyes.

"What?" Will asked.

"The war is over." Her reddened eyes told the story. "The Yankees won."

****

Erin and Brody settled in among the Union troops, to learn what tactics they were using against the Confederates. Shortly after, a cheer rose from a scattering of men nearby.

"Lieutenant, have you heard?" A young soldier poked his head into the tent. "I've just come from the trenches. Lee's surrendered."

Lieutenant Jamison, who'd been answering their questions, stood and squinted at the man. "I've received no official word of this, soldier."

"Word's spreading through the trenches, sir. The war is over."

The lieutenant exchanged glances with Erin and her companion.

"Could this be a trick?" Brody asked.

"I don't know, sir," Jamison said, "but I'll sure as hell find out." Blushing, he tipped his cap in Erin's direction. "Pardon my language, ma'am."

"No offense taken," she said. "Just find out what's happened."

The lieutenant nodded, then strode off.

She looked at Brody. "If the war *is* over, do we have a scoop for the *Dispatch*."

"Scoop of ice cream?" He frowned.

"Story," she corrected. "Guess they didn't use the word 'scoop' in this time," she muttered.

"Pardon me, ma'am?"

"Never mind, Brody." She smiled and rose. "Let's go see what's going on."

They left the tent to find more blue clad soldiers cheering, shouting, and racing about.

"Lee's surrendered. We won!" one soldier yelled lifting his rifle over his head.

****

Union troops escorted Erin and Brody into Petersburg. They found Confederate soldiers, looking not much better than scarecrows, in the process of handing over weapons to Federal soldiers, who in return, offered water and rations.

Seeing the state of the Confederate soldiers, Erin worried over Will's fate. Months had passed since she'd laid eyes on him. Mrs. Driscoll had assured her he'd live if she went to him, but what if she'd arrived too late?

The pair went from house to house, inquiring about wounded soldiers. At the house of a middle-aged woman named Claymore, Erin learned a few soldiers remained in residence.

"I'm looking for Will Montgomery," she said.

"Oh, the captain. Yes, he's here."

Erin's breath hitched. "I have to see him. Is he all right?"

The woman frowned, her eyes clouding over. "I'm afraid he's bad off. The doctor's in with him now."

"Take me to him, please." She glanced at Brody's perplexed expression. "I know the captain," she explained.

"Obviously," he said. Mercifully, he didn't ask any questions.

Mrs. Claymore led them to a downstairs room off the kitchen. A gangly man leaned over a stretched-out form on a bunk. The man straightened and turned in their direction. Erin sighed in relief.

"Doc."

"Erin!" He embraced her.

She turned her attention to the form on the bunk. He lay so still. Her eyes stung, and her throat constricted. "Doc, is he...?"

After a glance at Will, Doc turned back to her, pain etched on his haggard face. "I don't know if he'll pull through. He was buried alive in the trench. One of his men found him and pulled him out, but he broke his leg and a couple of ribs. I thought he was nearly healed, but he's developed an infection from a deep cut in his leg. He's feverish and has been in and out for days."

"I don't know if he'd even want to see me." Her breath caught.

"Believe me, not only will he be happy to see you, but he told me—"

"What?"

Doc grinned. "He told me he loves you and should never have sent you away."

Relief washed over her. "Can I talk to him?"

"Go." He gently propelled her to the bunk, then stepped back to stand beside Brody.

She knelt and touched Will's face. His eyes, dark and sunken, and his features stood out in sharp contrast on his pale, thin face.

"Oh, Will." She ran her hands along both his cheeks, where a new growth of stubble had sprouted. "You can't die on me now. Not after what I've gone through to find you."

He lay still. Only his breath against her fingers and the slow rise and fall of his chest under the sheet showed he still lived. She kissed his dry, parched lips, then turned back to Doc. "He's so cold. Will he wake up?"

"Talk to him. Maybe the sound of your voice will pull him back."

She nodded and started talking. She told him she loved him, talked about her job at the paper, the mysterious Mrs. Driscoll, the trip to his home, Jenny's baby, and the news of the war ending.

"Now you can come home," she told him.

Silence met her words. She laid her head against his chest listening to the slow beat of his heart.

Then it stopped.

Chapter Thirty-seven

Gentle currents lapped at Will as if he were floating in water. Voices called to him. Voices he hadn't heard in a very long time.

"Sam? Is that you?" The other voice was female and very familiar. "Anne?"

Am I dead?

He tried to open his eyes, but his eyelids wouldn't obey. He couldn't move or feel anything, but he could hear.

"Anne, is that you?"

"Yes, it's Anne." Her voice was low and melodious.

"Am I dead?"

"No, it's not yet your time. You have to go back. Amanda needs you, and you have the chance for love again."

Another voice penetrated the darkness. He focused and realized it was Erin. But how could she be here? She talked about a newspaper job, Jenny and Amanda, traveling on a train...her hands touched his face...then her warm lips pressed against his mouth. He longed to respond, to come back to her, but he couldn't move.

He drifted away from her, down a long, dark tunnel. Wanting desperately to find his way back, he tried to shake himself, to force his way.

His eyes opened, her beautiful face the first thing he saw. Tears glistened in her blue eyes. The generous mouth he'd thought never to see again, curved into a smile.

"You're back!"

He tried to form words, but his parched throat wouldn't allow even a croak. Pressing her fingers against his lips, she said, "No, darling, don't try to talk yet."

She moved aside. Doc leaned down to examine him.

"His fever's broke," he said aside to Erin. "Reckon he'll be all right."

"Thank God." She kissed his face and lips. "I love you so much. Don't ever leave me again. I couldn't bear it."

He longed to reach up, take her in his arms, and promise her he never wanted to be parted from her again. He managed to lift his right hand toward her. Taking it in hers, she lifted it to her face kissing and rubbing it against her smooth cheek.

"I love you," she said again.

I love you, he mouthed.

Seeming to understand, she smiled. Holding his hand, she reached her other hand toward Doc, who stood behind her.

"Thank you for taking care of him," she said. "For keeping him alive."

"You're the one who brought him back," Doc answered. "You're the reason he fought to live."

****

Days later, after receiving constant care from Erin, Will grew stronger. She'd sent her companion, Brody, back to York with the message she'd be staying in Petersburg a bit longer. She'd refused to leave Will's side.

He could drink, eat, and sit up. He had every intention of getting back on his feet and had a ton of catching up to do with the woman he loved.

She told him all about her time with the Quaker family, her trip to Pennsylvania, and the colonel, who knew her as a Yankee spy.

"I put on an Irish brogue, so he wouldn't suspect anything was up."

Will laughed. "I'd be liking to hear that, now,

241

lass," he said, in a very bad imitation of a brogue.

Erin shook her head and continued talking about the boarding house, her job at the *York Dispatch,* and Mrs. Driscoll.

"She knew I'd come from the future. She also told me I could go back, but if I did, you'd die."

"You gave up your future life for me?"

"You're my life now. What kind of existence would I have had back there without you?"

The extent of the sacrifice she'd made overwhelmed him. No one had ever done so much to protect him. He'd always felt he had to protect others, but this woman had shown him what love really meant.

"I also know," she went on, "that I've lived this life before. But the first time, I allowed you to die...and regretted it for the rest of my sad, lonely life. I was reborn in the future but couldn't find love there. I had to come back here and fix my mistake."

"You really believe this?" After all they'd been through, he was inclined to accept anything she said. As long as she stayed by his side.

"I know the whole thing sounds fantastic."

He traced a finger along her lower lip. She shivered in response. "If you say it's true," he said, "I believe."

"So, what do we do now?" Her eyelids narrowed mischievously.

"We go home...and get hitched."

Her blue eyes widened. "Married?"

"If you don't plan to ever leave me, I reckon that's for the best."

She smiled. "I'd like nothing better than to marry you, Captain Montgomery."

"Erin Montgomery...I like the sound of that."

"But wait...what about my new job at the paper?"

Will frowned. "My family is quite well-off. You don't need a job."

"But I like that job. I want to keep it."

"Whatever for?"

"It gives me meaning and purpose."

He reached for her, gathering her soft form into his arms. "I thought I gave you that."

"I'm serious. I feel a little bit like my old self when I'm working on a story."

"But you said it was in York...that's Yankee territory."

She shrugged. "The war is over. We can live anywhere we want."

Will sighed. Erin would not be a compliant woman like Anne, who'd been content to live in his parents' home. She was his new love, the woman he wanted to marry. He loved her spirit and outspokenness. If he wanted to keep her, he'd learn to accept her wants and needs. After all, she'd given up so much for him.

"Marry me," he said, "and we'll make our own way, our own space."

She nodded. "We'll live the life we were meant to have...the first time around."

Chapter Thirty-eight

Will was home again. He stood outside the parlor in his parents' house in Mason, surrounded by family. He adjusted his cravat and frock coat and nervously prepared for his wedding day.

Kevin appeared at his elbow, beaming. "I've never seen you so flustered, Captain, even when we faced Yankees on the battlefield."

"We're in-laws now, and you're the father of my niece or nephew-to-be," Will said. "Call me Will."

"Yes, sir...I mean, Will."

"That's better." He glanced toward the staircase where Erin would descend once his mother and Tillie, who'd taken her to Jenny's bedroom, had properly prepared her for the ceremony.

He'd asked Kevin to stand as his best man. Erin had asked Jenny to stand for her. Will's sister had been busy, crafting both Erin's wedding dress and a rose-colored sack coat to wear over her own dress to hide her advanced state of pregnancy.

And Amanda had been more than excited to be the flower girl. Throughout the entry way, she'd practiced spreading petals from the garden's flowers. Tillie had scolded her for making a mess, but his mother—so unlike herself—had only smiled.

When he arrived home with Erin, Will had been surprised when his parents welcomed them. Since they'd had to accept Kevin and Jenny's union now that she carried his child, his parents seemed to have mellowed. He suspected having the entire family together again was part of their transformation, as well as what the nation had just been through.

Last night, his father had asked to speak to him in his study. Will had expected a lecture or talk of the mess the government was in since Lincoln's assassination a month ago. But his father surprised him by extending his congratulations and blessings on the coming union.

"I believe you've chosen a fine woman." His father puffed on one of his cigars.

"I always thought you disapproved of Erin, because of her questionable background."

"I know she's had a hard life, but she's overcome a great deal. Amanda loves her."

"As do I."

"Of course you do, son." His father blew smoke rings above his head. "And that's all that matters."

So, although the war had been lost, Will had won. He had the woman he loved, who'd come to him from the future; his daughter now had a mother who loved her, and his family was accepting, at least for the time being.

He hadn't yet mentioned his plans to move north. But that news could wait for another day.

****

Erin brushed her hands over the skirt of the beautiful silk apricot gown Jenny had made for her. Will's parents had bought the material.

At first, she'd protested. She knew Southerners, even well-off ones, had a way to go to recover what they'd lost during the war. But Will's parents assured her they wanted and were able to do this. The acceptance of his family had made everything easier. While she still thought wistfully of the life she'd given up in the future, she knew she never would have been happy knowing Will had died.

"This is for you to wear, dear." Madeline presented Erin with a delicate silver-chain necklace from which a single sapphire stone dangled. "This is very old. It belonged to my grandmother." Erin leaned over so the shorter woman could reach around her neck to fasten the chain. She then moved to stand before Erin and admire how it looked.

"The stone is perfect for you. It matches your eyes," Madeline said.

"And," Jenny added, "it's old and blue. Your dress is new. So, all we need is something borrowed." She held out an embroidered hanky. "This is mine. Will it do?"

"It will be just fine." Erin's eyes stung when she accepted the handkerchief. Tears of happiness threatened to spill over.

This was the day she'd lived for her entire life, although she'd never known it. How could she have ever believed she'd have to travel one hundred and forty years into the past to find the man she loved?

Amanda pranced around in her short forest-green dress, trimmed in ivory lace. Her auburn hair had been arranged in ringlets falling past her shoulders. She also wore green and ivory ribbons in her hair and carried a basket of rose petals to spread in the hall after Erin descended the stairs.

Jenny had arranged Erin's hair in an intricate braided design. She'd also strung together a wreath of daisies for Erin to wear with long ribbons that matched her gown and trailed down her back.

Jenny adjusted the wreath and handed her a small nosegay to carry. Amanda beamed impishly at her.

"Miss Erin, you look beautiful."

"Thank you, Amanda. So do you."

Turning to Jenny, Erin said, "I think I'm ready. Is it time?"

"I do believe it is."

Mrs. Montgomery tapped Erin's shoulder. "Tillie and I will go downstairs. I'll send Mr. Montgomery up to escort you."

"Thank you, Mrs. Montgomery," Erin said, "for

everything."

"No need to thank me. You just take good care of that boy of mine."

"I will. I promise."

Madeline and Tillie left. A few minutes later, Zachary appeared in the doorway. He made a distinguished figure with his white hair and beard and impeccable black suit, gray vest, and white cravat.

"Shall we, my dear?" he asked.

Amanda and Jenny moved from the room. He waited until Erin took his arm. The small group moved to the head of the stairs. Jenny slowly started down. Amanda fidgeted at the top apparently impatient to perform her task. Once Jenny reached the bottom, Amanda pranced down. At the bottom, she glanced up at Erin and her grandfather, then spread rose petals from her basket across the hall to where her father and the others stood.

At the top of the stairs, Erin trembled.

"Nervous, my dear?" Zachary asked.

"A little," she admitted. "But mostly, I'm very happy."

After Amanda crossed the hall, Zachary said, "Shall we?"

"Yes, sir."

As she slowly started down the stairs on Zachary's arm, she caught Will's admiring gaze. A remembrance of the first time she'd descended these stairs came back to her. She nearly giggled at the thought of tripping down the stairs in her wedding gown.

Will's thick, dark hair had been recently trimmed, as had his mustache and chin beard. He was dressed as his father in a black suit, gray vest, and white cravat at his throat.

Once they'd reached him, Zachary put her hand into Will's. The love in his dark-eyed gaze made her want to cry. It had seemed like centuries ago when she'd first dreamed of this man. But Grandma Rose had been right. Will was her destiny. Her Rebel.

Epilogue

Philadelphia, Pennsylvania
December 1865

Erin looked on while Amanda tried to string more popcorn from the bowl the maid, Elsie, brought in from the kitchen. She noted with amusement the child ate more popcorn than she threaded onto the string.

"When's Papa coming home?" Amanda asked.

"He should be home soon, sweetheart," Erin said.

"But I want him home now." Amanda's blue eyes widened with excitement.

This Christmas Eve was the first since Erin and Will had married. They'd moved to Philadelphia, where Will had obtained a position with a local bank. She'd also found a job with the *Philadelphia Inquirer*. In a weird sort of way, she felt like she'd come home.

They had purchased a town house on Chestnut Street. Will had brought a tree home last night and trimmed it, and the house held the inviting aroma of pine and the cinnamon rolls Elsie had baked late this afternoon. She had a chicken roasting in the oven, and potatoes and assorted vegetables simmering on the stove.

"Momma," Amanda cried, "it's ready."

Erin smiled as the girl proudly displayed her string of popcorn. This was the first time Amanda had called her *Momma*, instead of *Miss Erin*. A sudden kick to her abdomen brought her attention to the new child growing inside her.

Once her pregnancy grew apparent, she resigned her job at the paper and, at Will's urging, was now writing fiction. She'd always thought she'd try that someday.

Hey, if Louisa May Alcott could do it, why couldn't she? This way she could be home to supervise Amanda and, hopefully, once the baby arrived, she'd be able to juggle them and her writing. After all, Elsie did all the housework and cooking. Amanda was now eight, old enough to attend school and help with the new baby.

The sound of the door opening brought a gasp from Amanda. "It's Papa."

Will stepped in, covered with snow that had started falling earlier that afternoon. He carried packages wrapped in brown paper and bound with string. He'd never looked more handsome. Amanda danced around him.

"What's in the wrappers?" she asked.

He looked at Erin helplessly.

"Amanda," she said, "come here and let your papa get settled."

The girl reluctantly moved toward her.

Erin pointed to the small wood bench Will had built and painted for his daughter. "Bring your bench over here by me, and I'll tell you a story."

"About what?" Amanda pushed the child-sized bench toward the fireplace, beside where Erin sat in a rocking chair.

"About the future..." She nodded at Will, who stealthily crept up the staircase with his bundles.

****

Hours later, after Amanda had been tucked into bed, Erin sat with Will on the settee before the fireplace. Elsie had gone home for the night.

The balsam pine had been adorned with popcorn, red ribbons, and candles set in stands on the ends of some of the branches. The candles made Erin uneasy, but Will assured her he'd personally make sure they were safely snuffed out before they retired for the night.

Jenny and Kevin now had a four-month old son they'd named Thomas. They, along with Will's parents, planned to visit over the holidays. Erin knew he secretly wanted a little boy, too, although he assured her another little girl would be wonderful. When the baby kicked, she lifted Will's hand, placing it on her stomach.

"Your son." She looked into his eyes.

He grinned. "How do you know it's a boy?"

"I just know."

Frowning, he said, "Is this something you know from the future?"

"No, silly." She laughed. "We were never together before in my past life. This baby will be a brand new creation. Who knows what he'll become?"

Will grew quiet, seeming to consider her words. "Do you reckon you'll be reborn again in the future?"

"That's quite possible."

"What about me?"

Erin considered. "I suppose you'll be reborn in the future, too."

"But will we find each other there? You didn't know me in your future life."

She recalled Mrs. Driscoll's words. "That's because our souls weren't connected before. Now, when we're reborn, we'll be able to find one another."

He frowned. "You're sure about this?"

"No." Erin laughed. "Of course not. But," she said snuggling against him as he reached an arm around her, "we've got this life to live first...we'll worry about any future lives when we get to them."

He brushed his warm lips against hers. She opened to him, and he deepened the kiss. His kisses continued to be as exciting as the first time he'd kissed her back in camp more than two years ago. The day she'd realized she was trapped in the past and had broken down in tears.

"You always know how to make me feel better,"

she murmured against his throat. His pulse beat reassuringly in her ear.

"Are you happy here in this backward century?" he asked. "Or do you miss the life you left?"

She shook her head. "No. There was nothing for me there, just gadgets and conveniences I've learned to live without. You're my world now. And Amanda and..." She patted her stomach. "Our son."

"I love you, angel." He kissed her hair.

"And I love you, too...for all my many lifetimes."

Will rose and snuffed out the candles, then reached for her hand to take her to bed.

A word about the author...

Susan Macatee has been writing toward publication for 13 years. Her stories range from sci-fi, the paranormal and history, particularly the American Civil War era.

She has one published young adult novel set during the Civil War and two Civil War romances in the works. Her interest in the time period stems from her husband getting involved with a Civil War reenactment group and pulling her right in. She and her husband are members of the 28th Pennsylvania reenacting group.

Her other loves are the paranormal and sci-fi, which she's incorporated into her most recent WIP. She lives with her husband of 26 years and three grown sons, as well as the family dog, a female Boxer named Kelly. She spends her free time watching her local baseball team, the Philadelphia Phillies, inhaling books and baking.

Visit Susan at www.susanmacatee.com

Thank you for purchasing
this Wild Rose Press publication.
For other wonderful stories of romance,
please visit our on-line bookstore at
www.thewildrosepress.com.

For questions or more information,
contact us at info@thewildrosepress.com.

The Wild Rose Press
www.TheWildRosePress.com

www.ingramcontent.com/pod-product-compliance
Lightning Source LLC
Chambersburg PA
CBHW070907180626
46817CB00003B/949